D1394775

For Mike Luxton
who helped with

Practise to Deceive

more than with any of
the others, but who must
not be held responsible for
any medical errors!

In gratitude

[signature] Dana Williams

Wentworth
August, 2003

Practise to Deceive

DAVID WILLIAMS

This edition published in Great Britain in 2003 by
Allison & Busby Limited
Bon Marche Centre
241-251 Ferndale Road
Brixton, London SW9 8BJ
http://www.allisonandbusby.com

A catalogue record for this book is available from the British Library

ISBN 0 7490 0671 4

Printed and bound by
Creative Print + Design, Ebbw Vale

DAVID WILLLAMS was born in Wales and educated at the Cathedral School, Hereford, and St John's College, Oxford. He founded and ran one of the UK's biggest advertising agencies before stepping down due to ill health. Since then he has been a full time writer and is the author of more than 20 crime novels. He lives with his wife at Wentworth in Surrey. They have two married children.

BY THE SAME AUTHOR

The Inspector Parry mysteries
Last Seen Breathing
Death of a Prodigal
Dead in the Market
A Terminal Case
Suicide Intended

The Mark Treasure mysteries
Unholy Writ
Treasure by Degrees
Treasure Up in Smoke
Murder for Treasure
Copper, Gold & Treasure
Treasure Preserved
Advertise for Treasure
Wedding Treasure
Murder in Advent
Treasure in Roubles
Divided Treasure
Treasure in Oxford
Holy Treasure!
Prescription for Murder
Treasure by Post
Planning on Murder
Banking on Murder

Collected Short Stories
Criminal Intentions

This one for Jill Swainson

O what a tangled web we weave
When first we practise to deceive

Sir Walter Scott, *Marmion* **can. VI** XVII

To begin with

He had been sure that he was dying. The paradox was that he hadn't minded.

It had seemed that he was being borne down gently into a narrowing cavern, with failing light giving place to a more devouring gloom. He should have been terrified but, again inexplicably, he had simply been numbed. His baffled mind had yielded to what he judged was a terminating experience that was incredibly comforting. It had been like succumbing to an anaesthetic, but one from which there would be no recovery. Even so, surrender had been easier than fighting back.

There was no gauging how long it was before this accepting of defeat became progressively facile to him, then ignoble, and finally monstrously unacceptable. In fact the whole episode had probably been enacted in a matter of minutes, something akin to a complicated dream. It is unlikely that his determination to retaliate saved his life. It is quite certain, though, that his voluntary resolution marked the arrest of the cerebral decline. Not even after the rational reawakening was there any sign that his limp, half-numbed body could do anything to reverse his physical demise. The new, positive intention was still solely in his mind.

'Christ,' he tried to utter now, except the word – which was a plea, not a blasphemy – was manifested only as an unconsonanted murmur from near his larynx. It registered neither in sound nor movement through his lips.

It was then that he began willing his blurred vision to concentrate on defining items immediately before him – the hemmed edge of a white pillowcase that was pressed against the foot of a wooden chair leg, both objects resting, like his own body, on dark blue carpet. Compiling that trivial inventory did something to strengthen his morale as well as his determination. The objects were all he was able to see. He could move his eyes a little, but his head scarcely at all.

'The rain in Spain stays mainly in the plain,' he recited to himself. 'In Hertford, Hereford, and Hampshire hurricanes hardly...'

He was ready to interrupt the memory test when, for the first time since recovering his regular awareness, he was conscious of exterior sounds louder than the beating of his own heart – sounds that, thank God, he could accurately identify.

There was the muffled thump of laboured footsteps on covered stair treads, and the buzz of voices coming nearer. Of the three speakers only one was female. One of the two men sounded confident and authoritative, the other, whose higher voice was warmly familiar to him, sounded worried, but less desperate than he had been earlier.

'Did my best...except it was hard to know what actually would be best. He looked terrible. Asked to use the loo, which meant getting him upstairs. The ground floor tenant's away,' he heard the second man say as he came closer. He was glad his friend was with him – except, for some inexplicable reason, he couldn't recall his name. It was only then that he fully recollected where he was – a fact that proved too much for his still struggling emotions. Either his mind suffered a relapse, or it was taking the easy way out as he briefly drifted into re-charging semi-consciousness.

When he rallied again, he was being carried downwards, but this time the experience was real, not part of a delirium. He was on a stretcher. He had been on one before, years ago, after a riding accident. How many years ago was it? Come on. It was six, wasn't it? No... seven. Yes, and in March, whereas today it was...September... September the third. He'd remembered the radio news announcer saying so this morning. That had been before breakfast when he'd been shaving – except breakfast now seemed so far away.

The constraints of the strapping on his left side were very tight, though there appeared to be none at all on his right. The sense of dangerous imbalance was acute. He wanted to cry out, to tell someone to take care in case he fell off. But he still couldn't speak. Instead, he tried to grasp the stretcher edge with his right hand under the blanket, but there was no response or feeling from that side, either in arm or leg. He made do by gripping even more tightly with the other hand. This still wasn't enough to make him feel secure, but it did something for his resolve if not for his safety. His restricted gaze was still mostly upwards. The white expanse totally filling his view was the sloping white ceiling above the narrow staircase.

Again he tried to utter, but the inward croaks he was making with such effort were still inaudible to anyone else, though the anxiety in his eyes must have been plain enough.

'Just relax, sir. You won't fall off. We're looking after you.' It was the unfamiliar male voice that had offered these comforts from behind the patient's head. The speaker's face became visible now, upside down, as he leaned forwards. 'We'll have you in the ambulance in no time.'

'And not so many are ready to play the Good Samaritan these days.' This came from the woman who had the other end of the stretcher. She was addressing the man, his friend, who was leading the sorry procession down the stairs.

The last words had confused the patient. And while he understood the response, it only served to perplex him more.

'I only brought him in, and did what I thought was best for the poor chap. Finding him like that on the doorstep was quite a shock,' his friend had claimed.

Chapter One

'Denis might have died, Dr Howell. It was a massive stroke. Massive.'

'A serious occlusion, yes, Mrs Ingram. But he did survive. And you'd be surprised how much courage that would have taken. It's not just a matter of self preservation, either. Oh yes, he's a fighter, determined to get back to work, both in the company and the charity. As you say, he probably feels he's let everyone down, which is nonsense, of course. As if he hadn't moved mountains already.'

Edwin Howell, the director and joint proprietor of the Howell Clinic, gave a smile that was more earnest than obsequious, but it was purposely that too, while he gauged the reaction to the words he had just delivered confidently and at some speed, in an ebullient voice with lingering Welsh intonations. He was a tallish, imposing figure – made more so by his straight-backed attitude whether he was standing or seated – and rugged, too, with large hands used, from time to time, to make unexpectedly delicate gesturing when emphasizing a point. His heavily hooded, dark blue eyes concentrated, but not unnervingly, on those of whomever he was addressing. The abundant dark wavy hair hardly helped to establish his real age, which was fifty-eight, but it did disguise an oversized, donnish cranium. Most people would have dubbed him commanding. The well-cut, subdued check suit enhanced the overall impression of prosperity as well as competence.

'But do you suppose he'll ever get back to work, doctor?'

'In time, certainly.' The hands separated to indicate, like the suddenly knitted brow, that the bold conclusion required corroboration. 'Though whether that'll be best for him we shan't know till he's had a chance to try. He's an important, and still ambitious, man. That's normally a good incentive to recovery.' He beamed broadly.

'If by that you mean he's craving the limelight, doctor, you're wrong.'

Howell's eyebrows lifted a fraction. He didn't much savour being told he was wrong, particularly in professional matters. 'No, I didn't mean that at all.' He leaned forward a little, then back again. 'It's more likely he feels... unworthy, perhaps, of the flattering things he must know have been said about him. He'll be feeling he needs to justify them. That's good. Better than giving up, which in his case would only nurture frustration.'

'Friends are very loyal, doctor. What Denis and I have achieved seems to have been appreciated.' The slim, ash-blonde woman, whom the doctor found strikingly attractive, responded in the same cool, sharp tone as before.

Howell had been waiting to see if his compliment about Denis Ingram should have been angled to include the man's wife, and was quietly amused that she had responded as though it had been. He had gathered that what Angela Ingram had accomplished in the eight months since her husband's illness had been pretty exceptional. But there had been a great deal before that too. If she responded as though her own and her husband's success had always been achieved jointly – that she had earned half the glory, not just been reflected in it – she was most probably right, and it was benign assurance, not vain arrogance, that had prompted the reaction.

She smoothed a hand down a bare forearm until her fingers engaged with the gold-banded wristwatch. The only other jewellery she had on were her rings, and a pair of pearl and gold ear-clips. She was wearing a half-sleeved, white linen suit with a low-cut, collarless neckline. The skirt ended just below her crossed knees – a length that was as elegant and flattering as it was purportedly modest, though making the best of a very good feature. Her entry in *People of Today* had included her age, which the doctor thought brave for a woman of 44 who could have passed for five years less. Her tapered fingers, and the well-turned ankles, indeed the whole of her well nurtured figure and delicate bearing added much to her authority.

Altogether, it was not surprising that Edwin Howell, as good a judge of human physical and mental acuity as most other consultants in his field, had come, on short acquaintance, to regard this unusual woman with respect, as well as with that degree of detached but acute sexual interest judged acceptable in one of his calling – or acceptable at least in his own judgement. He speculated that the studied coldness, epitomised perhaps by the arrangement of the hair that swept back to a large, tight bun, might melt quite quickly when the constituents of the bun were showered loose.

He opened the red folder in front of him and picked up a glazed sheet that showed four black and white cranial images. Silently he studied the scans, then turned his attention to another, similar sheet, before observing, 'As the second scan proved, there's no, as it were, mechanical reason why your husband can't recover further. A lot further.' Putting the two sheets to one side he picked up a closely typed letter from the file and read it with heavy concentration. 'Yes, and what's pleasing is there's no sign of any further intracranial flow problems around the blocked areas,' he added. 'You understand me?'

'Yes. Except the London neurologists promised that months

ago, on the evidence of the first test,' the woman responded, somewhat dismissively.

'So they were right, weren't they?' he replied promptly with a grin. Her emphasis on neurologists in the plural had not escaped him. He was well aware that Mrs Ingram had already tested a good many of the reputedly best men in his field in an effort to improve her husband's situation, and, in her opinion, with singular lack of success.

'But his recovery has still only been marginal, doctor.'

Howell looked up again from the letter. 'That's because you see the patient every day, Mrs Ingram,' he corrected with certainty. 'In that circumstance it's hard to gauge progress. I gather he wasn't walking with sticks four months ago, but he is now.'

She hesitated, before offering grudgingly. 'That's true, I suppose. He graduated from the wheelchair to a walking frame in January. He's managed with just the sticks only recently.'

The doctor gave a confirming nod. 'And with more than passable confidence, as I saw this morning. So he's making excellent improvement with his mobility.'

'Not to my satisfaction nor his own, doctor. And in any case, we're more concerned about his communication problems. The real frustration is with speech.'

Howell wondered which of the two people was the more frustrated. The patient, whom he had questioned and examined at length earlier, had been a touch more articulate when his wife hadn't been present, though articulate in this case hardly described the half syllables and grunts that passed for speech most of the time. Ingram had also seemed more philosophical in his attitude to the situation than his wife. But that was part due to the drugs he was taking. Possibly the wife had been coping for too long. Over time, the carer sometimes became more anxious than the patient – but not this carer. The patient was probably more nervous when they were both in the presence of others for fear that he was letting her down. No, Angela Ingram was certainly not anxious: impatient fitted her attitude more aptly.

'Lend him to us for six weeks, eight at the most,' said the doctor lightly, 'and I absolutely promise you a measurable improvement in mobility and speech. He's still relatively young.' He glanced down again questioningly at the report.

'He's forty-nine. No age, I agree,' the woman supplied.

'Precisely. I was going to say, he's younger than most stroke patients who come to us, and believe me, the younger the better in terms of recovery. Depending, of course,' he added quickly, 'on the degree of brain damage and where it happened. In your husband's case, the damage was substantial, but not in the area where his speech need be affected permanently. Of course, too few people appreciate that the brain injury during a stroke is irreversible. That damage can't be by-passed as it can after a heart attack.'

'I understand it well enough, doctor.'

'Of course you do,' he responded, believing her in a way he wouldn't have done with most lay people who couldn't distinguish between the two scourges. 'In any case, the way Denis's circulation has responded with medication since the stroke is more than satisfactory.' Which was precisely why he had promised a big improvement with such assurance. The signs were there to show that it might well be a matter of releasing the patient from whatever inhibitions had prevented him from achieving better progress already. His own clinical methods, not nearly enough respected by his contemporaries in the profession, were geared to removing such blocks. And if his success rate was not consistently

21

impressive, it was sufficiently so for his 'cured' patients to stand witness to his ability.

'And I can make overnight visits here at short notice, doctor?'

'At virtually no notice, Mrs Ingram. Feel free, though we make a charge for meals,' he added with an impish grin before continuing. 'Seriously, visits are very much encouraged, and, dare I say, of mutual benefit. As you saw, he's in a large twin-bedded sitting room on the ground floor, with a terrace onto the garden. The position will be a boon now the spring weather is on us. If a double bed is preferred, that's easily arranged.' He paused before adding, 'Simply, I er...I wouldn't advise your coming for more than one night during this first week.'

'If you're concerned that too much sex would be – '

'Oh, no, I didn't mean that. There's no problem there at all,' Howell broke in firmly, encouraged and surprised by her frankness. 'I meant only that the therapeutic regimen can be very tiring at the start.'

'And I was about to say,' she continued, equally firmly, 'that he's been virtually impotent since the stroke.'

The doctor nodded and clasped both hands together tightly. 'That's not uncommon, Mrs Ingram, even in patients whose general recovery is more advanced than your husband's.'

'So I've been told.' Except the woman's tone suggested that with more telling she was still some way short of believing.

'Well, it certainly needn't indicate anything permanent. The cause can be physical or psychological, or a mixture of the two. In time, you'll no doubt find the problem cures itself, after...after a great deal of loving care.'

'I'm not concerned on my own account, doctor.' The response was wooden.

'I understand, Mrs Ingram.' He hoped, even so, that she was still deeply concerned on her husband's account, if the matter was critical for him, as Howell already had reason to believe it might be. 'A stroke tends to destroy self confidence,' he continued, 'and that can show itself in any number of ways. The syndrome we're talking about is quite common, but needn't be enduring, particularly where a wife is prepared to play...to play an over-active part, as it were.'

He decided to interpret the lady's perceptible stiffening as implying that, for her, his comment had amounted to nothing so much as a lewd suggestion.

'It matters far less than other... considerations,' she answered.

'But perhaps not to your husband.'

'You've discussed this with him?'

'I touched on it peripherally, yes. His reaction, so far as he can presently put over a clear reaction, was ambivalent. I'd intended to pursue the point when he and I are... are better acquainted.'

'When you are, I think you'll find sexual activity has a low priority in his scheme of things. That's always been the case. If he's changed his attitude on that – '

'Which he may well have done, Mrs Ingram, in the sense that impotence can be a vivid and ignominious sign of a man's destroyed dignity.'

'If that's so with Denis, I'll do what I can to help, doctor.' Except the offer sounded less than wholehearted. 'If you feel strongly that he needs to reassert his manhood in that way, wouldn't one of these new drugs help?'

'In view of the ambulatory, not to say precarious, state of his arteries, I'd prefer a less... mechanical and, in his case, potentially hazardous answer to the problem, Mrs Ingram, but we'll see.' He construed that she had considered exactly how active an over-active wife's part need be, and had decided not to play it. 'Good,' he offered in a businesslike way, while inwardly beginning to question her instinctive sense of charity – no matter how incongruous it might be to suggest that Angela Ingram was lacking in charity.

The subject of these speculations glanced at the time, then crossed, and recrossed her admirable legs. 'My visits will be mostly at weekends,' she said, returning to the earlier point. 'While Denis is here, I can stay at the London flat for four or five days each week. It'll help me to reduce the backlog of work. I'll be going there tonight.'

'And you'll drive here to Llandaff at the end of each week?'

'Yes. Although I'll need to spend some time each trip at our Chepstow house.' She nodded her satisfaction. 'So if Denis makes the progress you predict, he can stay here as long as it takes.'

'Admirable, Mrs Ingram. But I honestly don't think it need be for more than the period I've suggested. By then I believe he'll be wonderfully improved.'

'That's very heartening, doctor. I do hope you're right.' She leaned over to pick up her handbag from the floor, as if she was preparing to go, but then looked up again, leaving the bag where it was. 'There's one other thing I wanted to mention,' she said, her movements implying even so that she had only just made the decision to do that. 'It'll please me and our undergraduate son Gerald a great deal if we can get Denis to an important event in July. It's a ceremony...in Buckingham Palace.' She swallowed before the next words. 'Very confidentially, he's to be knighted then by the Queen.'

Howell raised both arms in spontaneous delight, a sentiment equally reflected in his features. 'My warmest congratulations. An honour richly deserved, as everyone will agree, and the best thing that could happen to him. My word, what a terrific morale builder.' He leaned forward. 'Of course I'll respect the confidence. I assume it'll all be announced in...'

'In the Queen's Birthday Honours List in June,' she put in. 'I decided to tell you now because Denis is daunted at the prospect. You'd think it would have buoyed him up no end. On the contrary, it just fills him with dread.'

'At becoming Sir Denis Ingram, you mean?' He doubted that the new Lady Ingram would have any related misgivings.

'No. Of going to the Palace.'

'I see. Well, that's a predictable reaction, of course, in the circumstances.'

'We're not quite certain yet of the protocol, doctor. I imagine it's possible to shift the date, if necessary. I mean for him to attend a later investiture. Or to get the honour by – '

'B...bu...by...po...' a faltering, weak voice intruded on the conversation.

'By post you mean, darling?' Mrs Ingram had turned toward her husband who was propped in the now open doorway of the room. 'Yes, we've discussed that, but I meant by having the ceremony delayed until you're quite ready.'

'Your hearing is pretty acute, my friend,' said Howell with a loud guffaw. He rose imperiously and strode across the room to his new patient's side. 'But I shall strongly oppose postponement, Denis, or anything as defeatist as what you've just suggested. July it shall be, and a marvellous focus for everybody's effort, including yours. We'll have you ready and eager for the event long before then. Why don't you sit yourself down over there.' The speaker next turned to the breathless, white-jacketed and slightly built young man who had just appeared behind Denis Ingram. 'Thank you, Kevin. Mr Ingram will be staying here.'

'Right, doctor. Sorry, I had to go back for Mr Ingram's

book. We've had a good walk round. Er...Matron was arranging to see him in ten minutes. Shall I tell her he'll be delayed?'

'No, I'll look after that.'

'Very good, doctor.' The curly headed, thirty-two-year-old nursing auxiliary, Kevin Rees, handed a paperback to Howell, then gave a short bow to the lady. 'Good afternoon then, ma'am. Privilege to have met you,' he said. 'We'll look after Mr Ingram, don't you worry.' With that, he turned about smartly and left the room, closing the door behind him.

'Denis, I couldn't say so after Kevin had appeared, but warmest congratulations on your pending knighthood,' said Howell. 'Couldn't have happened to a better man... mmm, or a more deserving one.' He beamed warmly at the patient.

Ingram had already moved across to a chair beside his wife in front of Howell's desk. His lopsided but determined progress had been achieved through the not exactly rhythmic wielding of two walking sticks, but he certainly appeared to be in charge of his own movements. His right side was less easy than the other in its response. That he was a shrivelled version of the figure he must have cut before his illness was indicated by the way his clothes hung too loosely about him. The crinkled flesh on the face, neck and hands bore similar witness. He seemed to be several inches shorter than his wife when she stood to help him into the chair, except the perceived difference was accounted for entirely by his stoop. Although his eyes were alert, the lid of the right one drooped a fraction.

'Anj...' With his head pressing forward, Ingram had opened his mouth three times, as though he was attempting to unlock his jaw before he eventually succeeded in uttering the first syllable of his wife's name. The effort involved with each attempt had shown in his eyes to be as exasperating as it was evidently uncomfortable. In the end he gave up trying to speak, only the expression on his face was now urgently questioning.

'Yes, I felt it right to tell Dr Howell the good news, Denis,' Angela Ingram responded in a jolly-up, nanny sort of tone. 'We need his input on whether you should go to the Palace.'

'And I'm certain you should,' said the doctor.

Ingram shook his head, before taking a long breath. 'No...imp...imp...' was the best he could manage on the second try.

'Not important?' his wife supplied the words with the sureness of a practised carer. 'But I think it is important, darling. Certainly for me, and for Gerald. And don't forget the people in the company and the charity. They'll all be so proud of you.'

Ingram surrendered with an awkward smile as he looked across at Howell.

'S...so...'

'So no option, darling,' Mrs Ingram had guessed at the words and the sentiment he was seeking. The doctor judged her attitude to be one of humouring tolerance.

In fact the look of disappointment in Ingram's eyes had suggested that he wished she had kept quiet. Howell had noted that too. 'Well, I know you want to be on your way, Mrs Ingram,' he said, meaning that he judged it was high time some meaningful therapy was underway, particularly as he now knew he was to be working against the clock.

Chapter Two

It was six weeks later, at 8.15 a.m. on the third Sunday in May. Detective Chief Inspector Merlin Parry of the South Wales Police was accelerating his venerable soft-topped Porsche up the ramp from the communal garage under his rented flat in Cardiff's central Westgate Street. Detective Sergeant Gomer Lloyd, sitting beside him, was straining to maintain a conversation on a mobile telephone. He blinked when they emerged into the sunlight.

If these permanent members of the South Wales Major Crime Support Unit were feeling put upon for having to work on the expectedly first dry weekend since mid-April, neither was showing it. Lloyd, in any case, put no more trust in weather forecasts than he did in railway timetables, racing tips or politicians. So a day forecast to be sunny and cloudless that produced unseasonable and persistent hail storms from dawn onwards only served to confirm his prejudices. Parry, for his part, had just taken a week's holiday in Spain and was only too pleased to have missed the rain that had brought out more of the City's corporate, patriotic daffodils in his absence.

Both men had worked late the day before, and the sergeant had spent the previous two hours with a team interviewing witnesses in a case of suspected arson at a Cardiff Bay hotel. He had joined Parry from there, after both had been assigned to a case of a suspicious death that had just been reported.

After they had crossed the Taff River Bridge, beyond the Castle walls, the chief inspector turned the car northwards into the almost deserted Cathedral Road. The tenants of the affluent looking stone-built Victorian villas at the start of the wide thoroughfare were doing nothing to spoil the Sabbath stillness. The establishments that had not become small hotels or guest houses, busy in the week but not at weekends, had long since been converted into professional chambers or consulting rooms. Members of the callings who toiled here from Monday to Friday – and the most avaricious of them on Saturday mornings as well – lived in less ponderous residences in the City's leafy or seabound outer reaches.

Parry's destination was the Howell Clinic, two miles distant, near Llandaff's Anglican cathedral. He had opened the car roof before they had set off. Lloyd, who had been making notes with one hand, while holding the mobile in the other, had only a little finger to prevent the surviving front lock of his hair, which needed cutting, from blowing into his eyes and up his nose, though his well nurtured moustache provided some protection against the last hazard.

'Well, it's a pretty respected outfit, boss,' offered the overweight, avuncular sergeant, switching off the phone. With difficulty, he began pushing it under his seatbelt, and into the side pocket of his tweed, herringbone jacket. Most of what he was wearing was predictably more than a touch too heavy for the expected scorcher of a day.

'Pricey private clinic, is it,' Parry commented rather than questioned.

'Like you thought, yes.' Notebook now in hand, Lloyd squinted briefly at the sun to their right. He grudgingly calculated there wouldn't be time for him to grow a melanoma on his forehead before they reached Llandaff. He had left his cap in his own car at Parry's place. Probably it would have blown off anyway. 'Only they do take National Health patients by arrangement,' he added.

'With the NHS footing the bill?'

'I expect so. Elan didn't say.' The Elan referred to was a well informed senior nursing sister at the University Hospital, who had lived next door to the Lloyds in Fairwater, a western inner suburb, before their recent move further out of the city. It was Fairwater Police Station that housed the eastern division of the Major Crime Support Unit. The sergeant had called Elan after Parry had asked about the status of the Howell Clinic. 'It's devoted to reha-bilitation. For people who've had strokes, or other kinds of brain disorders. Very nasty things, strokes.' Lloyd paused to press a peppermint into his mouth, the brief silence serv-ing to invest his last commonplace observation with the greater seriousness he'd intended. 'Seems the Howell Clinic gets patients from all over the country, and abroad,' he continued. 'Dr Howell's a maverick. Well, he can afford to be. His wife's supposed to be loaded. She's a doctor as well. They own the place. I gather he fell out with the neu-rological establishment years ago. Never got a senior con-sultancy.'

'So he established one of his own,' Parry commented.

'Seems like it, yes. Has his own methods. Unconventional but effective. Well, that's what Elan's been told. His name's Edwin Howell. Dr Edwin Howell.'

Parry gave a sniff. 'Strange neither of us knew anything about the place.'

'Except where it is, boss. The only time I've come across it was when I parked my car by the gate, against regulations, as I remember. Gracie and I were late for a memorial service in the cathedral. That was a few years back. From outside you'd think it was just another nursing home, with better security than most.'

Parry nodded. 'Expect they have physiotherapists,' he offered ruminatively.

'Sure to,' Lloyd agreed, and went on, 'Perdita would know the clinic, would she?'

'Might do, yes, but she didn't do that much private work in the Cardiff area when she was a physio.'

The thirty-nine-year-old widowed chief inspector was engaged to marry Perdita Jones later in the year. She had gone back to studying medicine, which she had earlier abandoned, to qualify instead as a physiotherapist. At the time the change had been prompted by her pending first marriage – which had recently ended in divorce. Perdita was sitting her final examinations at St Mark's, the London teaching hospital, in June. She had also been expecting a baby in the autumn, except she'd miscarried at the beginning of May, which was why she and Parry had taken an unscheduled holiday so close to her finals.

'Well, that was a smooth drive. Sunday, of course,' said Lloyd, two minutes later, as Parry waited for a racing cyclist to pass the other way before turning the car right into the short, shop-lined Llandaff High Street.

'Mm,' the other man responded, his mind on something else. 'Tell me, Kevin Rees, the victim, he's described as an auxiliary. That's a trainee nurse, is it?'

'More a nursing assistant, boss. A fetcher and carrier, like. We don't know yet what this one's duties were. But he was single, and lived on the premises.'

'And the sharp metal object stuck in his back?'

'Was some kind of garden hand tool.'

Parry nodded. 'What time was he found?'

'7.32 this morning. On the steps of a cricket pavilion in the grounds,' the sergeant added for good measure, scowling at his notes. His own briefing on the telephone had to do for both of them. Parry, on stand-by duty, had been called in only after a fellow DCI had been prevented from leaving another case.

'Is cricket one of Dr Edwin Howell's maverick rehabilitation methods, I wonder?' Parry mused as they moved past the parked cars on the upward sloping street, following the route to the cathedral.

'No, I think the pavilion is a leftover from a previous use of the site, boss. But Elan did mention the treatment puts a lot of emphasis on physical exercise. Good thing too, I expect.' The Lloyds had a rarely used exercise bike in their bathroom as witness to the sergeant's belief in the principle of physical fitness. It was the same principle that had moved him to give up smoking five years before this – which was when he had become heavily addicted to peppermints. 'The uniformed constable who answered the 999 said it's a wooden pavilion, standing close to the main building,' he continued, looking up as the car changed direction.

They had now reached the near end of the cathedral close. Unusually, this was set high above the cathedral itself, so that only the tops of the two western towers of the great, low lying edifice were at first visible. Here Parry pointed the vehicle onto a straight and steeply plunging lane bounded by four foot stone walls on both sides.

The lane ran down the defile and widened in front of the west front of the magnificent, largely 13th Century, cathedral – on the same site where the original 7th Century shrine had stood, under the high ground that had sheltered it from the view of marauding, pillaging Norsemen in the Bristol Channel.

'Police surgeon is probably ahead of us, boss,' Lloyd offered, and added, 'DS Mary Norris has been the officer in charge since 8.05.'

'Well, let's hope she's got the case buttoned by now.' Parry grinned as the route, descending again, but not so steeply, narrowed before it carried them on past the back of a white-painted cathedral outbuilding. A few yards beyond this the forward landscape changed abruptly. With the wooded hillside now behind them, in front was a broad and verdant plateau. The cement surface of the lane ended with a turning area abreast of the entrance to a wide, imposing driveway on the left. The lane itself continued straight onwards, but was here reduced to a narrow footpath which both policemen knew would shortly reach the winding River Taff and its adjoining pathway, both features now masked by a line of trees.

The Howell Clinic's black-painted nameboard with gold lettering, which the sergeant had mentioned earlier, stood to one side of the driveway, and a pair of electrically operated wrought iron gates. In addition, the grounds were protected by a five foot high, green wire-mesh fence.

The young, uniformed policeman on duty at the gate recognised the car and saluted Parry. 'Follow the drive round the house at the top, sir, and the front door is on the right. DS Norris has arranged for police parking just after that,' he explained. 'Oh, and the scene of the crime is on the far side of the building, sir. You'll just see the pavilion at the top of the lawn on the right as you get a bit nearer.'

'The Scenes of Crime team has arrived?' Parry questioned.

'Yes, sir. Five minutes ago. DS Wilcox in charge.'

'Thank you. It's PC Hopkins isn't it?'

'That's right, sir.' The unexpected recognition brought another, and involuntary, salute.

Parry crunched the car forward on the loose-gravel surface toward the main redbrick building which turned out to be smaller than he had expected. A mish-mash of architectural styles, it was topped at roof level by a Georgian, light-weight stone cornice, punctuated in the centre, on the visible eastern aspect, by a much more substantial, unsupported pediment.

Curiously, these and other disparate features seemed to meld harmoniously enough with the churchy, Gothic-arched windows on all three storeys. The whole stood at the far end of the hundred yard drive which was skirted on the left by a line of budding Spanish oaks and on the other side by tallish shrubs. The shrub cover allowed for only fleeting glimpses of an impressively large lawn running up to the terraced frontage. Where the miniature oaks ended, the route curved around the narrower south side of the building, passing a single-storey, twin-gabled cottage on the left, before reaching the main entrance to the clinic in the western elevation.

The centered, double front door had white, fluted Doric pilasters and was set above two wide, shallow steps, probably intended, in the less socially responsible time of their fashioning, to add dignity. This had later been diminished by a cement ramp placed over part of the steps to allow for wheelchair access.

At this point the drive expanded into an impressive semi-circle fanning from the door, and edged by empty flowerbeds evidently prepared for new plantings.

Yellow blooming bushes at the rear of the beds fronted two elderly chestnut trees which seemed to mark the western end of the clinic grounds. There were already more than a dozen vehicles parked in the crescent. Half of these were glistening with dew, indicating that they had probably been in position all night. Another, even younger, uniformed policeman, a cadet, was finishing the task of writing down the registration numbers of the overnight stayers. He didn't recognise the approaching Porsche or its occupants, but he saluted them anyway, to be on the safe side.

The chief inspector drew up close to the farther end of the building, beyond a Ford Transit van and a twenty-four-seater bus, both parked longways and painted in police livery. He and Lloyd pulled plastic covers over their shoes before getting out, then followed the drive to the next corner of the building, ducking under the yellow and black police tapes that were cordoning off the area.

'Morning, sir.' Dark haired, petite, twenty-five-year-old DS Mary Norris, looked less than her usual crisp and efficient self because, perforce, she was dressed in a voluminous white SOCO outfit. As always this regalia was too large for her, although the hood, before she self consciously drew it back, had been enhancing her over-youthful, elfin appearance. The stern expression on her face was the one she adopted on these occasions to emphasise her senior function as well as her actual rank.

'Morning, Mary,' Parry greeted her affably. 'I understand the body was found on the steps of a cricket pavilion.'

'Yes, sir. The pavilion's further along this way.'

'We saw it, yes, coming up the drive,' offered Lloyd.

'Actually, the body was just below the steps on this side,' the woman sergeant completed in the important cause of strict accuracy. She led the way for the two newcomers, passing a service entrance, close to which the contents of four large, wheeled refuse bins were claiming the attention of more white-clad police personnel.

Just beyond the bins on the left was a substantial timber tool and garden machine shed with entrances at both ends. A tall, weather-beaten man, in shirtsleeves and soiled grey trousers, and seemingly in his late twenties, was standing beside the open door to the tool section, with the resigned demeanor of someone who had been asked to do just that. More uneasily than just impatiently, he was eyeing the two members of the SOCO team who could be seen engaged inside

A long rectangular greenhouse came next. It was currently

wholly given over to propagation – evidenced by the stacked trays of young potted plants visible from the outside. It lay just forward of the north-east corner of the clinic, and several yards to the left of it, with its longer sides set to catch most of a good day's sunshine.

'Dr Maltravers got here the same time as I did, sir. He's examining the body. We're keeping to the path for now.' DS Norris had offered the coded admonition to deter the newcomers from straying onto the edge of the wide lawn which was bounded by a well rolled grit-and-sand pathway around three sides of its perimeter. The path was punctuated by benches placed in what would be, in a few weeks, morning shade from the leaves of some elderly chestnut and copper beech trees on the left, and in the afternoon by the Spanish oaks on the right. There were also flowerbeds, again empty but ready for replanting, behind the path at numerous points.

More police were moving in lines of four or five along the grass next to the path and across the wide terrace in front of the building, searching for putative bits of evidence.

It was now that the apparently fit but still breathless Detective Sergeant Glen Wilcox, an officer of few words, joined Parry's group. 'No doors or windows forced anywhere, sir. No disturbances at the area fences either,' he began, without any preliminary greeting. He too had pushed back the hood of his SOCO overalls, exposing a head of short cropped red hair and a sweating forehead. 'Main gate electronic locks are intact,' he continued. 'If it was a burglar with heavy transport he must have known the combination. The loose gravel on the drive is thirty milles deep, but with no recent heavy indentations on it, or wide ones either. We checked that on foot before we brought in the two personnel transporters.'

'So they didn't bring a pantechnicon this time, Glen.' Parry gave a sour grin as he spoke. Both men had been investigating the violent case of an as yet unsolved burglary the week before where a van load of fine pictures and antique furniture had been removed from a country house in broad daylight, and the owner and his wife badly battered. 'You're doing the grass now ?' he added.

Wilcox had matched the initial grimace. 'That's right, sir. We did from the front door to here first, including a first run-through of the pavilion. The broken piece of handrail found near the body has been done for dabs and bagged already. Could be one of the weapons used. Nothing else important-looking so far though. We're starting on the upper part of the lawn and the stone terrace now. The detailed search of the pavilion and area can go ahead as soon as the doctor's finished. '

'Good. Fast work, Glen. Carry on then,' Parry replied with a smile. Wilcox disappeared with the same alacrity that had attended his arrival.

Parry and his two companions were now covering the ten paces that would bring them to the pavilion which was set forward of the greenhouse, and angled to face the opposite, distant corner of the lawn. It was a white-painted, clapboard construction in fair condition, despite its probable age. Parry, still a handy spin bowler and a player once trialed for the Glamorgan Juniors, noted its appearance with approval. It might, he thought, have been the prototype – or at least a worthy survivor – of those cricket pavilions that had graced pitches from the middle of the 19th Century wherever in Britain or the British Empire the game had been played. It was a seemly contrast to the prefabricated, flat-roofed and often garishly painted modern versions of the species. This building had grace and style, with a verandah and steps to it at either side – even allowing for three feet of missing handrail at the near end. It also sported a high-pitched, green slate roof, gabled at the sides, and foreshortened at the front to make room for a balustraded balcony. Set under a cupola, on the roof ridge, was a working clock which, in its heyday, had overseen a sport whose leisured pace was a monument to time's lack of essence – a game whose invention might well have been contrived, by the puritanical but not overtly religious English, to provide a truly comprehensible manifestation of eternity. Happy days, Parry thought.

'Morning, Merlin,' puffed the ageing, bluff Dr George Maltravers from a kneeling position. Beside him was a hard-sided black leather case, standing upright with its divided, hinged front open to reveal a series of pull-out compartments that contained a variety of medical accoutrements. It reminded Parry of a doll's house a girl cousin had inherited in their youth which had operated on a similar principle but with less complicated contents.

The chief inspector had come upon the police surgeon beyond a screen of orange coloured plastic sheeting. The body of a man lay chest downwards, face revealed, four feet from the three steps that led up to the pavilion. The blue checked shirt the deceased had been wearing was badly blood-stained in the section below the left shoulder blade.

'So, anyone for cricket?' the doctor added grimly, but without looking up again.

'Not Mr Kevin Rees, that's for sure,' Parry replied, studying the body as he settled on his haunches beside Maltravers.

'No, nor anyone else here, as it happens, Merlin.' The speaker offered, while continuing to busy himself with what he was doing. 'Of course, this was all cricket fields forty years ago,' he went on, giving a wave of a happily still spotless steel probe vaguely to illustrate the extent of the territory involved. 'That was when this section was carved off for putting up a multi-use diocesan building. Sort of residential conference centre, I believe. It eventually proved too small for the job, and possibly liable to flooding. Should have known it'd be too small in the first place, of course.'

He shook his head while labeling a small specimen bottle before placing it within the confines of the case. 'It was about eight years ago when Edwin Howell and his wife got the place for a song to use as a clinic,' he continued. 'On a medium lease. Extra grassed acres thrown in, of course, because the local planning authority wouldn't allow any more building here, and there was the cost of care and maintenance to think of. Howell was lucky to get it, really.'

'You know him, do you?' Parry asked.

The doctor seemed to consider the question, as he measured the small graze on the dead man's left cheek. 'Mm, yes,' he responded eventually. 'Not all that well, but for quite some time. He came from near here originally. I think the Church in Wales took that into account when they accepted his bid for the lease.'

'They owned the place?'

'Yes, and the freehold still, I expect. They liked the idea of leasing it to an enterprise whose objects were compatible with Christian purposes. Unlike the surprising number of commercial outfits who put in for it.' He chuckled. 'I understood they were all involved in "financial services" which the then Archbishop defined as usury by another name.'

'And the pavilion dates from the cricket field time,' said Parry.

'Yes. I remember it well from my college days. Had tea in it many times. It used to stand on its own then. Looks a bit incongruous now, next to the main building. Glad it wasn't pulled down. Wouldn't have been easy to shift, of course, and it never will be now I hope, but bits of it are falling away.'

'Like that piece of handrail?' Parry indicated the splintered piece of white-painted wood sealed in a transparent evidence bag behind the doctor.

Maltravers considered the item for a moment. 'Maybe. We've kept that here for you to see, Merlin. It was lying more or less where it is now. Could have been torn off by our murderer, or the victim perhaps. They've dusted it for fingerprints already. That Sergeant Wilcox keeps his workers moving, doesn't he?' He glanced about him, as a way of easing his stiffened neck, while needing to lift his hand to shade off the sun. 'Pavilion was put up facing south-east. That used to keep the morning and afternoon sun in the scorers' eyes, I remember. Well, you can't think of everything, of course.'

The doctor now fully straightened his back, and his more serious expression presaged that he was at last ready to turn to the business on hand. 'So, there's your almost certain cause of death, Merlin.' He pointed to a small implement with a shaped, black plastic handle and a cylindrical, five inch, thin aluminium blade that tapered nearly to a point at the end. This was also encased in a sealed and labelled bag lying on a plastic sheet next to the body.

'And he was stabbed in the back with that?' Parry said, but without querying the doctor's reservation about the implement being the *almost* certain cause of death.

Maltravers was famous for his professional caution, insisting that he was a humble police surgeon not a Home Office Pathologist. He was given to cautioning that intended victims had been known to die of shock a second before being garroted – or being trampled on by stampeding elephants. The law required allowance to be made for such rare possibilities, a knife in the back of a dead body notwithstanding.

'The blade must just have missed the spinal column, but it certainly pierced the heart.' The doctor levered himself onto his feet. 'If he'd been wearing more clothes, a jacket and sweater say, instead of just a shirt, the penetration mightn't have been so deep. He bled a bit, even though the blade stayed in him.'

'So he survived a while, did he? For how long, doctor?'

Maltravers shrugged. 'Not long. A few seconds probably. Difficult to tell. As you can see, he's got a graze on his forehead. There's also bruising behind the left knee. So he could have been in an accident recently or...'

'In a fight?' the chief inspector questioned.

'Well, the injuries were recent. The graze could have been caused by falling down those steps before he was stabbed.'

Parry's nose wrinkled. 'But if he'd been coming from the pavilion he was pointing the wrong way when he copped it.'

'Except if he'd slipped when he broke off that handrail, he was still most likely to have been leaving than arriving,' the doctor offered, before adding, 'Well, that's a puzzle for you lot, especially if his dabs are on that bit of wood. Anyway, it wasn't assault and robbery. There was nine hundred quid in his trouser pocket. Wilcox and I counted it together. He's bagged that too. His evidence lady's taken charge of it.'

'A thief might have been disturbed, of course,' said Parry. 'In any case though, you reckon the stabbing was the cause of death?'

'It's what I'd expect the autopsy to show, Merlin, yes,' came the careful reply.

Parry nodded. 'That tool's called a dibber, isn't it? For making holes for planting.'

'That's right, boss,' put in Lloyd who had been standing behind him with Mary Norris, both of them making notes. 'Except the commonest sort is a solid wooden shaft with a pointed end, not a rounded blade. That's for general planting. This one's made for putting small bulbs in soft ground at shallow depth. Crocuses and miniature daffs. When you pull it from the ground, a plug of earth comes up with it.'

'Which you push back when you've dropped the bulb in the hole,' the doctor completed with a nod at the sergeant – one knowing gardener to another, although the breeding of exotic pigs was Maltravers's serious hobby.

'So the blood flowed back up to the handle, because the blade made a conduit,' put in Mary Norris, who was no gardener but a good policewoman.

'No more than it would have done from an ordinary knife wound,' the doctor corrected. 'Very little tissue came with it when I pulled it out. Incidentally, the thrust of the blow was downward. Angle of about forty degrees.'

'Time of death, doctor?' Parry enquired, as always in these cases, with more hope than certainty of getting a really useful answer.

Maltravers made a pained expression. 'Before midnight, I'd say, and not within the last few hours. There was no frost last night, and although he was in the comparative shelter of the pavilion, I mean from what there was of the prevailing wind, he was stone cold when I got to him.'

'Who found the body, Mary?' Parry asked.

'Mr Phil Collit, sir. He's the gardener. We passed him outside the toolshed. He got here at 7.30, his usual time on weekdays.'

'Although it's Sunday?'

'It was a question of ventilating the greenhouse, sir. He didn't intend doing a day's work. He says he was here at 10.45 last night.'

'Again to ventilate the greenhouse?'

'Yes, sir. Well, to check the thermostat he says.'

'Did he see the victim when he was here?'

'He says he didn't, sir. Except they were together from about 9.35 to 10.20 last evening at the Eight Bells, the pub in the High Street.'

'But they didn't come back here together afterwards, Mary?'

'No, sir. They'd had a disagreement which went on outside the pub after they left it.'

All three men looked at the woman sergeant in surprise.

'Mr Collit volunteered they'd had an argument?' Parry demanded.

'Not exactly, sir. But it came out when I questioned him. That was just before you arrived. I thought you'd want to see him. He's been asked to wait,' the speaker completed in a gently confident voice.

Lloyd smiled at the diminutive detective. It seems she might have had the case sorted after all.

Chapter Three

'So you and Kevin Rees had a regular syndicate going on the National Lottery, sir?' Lloyd asked. He and Parry were questioning Phil Collit. The three men were standing just inside the greenhouse whose floor, long wooden tables and slatted shelves were packed with plants, some of them showing their first seasonal blooms.

'We've been doing the Saturday lottery, not the Wednesday. I couldn't afford both.' The reply had been in some way grudging, as if the speaker had resented having to answer questions at all, and had done so this time only to make his last point.

Parry nodded. 'But you both put ten pounds in every Saturday, Mr Collit?'

'Definitely, yes. Every Saturday since before Christmas.' The claim came with an aggressive insistence. 'We've used the same numbers too. Always.'

The twenty-eight-year-old gardener was tall and burly. He wore his long, jet black hair tied back in a short ponytail. His shirt sleeves were rolled up, his muscular arms folded in front of him as he half-perched on the edge of the table behind him. There were silver rings in the lobes of both his ears, and a silver necklet glinted below the open shirt. His face was weather-beaten, and the pronounced nose matched the deep hollows of his dark and presently wary eyes. His thick lower lip opened very little when he spoke, the low-pitched words emerging sometimes with emphasis, but in a tone that Lloyd, for one, was finding deeply monotonous.

'And Kevin always bought the tickets?'

'Yes. At the post office. It was...it was easier for him.' The gaze darted from the chief inspector to the sergeant, and back again.

'Just easier, sir. No other reason?' Lloyd put in, noting the hesitation.

The big man ran an open palm across the lower part of his face, in the process exhibiting a raw knuckle. 'It's partly because of my wife. Megan.' It was another slow, diffident response. 'She doesn't hold with it. The lottery.'

'Because it's gambling,' the sergeant observed with an understanding grin.

'No, not that,' Collit offered, then paused before he added. 'She thinks the chances of winning are too small. We used to buy Premium Bonds. Never won once though. We've had three numbers up twice with the lottery. Not much, but it's something. We're saving for a baby, see?' The last claim had been his first nearly enthusiastic utterance. For a moment, even, it looked as is if he was intending to enlarge on the point, but had then thought better of it.

'So the tickets were always in Kevin Rees's possession, sir?'

'That's right. I trusted him.' Lloyd noted the earnest emphasis in the last words.

'But you say it was the ownership of yesterday's tickets that caused the argument in the pub last night?'

'Yes. Because he was cheating me. I don't want to speak ill of the dead, but...well, there was no other way of explaining it.' The speaker shook his head, sighed, then continued in a voice that was now showing mounting emotion. 'Kevin was a good mate. Or supposed to be. Yesterday we'd had five numbers up. That meant we'd won two thousand quid. More probably. I expected him to be over the moon, which he was. But only for himself.'

'How exactly did he cheat you, then?' As he spoke, Lloyd was searching in his jacket pocket for peppermints.

'Like I told the woman officer, he said all the winnings were his. Because I hadn't paid him for the previous Saturday he thought I'd packed it in. He'd put twenty pounds in yesterday, he said, like always, but just for himself. I couldn't accept that.'

'Which part of it, sir? His claiming you'd packed it in, or the twenty pounds being just for him?'

'Both. It was...' He paused to swallow. 'Well, there's no getting round it, it was bloody lies.'

'But you still hadn't paid up for the previous Saturday, Mr Collit?' Parry spoke over his shoulder. He'd moved further into the greenhouse, and was absently fingering the leaves of a well-formed geranium plant.

The gardener hesitated before answering. 'Well...no. Not at that point. But it was crazy to say that proved I'd packed it in. If I was going to do that, I'd have told him straight.' He let out a breath in exasperation. 'Look, Kevin and I always met to settle up in the Eight Bells on Saturday nights. Over a pint. Around half-nine. Only the previous Saturday Megan and I'd been in Treorchy, staying overnight with her parents.'

'So you couldn't settle up then, sir. But you didn't do it later, either? In the week, like?' As he spoke, Lloyd had offered Collit a peppermint which the other man refused with a shake of his head before answering. 'I had the money for him last night. Twenty quid. For the two weeks. OK, I'd meant to give him the ten I owed him earlier, but I forgot.'

'And Mr Rees hadn't reminded you, Mr Collit? I mean, you must see him often enough in the week.' Parry had put the question from a pace further along the plant packed aisle.

'Not last week I didn't. I was too busy outside every day. Never saw Kevin once.'

'You sometimes work inside the clinic, do you?'

'Yes. In winter I do basic care and maintenance on the

building as well as the gardening. In late spring there isn't time for both, with all the planting to do. Anyway, what's this got to do with Kevin being killed? You don't think I did it? It was me found the body. That was a terrible shock. Still is.'

'Quite so, sir. A bad thing to happen, all right,' Lloyd put in sympathetically. 'Of course, by the time you met up with Mr Rees in the pub, the winning numbers in the Saturday lottery had been announced on TV. You'd seen them, had you?'

Collit gulped, staring hard at his questioner. 'What if I had? Yes, all right, I'd seen them, and I knew we were in the running for a prize.'

'A big one, sir?'

'Perhaps. But if you're going to say that's why I went to the pub you'd be bloody wrong. I went like I always go that time on a Saturday, to pay Kev the money I owed him for the tickets. Twenty pounds last night, not ten, because I owed him for the week before. And that's the truth. You can ask Megan, my wife.'

There was several seconds silence while all three men, Collit not least, recognised the naivety in the last invitation.

The chief inspector had moved back closer to the others. 'Mr Collit,' he said, 'on your own admission, you and Kevin Rees had an argument in the pub last night, which later led to...to a further altercation outside in the street.'

'Sure. I was angry. With justification.'

'Were there blows exchanged? Is that how you damaged your fist?'

In a reflex movement, Collit covered the reddened knuckle with his other hand. 'No, it wasn't. I did that putting my bike away. I pushed Kevin out the way, that's all. It wasn't a fight. And I didn't stab him later up here, either. Good God, would

I have told you we had a...a bust up if it had ended with me killing him? Don't be daft. The last I saw of him he was heading back to the clinic, and I was riding home in the opposite direction.' Collit shifted his weight off the tabletop and stood his full height, glowering at the policemen, arms hanging limp at his sides, fists clenched.

'That would have been at what time?'

'About twenty-past ten.

'And you didn't see him when you came back here. That was at 10.40, you told Sergeant Norris,' Parry pressed.

'No, I didn't see him then. Nor anybody else. We heard on the news there was going to be frost. I had to come back up to see to the heating in here. I'd promised Dr Janet I'd do that if there was a frost.'

'That's Dr Janet Howell is it? Dr Edwin Howell's wife?'

'That's right. She's in charge of the gardens like. Problem's been that the thermostat's been acting up. I couldn't risk losing any plants. There were some I'd put in the cold frames outside, as well. They needed covering.'

'Except there wasn't a frost,' said Lloyd.

'No. And if I'd known that I wouldn't have been here last night at all. But I'd promised the doctor, like I've said.'

'And this morning you arrived at 7.30 was it, sir?'

'Thereabouts, yes. Because there was no frost, I needed to lower the heating and get more air in here, didn't I?'

'After which, you went to the pavilion – '

'Only after I saw a body through the glass. Well, it looked like a body. I couldn't believe it.' The interruption had sounded heartfelt.

'You saw what he was stabbed with, sir?'

'Yes. A dibber.'

Lloyd screwed up his eyes as he checked a note. 'Actually you told Sergeant Norris it was your *bulb* dibber, sir.'

'Because that's what it looked like. I thought I recognised the handle.'

'And the dibber would normally have been locked in the tool shed, would it?'

'If it hadn't gone missing in the week.'

'You'd noticed it had gone, Mr Collit?' put in Parry.

'From its place in the rack, yes. It's not something that gets used much this time of year. But I noticed it was missing, Friday morning I think it was.'

'And you keep the tool shed locked?'

'At night, yes. Not in the daytime.'

'I see.' The chief inspector ran his tongue along his lower lip. 'So, how long had you known Kevin Rees?'

'Since he came to work here in October. We chummed up after a bit. He was Welsh, but not from around here. He didn't have any friends. Megan liked him. We've had him over for supper a few times. He made Megan laugh. Well, both of us.'

'If we accept your account of last night, can you think of any logical reason why he was trying to do you out of your winnings?'

Collit shrugged. 'I've been thinking about that. It has to have been something big. God's honour, he was lying to me. But to try swindling a close friend, he must have been desperate.'

'And stupid with it?' Parry queried. 'For instance, would you have lent him your winnings if he'd needed them badly enough?'

Collit seemed surprised by the question. 'Yes, I suppose. If he'd been that strapped.' Except there had been a noticeable hesitation before the start of the reply. 'Did he have any enemies you know of?'

'Don't think so, no.'

49

'Was he in debt, perhaps? Or did he have expensive girlfriends? Was he on drugs? Could he have been appropriating money, and needed to replace it in a hurry?'

'No, nothing like that.' The gardener had shaken his head after each suggestion. 'Not so far as I know. But perhaps I didn't know him well enough. Seemed to Megan and me he led a pretty lonely life, but nothing abnormal. She's going to be very upset.'

'Perhaps your wife can give us a better idea of him,' put in Lloyd carefully. 'The ladies are sometimes more knowing in matters like that.'

'Maybe.' But the single word reply lacked conviction, just as the speaker's sunken eyes still reflected deep suspicion – and, Parry thought, perhaps guilty nervousness.

'The grounds are very well kept, Dr Howell.'

'My wife would be glad to hear you say that, Mr Parry. What a glorious day to be wrecked by such a dreadful tragedy.' The director of the Howell Clinic made a tutting noise, then took a deep breath, and squared his shoulders. He motioned Parry to one of the green leather upright chairs on the other side of the desk, before sitting himself with his back to the window that overlooked the main drive. The room had been immediately to the left of the front door after the chief inspector had entered the clinic.

'Interesting building, too, doctor.'

'If you mean it's an architectural oddity you'd be right. I'm told the man appointed to design it originally came up with something aggressively modernist, or what passed for modernist in the nineteen-sixties. The plan was rejected by his client, a committee consisting mostly of clerics. He then returned with something blander, and, in his private view, entirely lacking in artistic integrity. The committee recognised this as a sound Welsh compromise, and approved it instantly.' The speaker's hands sprang apart like a conjurer's at the end of a successful trick, and to the accompaniment of a throaty chuckle. 'The result from the outside, as you've seen, is perfectly seemly, better than most starkly institutional boxes erected at the time, so there's no immediate danger of anyone wanting to tear it down.' He completed with a knowing lift of his eyebrows.

'So much for artistic integrity, perhaps?' Parry rejoined.

'Or the durability of pseudo-classical blandness?' the doctor offered in a serious voice, then leaned forward over the desk. 'So, mister...chief inspector, what's the news?'

'Well first, I'm sorry we're having to disrupt the peace of your clinic, doctor.'

Howell made a sharp dismissive gesture with one hand. 'That's inevitable, of course. Or I assume it is at the start, at least. Naturally, we try to avoid anything that destroys the...the even tenour of our ways.' He gave a brief smile. His manner was infinitely more businesslike than it had been when he had interviewed Angela Ingram. 'A sense of normality is fundamental to our therapies, and, of course, that goes further than trying to avoid abnormal interruptions. A murder on the premises is pretty upsetting all round. I suppose it is murder?' he completed abruptly.

'Murder or manslaughter I'm afraid, yes,' the policeman replied.

The other nodded. 'So, will your enquiries take long? I mean, if it was a burglar poor Rees disturbed, I imagine there won't be much to detain you.'

Parry looked doubtful. 'If it was a burglar. But there's no evidence so far to suggest it was. No sign of a forced entry anywhere. Mr Rees had a large quantity of cash on him which wasn't taken, and nothing else has been reported stolen.'

'Which is hardly conclusive is it, Mr Parry? Intruders in a medical establishment could be after something other than money. For instance drugs or expensive equipment. That's why we have fairly high fencing around the perimeter, and electric gates to keep out unknown vehicles.'

'Oh, could you tell me how the gates are controlled, doctor?' Parry interrupted.

'Certainly. They're kept open every day between eight a.m. and six p.m. The rest of the time the duty sister opens them by remote control in response to a voice request. Regular employees know the code and can let themselves in whether on foot or in cars. The code is altered from time to time. Perhaps it's not a perfect system, but it's practical.' The doctor nodded in support of the spoken assurance, then went on. 'We're not overly concerned about inside security, like locking windows, except, of course, ground floor windows of rooms not used at night. The dispensary is on the first floor and is totally secure at all times. So, you see, if Rees did challenge an intruder, and got killed for his pains, the chances are the culprit fled before he'd had a chance to lift anything.'

'That's always possible, doctor, but I'm afraid we have to work on a parallel assumption. That it's conceivable Mr Rees was attacked by someone who knew him.'

'By that I suppose you mean Phil Collit? Because of an argument in a pub over lottery winnings.' Howell cleared his throat. 'That's not on, you know? Not murder.' He glanced down at a brass paperknife lying by his hand, picked it up, put it down again, then lifted his gaze firmly to re-engage Parry's.

'May I ask how you knew about the argument, doctor?'

'Certainly. A senior member of staff was in the pub too. It was the Eight Bells, I think.'

'The other staff member being ?'

'Mrs Sheila Radcliffe, the clinic secretary and accountant. She's not here today, which is why she needed to call Eve Oswald, our matron, about something after she got home last night. I gather from Miss Oswald that, quite in passing, Mrs Radcliffe mentioned the er...the little spat between Rees and Collit. Matron didn't feel there was much to it.'

'I see, doctor. We'll need to follow that up, of course with both ladies.'

Howell's only response to this was a dismissive shrug of his shoulders as the speaker continued. 'You said Mrs Radcliffe wouldn't be here today. I expect we can reach her at her home. Does she live locally?'

'Yes, but Miss Oswald told me she left early this morning to be at some jamboree or other. Home this evening though. Meantime you could try reaching her on her mobile. The duty sister will have the number.'

'Thank you, doctor.' Parry completed a note before he next asked. 'Would you have any reason to think Mr Rees was desperately short of money?'

'No. But then, if he had been, he wouldn't necessarily have told me.'

'Except you were his employer, and, I gather, a popular and understanding one?'

Howell's immediate response to the compliment was a non-committal expression. 'We're a small outfit,' he said. 'I suppose people do tend to come to the owners with their problems. At least with their professional problems, but less often with off-duty ones. If it comes to money, though, I think it's more likely they'd approach my wife, not me.'

'And Mr Rees hadn't approached either of you, doctor?'

'That's right. You believe he was hard up, do you? That he really was trying to swindle Phil Collit?'

'So far it's too early to make a judgement on that, sir. Mr Collit's account of what happened seems reasonable enough.'

Howell hesitated, pursing his lips, before his next comment. 'I can tell you Kevin Rees was a moody chap. Up one moment, down the next. A manic depressive in the making, but that may be putting it too harshly. He was the opposite of Phil Collit who has a contemplative disposition. Goes with being a gardener, perhaps.' He paused for a second as though testing his statement for professional credibility. 'Incidentally, he's properly qualified for the job. Training certificates and all that. My wife will have the details.' He hesitated briefly again before adding, 'If Rees got it into his head that Collit was playing silly buggers, I mean over making his contribution to their stake, he could possibly have taken the stand he did, just to teach him a lesson.'

'And afterwards he'd still have paid Mr Collit his winnings?' Parry questioned.

'Just possibly, yes. Alternatively, Rees might have been telling what he believed to be the absolute truth. If so, Collit may well have tried the same ploy before. Conveniently forgotten to pay up his ten pounds until he knew they'd won something. If you ask me, Rees was pretty trusting not to demand the money in advance each week.'

'But if Mr Collit had been making a habit of forgetting to pay at the right time, doctor, isn't it likely that's just the action Mr Rees would have been taking already?'

The doctor considered for a moment, then shrugged. 'It's all supposition, of course. My central point is still that Collit wouldn't have committed murder. Certainly not with that piffling degree of provocation.'

'He admits to pushing Rees aside when they left the pub,

doctor. And I'd have thought being cheated out of a thousand pounds or more was provocation enough.'

Howell frowned while studying the fingernails of one hand. 'If, in his heart of hearts, he really believed he'd been cheated,' he said, looking up. 'He must have known he was partly in the wrong, at least. Rather than murder Rees after they'd left the pub, it's more likely he'd have gone home, talked to his wife about it perhaps, and then approached Rees today, admitting he'd really been careless and forgetful, and begging him to reconsider things. That would have been more his style.'

'And you think Rees would have listened, doctor?'

The other sniffed. 'Very possibly.'

Parry nodded slowly, while inwardly deciding he needed more convincing. 'And Mr Rees lived on the premises, doctor, in a room on the top floor overlooking the yard and the tool shed?' he asked.

'Yes. He and the matron are the two members of staff who live in. Except, of course, my wife and I occupy the garden cottage.'

'That's the single storey house on the left of the drive, doctor?' Parry nodded toward the window.

'Over there, nearly opposite, yes.' The speaker had gestured over his right shoulder. 'You passed it as you came in. We prefer to have our own place, but we're both just as instantly available to patients from there as we are from here.' He tapped the pager clipped to the top pocket of his light tweed jacket.

'And your wife is also a doctor, a neurologist like yourself?'

'Yes. Actually I'm a neuro-psychiatrist. We're a team, chief inspector. Have been since hospital training days in London.'

'Indeed? Which hospital was that, sir?'

55

'St Mark's. Regrettably, my wife's been confined to a wheelchair since an appalling car accident eight years ago.'

'I'm sorry.'

'Thank you. But she's been fully active in the clinic for many years now.'

Parry nodded. 'The clinic is very celebrated in its field, of course.'

'You do us too much honour, chief inspector. Yes, we're pretty well-known, I suppose, but very small. We have seven patients here at the moment, and rarely ever more than ten. In proportion to that, the medical, professional staff is relatively large. All chiefs and no Indians, you might say, though the other doctors involved are part-time. We work one-to-one with individual patients throughout their stay here. That's why the treatment is expensive, and, dare I say, effective.'

'I understand, doctor.' It seemed to Parry that in relation to the reason for the police presence, the clinic director was a little too keen to promote the virtues of the establishment. 'So, can you tell me who would have been here from, let's say, 10.30 last night?' he asked.

'Apart from the patients, you mean? Well, there was Ruth Tate, one of our two full time nursing sisters. They take it in turns on the night watch, as it were. Sister Tate lives locally, and is married to an airline pilot. She came on at eight. My wife and I were here too, of course, as well as the matron. I did my usual informal round of the patients. That starts after dinner at about nine, and finishes usually around ten. Last night it was more like 10.30. It's not quite like a hospital routine. If patients want to talk then, I encourage them. One usually knows which those are going to be, and I visit them last. Patients like to discuss their progress when they've made some – or even when they haven't.' He gave a ruminative grin. 'It's all part of the therapy, you understand?'

'Of course. Were you perhaps with one patient last night between, say, 10.15 and when you finished your rounds?'

'Yes, I was. It was Denis Ingram and his wife. She was staying the night, as she's done on the last few Saturdays. When she's here, I've made a habit of dropping in on them at the end of my rounds. They're both late birds, as I am, and we have a nightcap together. My wife joins us sometimes, but she couldn't last night. It was more of a social visit than a professional one. He's had a bad stroke, but his recovery while he's been with us has been quite...quite phenomenal.'

'And you dropped in on them at what time, doctor?'

Howell's face screwed up as he calculated. 'Hm, I'd say it was about five-past ten.'

'And you left, as you said, at 10.30?'

'That's it, yes.'

Parry checked his notes. 'What about the non-medical staff, doctor? The catering people, for instance? Do any of them live in?'

'No, they don't.' Howell brushed a speck of something off his jacket sleeve. 'The kitchen closes at ten. Up to that time, hot drinks and light snacks are available to patients in their rooms. We find there's very little call though. Most patients are usually in bed and ready for sleep by then, again because they've had a long hard day, weekend days included. Yes, the courses are usually very tiring. Virtually no respite between nine and six, and even after that there can be what we term evening homework. We do kick off an hour later on Sunday mornings.'

'And Kevin Rees was ready to do any fetching and carrying, as required, last night like every night?'

'Yes,' Howell had elongated the word. 'His contract didn't specify as much, but since he slept in, and was such a willing chap, that's the way things worked. His duties were less arduous than they sounded. Certainly in that connection. We rarely have real emergencies, and if we do they call for qualified expertise not, as you say, for a fetcher and carrier.'

'I gather Mr Rees had no qualifications?'

'That's right. Dependable chap, and a born nurse, but he's never stayed anywhere long enough to get qualifications. Not in either of his previous posts, for instance.'

'And where were they, doctor, do you know?'

'Yes, both in London. The first was as an auxiliary nurse at St Mark's.'

'Your old hospital?'

'That's right. From there he joined the London Ambulance Service. Coming here to a post outside the NHS wasn't going to get him any qualification, either. Still, he was willing and ready. We tend not to be union-minded, if you follow me? We like people who'll get on with whatever has to be done, and don't stand on their rights, real or imaginary. Our pay rates are good, of course. Well above the going NHS minimums.'

Parry thought they probably needed to be. 'I gather Mr Rees would normally have reported to the night sister when he returned last night,' he questioned.

'That's right. To establish he was back on the premises. Not really necessary. He has a bleeper like everyone else. Just good manners really. The sister would have been in the nurses' open office near the first floor landing, that's unless she was with a patient. He might also have told the matron that he was back except he didn't. I asked her. Her room is on the second floor, like his, but it overlooks the main lawn.'

'Yes, I gather he looked in on the sister, doctor. Would there have been any special reason why he'd have gone out to the pavilion after that? I mean, was he involved with the place on a day to day basis?'

'Depends on the season. You've been inside it?'

'Yes. It's used to store garden furniture and sports equipment.'

'Mm, our croquet and bowls sets. Both popular with the patients in the warmer months. Rees had recently taken to looking after the stuff there. Even so, I wouldn't have expected him to be in the place late at night. Not at this time of year.'

'Perhaps he assumed you and your staff would think that, doctor.'

Howell chuckled. 'That's too deep for me, chief inspector. Are you suggesting he was using it for secret activities? Assignations, perhaps?'

'I gather he had a key to the pavilion, sir,' Parry commented with a smile, but without answering the question. 'Was anything else stored there besides the chairs and sports gear, do you know?

'Could be. But nothing that Rees was involved with. Well, not so far as I know. I don't believe it's been used to store gardening equipment for instance, though Collit would have charge of that. He may have a key too.'

'He says he doesn't, doctor.' Parry shrugged, then added. 'Apparently the only other key is on the locked board in the nurses's office.'

'Ah, well that's quite possible, and...and practical.'

'So the pavilion has been part of Mr Rees's domain more than anyone else's?'

'You could put it that way, yes.'

'It's how Mr Collit describes it,' said Parry, adding: 'Do you know there's a cupboard at the back of the upper floor, doctor?'

'Yes. I believe it was the drinks store in the old days. Was Rees using it? I know it's not locked because the lock's broken.'

'It's got a new lock now, sir. Mr Rees had the key on a ring in his pocket. I assume you don't have a key as well?'

'You assume correctly. This is all news to me. If there is another key I imagine Collit might have it.'

'He says he doesn't, doctor, and that he didn't know about the new lock either. I'd guess that the cupboard was strictly under Mr Rees's control.'

Howell nodded slowly. 'Perhaps you're right. I assume you've opened it. So what was inside?'

'If we could come back to that in a second, sir? I wanted to ask if you'd seen Mr Rees or Mr Collit after they both got back here last night?'

The doctor shook his head. 'I didn't, as it happens. I think I may have heard Rees's voice coming from near the front door, but I can't be sure. That was when I was leaving Mr Ingram's room. Mrs Ingram was with me.'

'Did you hear what the voice was saying?'

'Afraid not. It was certainly a man.'

'But you don't know who he was speaking to?'

'No, and it was only the one voice I remember. Mrs Ingram may be able to help. She and I walked to the front door together.'

'Thank you, doctor. Now, just for the record, would you mind telling me exactly where you were yourself from after you left Mrs Ingram until midnight?

The other's eyebrows lifted again in what registered as mild, if tolerantly amused, surprise.

Chapter Four

'Dr Howell couldn't have been too pleased, boss. Not when you told him his cricket pavilion was used for storing ecstasy tablets ready sorted in packs of tens, with a total street value of around seven thousand pounds.'

'No. Finding what he called a "born nurse" had been flogging illegal drugs made it a lot worse, too,' Parry responded to the sergeant's comment. 'Not that the ownership of the stuff is proved yet, not for certain.' He turned from the single window of the quite large patient's bedsit they were in. It was on the ground floor.

The window offered only an uninspiring view of the near end of the greenhouse and, partially, of the rubbish bins – the reason, possibly, why the room had been available, though presumably the bins were moved out of sight if a patient was installed here.

'Except Rees had the key to that cupboard in his pocket. Even the CPS would take that as proof the ecstasy was his, surely?' Lloyd was seated at a small, circular dining table, while consuming coffee and biscuits supplied by the clinic. He had a low opinion of what the Crown Prosecution Service accepted as sufficient proof to justify arrest and trial. He believed, from bitter experience, that the CPS was altogether too wary of being blamed for the dissipation of public funds on cases that ended in acquittals through an alleged lack of admissible evidence. He was inured to the fact that incontrovertible and damning evidence, painstakingly gathered, could be made to look the opposite after it was manipulated by a spry defence lawyer, especially one with an eye for the openings offered by political correctness.

'What if the murderer planted the key in Rees's pocket, Gomer?' Parry questioned, and being purposely perverse. His view of too many CPS decisions coincided pretty well exactly with the sergeant's, but he was more realistic about the chances of such decisions prevailing.

'Passing up seven thousand quid in the process, boss?' The sergeant registered his dogged disbelief in the justice of the proposition .

'I agree, but a jury might not. Anyway, at the moment we're investigating Rees's murder, not his criminal activities.' Parry gave a ruminative sniff, sat down, and poured himself some coffee. 'At least the drug business gives us a solid reason why Rees needed to hang on to those lottery winnings. On his salary, he'd have been in hock up to his eyebrows paying for that kind of a statch.'

'Probably meant to move the stuff on pretty smartish, boss, for cash.'

'Sure, but he must have had to pay for it, and I doubt if he was planning to move it on last night either.'

'True.' The sergeant shrugged. 'And there was no cash in that cupboard, or in his room. Except we're taking another look there now.'

Parry rubbed the back of his neck. 'My guess is he'd overreached himself, and the lottery would have been a godsend, especially if he was keeping it all.'

'Seven thousand quids worth of ecstasy was pretty good going for a small time operator, boss.'

'Seven thousand in street value, Gomer. His outlay could have been half that, perhaps less. Well, you know the scene better than I do.'

Any sympathy Lloyd had felt for the dead Kevin Rees had already evaporated. He had served on the Drugs Squad for a period in his career, an experience which had left him with an enduring and ferocious loathing of all drug peddlers, even greater than the one he harboured for slick defending barristers. 'Anyway,' he said, 'the drugs open up a new line of enquiry on the murder.'

'Granted. Unless Collit was in it with him. They'd co-operated over the lottery so far. Were they doing the same with the drugs?'

'Collit was pretty firm about that, wasn't he, boss? Insisted he had no knowledge of the drugs. Said drugs were against his principles. But was the surprise when we found the ecstasy tablets genuine?'

Parry took a sip of coffee. 'I thought so, yes. He looked totally astonished, didn't he? Could be a better actor than I'm giving him credit for, of course.' Collit had been present when the pavilion cupboard had been opened after he'd identified all but one of the keys in Rees's pocket – the remaining key being the one that fitted the new lock. 'They could have been in it together,' the chief inspector continued, 'till Rees saw the opportunity and the excuse to go it alone after the win yesterday?'

'That fits, boss. But if lottery winnings were always intended to pay for drugs, wouldn't Mrs Collit have to have been involved? According to Collit they're saving for a baby. Everyone in the pub knew about that win, so it'd be difficult to keep it from her, wouldn't it?'

'Probably. Yes. Good point, Gomer. If Collit was trafficking along with Rees, then the wife almost had to have known.'

'So do we take him in for more questions, boss?'

'Not yet. He's not going anywhere while he thinks there's a chance we won't arrest him. Not on the present evidence. Mary Norris is interviewing Mrs Collit now, is she?'

'At their house, yes,' the sergeant replied.

Parry rose from his chair, marking the end of their coffee

break. 'So what's happening about an incident room?' he asked.

'Miss Oswald, the matron, she wasn't keen on us setting one up inside the clinic, boss. Not that there's a free room big enough in any case, except possibly for the pavilion.'

Parry shook his head. 'Not suitable. Not in the circumstances.'

'I thought that, too, boss. Incidentally, hasn't the title of matron gone out in hospitals years ago?'

'Yes, but I suspect Dr Howell is old school in that connection. Or maybe his matron is. What's she like?'

'Quite a surprise. You'll see when you meet her,' Lloyd responded with a chuckle. 'Lovely lady, who packs an iron fist in a velvet glove. I reckon she probably runs the whole place. Not that old, and quite a looker. Anyway, our incident van's ready. Be here and working within the hour. Oh, and Miss Oswald says we can keep this room for interviewing and such for as long as we like. They don't use it much for patients. Might be the smells from the kitchens.'

'So you made your number with Miss Oswald.' Grinning, the chief inspector looked about the well curtained and carpeted room. It had its own bathroom, but was presently bedless and the absence was notable since no effort had been made to re-arrange the remaining furniture. There were two low armchairs besides the four upright ones around the table, with a writing desk in one corner, a free-standing television set, and a wall of built-in cupboards. 'OK,' he continued, 'let's have the incident van just inside the gate for today at least, Gomer. That won't upset the patients, but it'll be a police presence if anyone wants to talk to us. Better to go through the motions, I suppose.' Even so, both men were close to the view that the case would not be so long in the solving as to justify more than the minimum of police paraphernalia.

'So no witnesses yet. Not to anything useful,' Parry remarked, flicking a biscuit crumb from his tie.

'No. Seems most of the patients turn in early, like the doctor said.'

'What about Ruth Tate, the night sister? Rees reported to her.'

'That's right. At ten-thirty-one.' The sister had been another member of staff interviewed by the sergeant while Parry had been with Dr Howell and then for some time on the telephone to their Divisional Superintendent. 'She noted the exact time in her log,' Lloyd added, 'but she never saw him again. Had an undisturbed night, she said. Seems she's not required to do rounds or anything. Slept from midnight to six o'clock on a day-bed, but fully clothed and ready for action, like. That's the routine.'

'Is she a good looker too, Gomer?'

'She is, as a matter of fact, smashing redhead. She told me Miss Oswald recruits attractive female staff on the doctor's instructions. He says they're good for the male patient's morale.'

'Good for the doctor's too, probably,' Parry countered, and wondering how true the comment might be. He looked at his watch. 'Right, let's see what the celebrated Mrs Angela Ingram has to tell us, if anything. Our audience with her was timed for ten-thirty.'

*

'So Mr Collit here got home from the pub at 10.20 last night, Mrs Collit?' DC Mary Norris, now in street clothes, enquired gently of the still watery-eyed woman. The sergeant's pencil was poised over the notebook that was resting on her crossed knees.

She was seated on a sofa beside Megan Collit, facing the empty fireplace. The sofa and two matching armchairs were draped in over-laundered, loose covers printed in an autumnal leaf design that clashed with the original red moquette underneath. This was revealed where the covers were stretched at the lower corners and in several places along the seams. Phil Collit was slouched at right angles to the others in one of the armchairs, his back to the window.

The furnishings in the room offered scant witness to the passing of the third quarter of the 20th Century, let alone the fourth one, except for a television receiver with a small gold plaque bearing the word 'digital' in gold. There was a colour group photograph taken at the Collit's wedding in a large frame on top of the TV with Phil Collit looking only a fraction less contented than he was now, but with his new wife wearing an expression of apparent surprised relief.

'That's right, isn't it, Phil?' Megan Collit sniffed, looking for more than simple support toward her husband. He had returned to the house only minutes before this and told her about Rees's death. He had then scarcely begun his account of his police interview at the clinic before the woman detective sergeant had arrived on their doorstep. The wife's continuing shock and tears over the news of Rees seemed genuine enough, her grief appearing deeper than Mary Norris had expected – a lot deeper.

At twenty-six, two years younger than her husband, Megan was assistant manager at the small, independent supermarket in close-by, affluent Bryntaf. Her title denoted very little in terms of genuine extra status – only that its conferring had excused anything at all in terms of extra salary from the store's canny and frugal owner. Megan was hardly managerial material. Of medium height, slight build, and timid manner, she had a pretty face, with short darkish hair and brown eyes which were now beginning to show apprehension as well as enduring sorrow. Her sight was poor, which accounted for the heavy-lensed spectacles she wore at all times. The light blue tracksuit she had on revealed nothing of the figure underneath which was slim but without many discernible curves. There was a white towel wrapped around her neck which further evidenced that she had been prepared to go jogging with her husband on his return.

The three were in the front room of the Collit's neat Victorian, semi-detached home which they shared with Phil Collit's widowed mother who owned it. The small house, well decorated and modernised, notably in terms of its plumbing, was in Mary Street, Llandaff, a little over a mile from the Howell Clinic. Like its neighbours, it had a bay window on the ground floor, and was set back twelve feet from the pavement behind a low wall and iron gate with, in this case, carefully pruned rose bushes set in the area under the window. A tiled path, on the left, led to the covered porch, and a front door, its upper half patterned with stained glass panels depicting open tulips in a variety of poses and colours. The room offered an uninterrupted view across the road to the railinged municipal Hailey Park which the River Taff bounded on the far side, on its winding way past Llandaff toward Cardiff.

Because Collit had volunteered only a nodded assurance to his wife's anxious question about agreeing the time he had returned from the Eight Bells, the woman detective had supplied reassuringly, 'Mr Collit told us earlier the time he got back, Mrs Collit. I just needed your confirmation.'

'I see. You can call us Phil and Megan if you like,' the other woman volunteered in a still broken voice, while wiping her eyes again with an already soddened tissue, and before registering her husband's frown at her suggestion.

67

'OK...Megan.' The sergeant smiled. On her arrival she had debated whether she should have left the two alone for a while when it was clear that Mrs Collit's distress was so profound. She had decided against doing so for police, not compassionate, reasons. Originally it had been her intention to reach Mary Street by car, ahead of Phil Collit who had set off there on his bicycle. That way she could have broken the bad news to Megan herself and hopefully witnessed her reactions to it, unaffected by the presence of her husband. But the sergeant had been delayed. Her stony interest now was to discern whether the depth of Megan Collit's unhappiness was solely due to the sudden death of a close friend, or conceivably because of her known or imagined involvement of her husband in it. 'And then you both watched the end of the news on TV?' she finished.

Megan swallowed. 'The weather forecast, yes. On BBC1. It's why Phil went out again.' The speaker sat up straighter than before, and moistened her thin lips. 'It said there was going to be a frost. He had to see to the greenhouse at the clinic.' She leaned forward in her chair, a movement that prompted the black and white Welsh spaniel, lying across her feet, to lift its head enquiringly, and then to drop it again. 'I mean, he didn't have to go,' she went on, 'but he's like that, see? Ever so conscientious, aren't you, love?' She gave her husband a tentative encouraging smile.

Assuming, correctly, that there would be no recordable, audible reply from Collit, the sergeant continued: 'And you hadn't been to the pub with him?'

This time Megan hesitated before replying, glancing first at her husband. 'No. I do usually on Saturdays,' she said. 'Except Phil's mam isn't too well, and I didn't like leaving her. I was sorry I couldn't go because...because of the lottery win. It was going to be a celebration.'

'So you both knew your numbers had come up?'

'Yes. We saw that on the TV earlier. We were thrilled to bits.' She sighed and shook her head slowly at the recollection.

'But you still didn't go with him?'

'Well, like I just said, his mam wasn't well.' Her tone was gaining a little in confidence, and well as resonance.

'It wasn't because you both expected there might be a problem with Kevin Rees? Over your share of the winnings?'

'Certainly not,' Collit intervened loudly. 'It was like Megan said. We didn't want to leave my mam on her own.'

'Is your mother-in-law better now, Megan?' The sergeant had ignored the comment from Collit, pointedly addressing the question to his wife.

'Not really. She's upstairs now, still in bed. I took her up her breakfast. Weekend treat really. She's been poorly for some time. And Phil's right. Kevin's attitude was, well, unbelievable. The last thing we expected.' She gave a long sniff, and it seemed for a moment that tears were welling again.

'I see. Going back to Mrs Collit senior, presumably you have to leave her when you're both out at work?'

'Well, that's different, isn't it?' Collit put in. 'She doesn't get so lonely in the daytime, and there's plenty of neighbours handy then if she's in trouble. Anyway, we definitely weren't expecting a problem with Kevin? I've said already, at the clinic – '

'Yes, Mr Collit, but if you don't mind it's Megan I'm questioning now.' DC Norris interrupted firmly, looking across at the woman. 'Were you expecting Kevin might be difficult, Megan?'

Mrs Collit began rubbing the palm of her left hand to and fro over the back of her right hand which was still grasping the tissue. 'About Phil owing for two weeks? Not really,' she said, her delivery quickened because of an impatient sigh from her husband. 'See, a week yesterday we'd been staying the night with my parents, so Phil couldn't have paid Kevin his ten pounds then.'

'So you didn't expect the meeting last night to be embarrassing?'

'No, of course we didn't. And it wasn't the reason I didn't go to the pub. Really it wasn't.' The expression on Collit's face indicated that his wife had at last given the reply he wanted.

'Your husband's told us that you befriended Kevin Rees. Were you angry when Phil told you what happened in the pub?'

'I was shocked and...disappointed, I suppose.'

'I know you were both friends of Kevin's, Megan, but were you and Kevin closer friends than Kevin and Phil?'

Without warning the woman broke down again, sobbing loudly, and covering her face with her hands. The spaniel jumped up and began pawing at her knees.

Chapter Five

'At least he didn't ask if any of the patients had homicidal tendencies,' Edwin Howell commented drily to his wife in an unusually deep, and seriously reflective tone. He had several slim files of patient notes under his arm.

'A detective chief inspector would have known better than that,' Janet Howell responded firmly, while speedily and fairly silently propelling herself to the other side of the room. As always, the arrangement of her short, professionally styled black hair, and the application of her light make-up were both impeccable. She was dressed in a well-tailored, dark blue trouser suit worn over a starched, lace collared white blouse.

Her matching blue shoes were fashionable as well as 'sensible', despite being an item of apparel she never had the opportunity to wear in let alone wear out. With a strong, upright build still, as a young woman, her natural agility had been matched by a formidable athletic prowess, notably at tennis – in addition to a fetching face and figure. Now at fifty-six, although misfortune rather than age had robbed her of much more than was fair, it had also added to her personality that special grace nurtured often by stoicism.

The couple were in the sitting-room of their cottage, and had just come from finishing a very late breakfast in the kitchen. The meal was usually taken at eight on Sundays, an hour later than weekdays – and that was after Howell had visited, with the night sister, any patients under special observation. It was immediately after breakfast each day that he and his wife went over clinical notes at home, ahead of a short staff meeting in the clinic. This morning the routine had been upset and the staff meeting cancelled after the discovery of Kevin Rees's body. Breakfast, always prepared by Janet, had been deferred until her husband had returned from his encounter with Parry.

The room was set out with as much ingenuity as good taste. It was big enough to allow for the manoeuvering of a quite large, state-of-the-art electric wheelchair (what Edwin Howell had christened his wife's 'Sputnik') but without that necessity being permitted to govern a creative ordering of the furnishings. This was due to the artifice of Janet Howell, and was equally evident in the matching arrangements in the rest of the house, allowing that, in the kitchen and her own bathroom, equipment had been modified or contrived for her specific use. In the main, it had been her objective to ensure that her husband's domestic living space was set out in a way that did not perpetually remind him and others that he shared it with a seriously disabled partner – a description which, despite its evident justification, she would not have accepted fitted her in any case.

Gardening had become Janet's hobby, and her management of the clinic grounds was subject to strictures similar to those she applied in her house. In this other context, though, she was more than ready to cater for mobility problems in the clinic's patients, even though, in terms of their severity and often their permanency, these handicaps often fell short of what she termed her own 'little challenges'.

Altogether, Janet Howell was a paragon of a wife, as well as being a neurologist of repute, though she insisted on placing herself at a lower level of achievement to that of her husband. The motoring accident, eleven years before this, that had effectively paralysed her below the waist had, on what she called the 'upside', resulted in the award of record-breaking insurance compensation. This, in turn, had provided the funding for the private clinic that the Howells had founded since their marriage.

'We've been described as some kind of loony-bin before now, you know?' Howell commented next. 'People are still so fearfully ignorant about the nature of strokes.'

'Except I'm sure that high-powered policemen are much better informed these days,' his wife allowed.

'I don't know how highly powered this one is, but he's intelligent. Doesn't miss anything.' Even so, this response had been grudging.

'Well, I look forward to meeting him. That's if he hasn't solved the crime and left before lunch. Of course, I'll be no use to the cops anyway because I was at home and asleep when poor Rees was killed, wasn't I? Incidentally, you were very quiet when you came in again last night.'

'Didn't want to wake you.'

'Which was why you slept in the guest room. You are a darling. Actually I was just dropping off. I needed a good night.' She sighed.

Her husband smiled and glanced at the time. 'I told you, didn't I, your highly powered chief inspector isn't the least bit ready to accept Rees was killed by a burglar?'

'I suppose that's because burglars rarely murder people. That doesn't stop it happening occasionally all the same, usually because someone panics. You should follow *CrimeWatch* on the telly.' Janet was hurriedly rummaging through the drawers of an *escritoire*. It happened she had seen the regular television programme for the first time in months the week before. Neither she nor her husband watched much television. Both were classical music buffs, and she was a voracious reader of biography – and crime fiction.

'Yes.' Howell drew out the affirming word which meant that he was not sufficiently interested in the ways of burglars, nor, for that matter, the benefits of television viewing, to have disagreed with his wife's directive. 'What have you lost?' he asked.

'Nothing important.'

He dropped into an armchair, and opened one of the files, but before studying its contents, raised his eyebrows and went on. 'If the investigation is prolonged, they'll probably want to interview all the patients. I shall oppose that, which will no doubt involve arduous justifications.' He sighed. 'Faced, as we are, with a murder on the premises, it'd almost be easier if we were back in the days when most people assumed a stroke – '

'Was a debilitating kind of heart attack that stopped the sufferer from even getting out of bed let alone stabbing victims on pavilion steps,' his wife chipped in. 'Yes, that would have reduced police interest in our little group. Ah! I knew I'd hoarded one of these.' She held up a black, inch-long object, half handle and half probe. 'It's one of my father's extricators for cleaning wax out of expensive hearing aids. They're such fiddly implements, the extricators, I mean, not the hearing aids, though they're fiddly too. Algernon Justinian Claverhouse the Third has lost his last one. He'll be delighted when I give him this. His hearing's important to him now he's joined the world again. You know he threaded a needle for Eve Oswald yesterday, mainly using his right hand? She said he was quite ecstatic. You'd have thought he'd split the atom. Getting his speech back has released his movement inhibitors as well. You said it might.'

'Lucky guess,' her husband offered in a deprecating tone. He was still preoccupied with other matters.

'Nonsense. I clearly remember your smoking out his problem the day after he got here,' Janet insisted. Her father had died four years before this. They had inherited the *escritoire* when her mother had moved to a smaller house.

A.J.Claverhouse was a sixty-four-year-old American patient, a distinguished and affluent lawyer with a married daughter living in England. It was his daughter who had persuaded him to come to the clinic in Wales after the incapacities following his stroke had defied the ministrations of his American doctors. Six weeks earlier the now fast recovering patient had begun retrieving his speech to the extent of being able to announce his name – loudly, proudly and in full to the extreme satisfaction of himself, and the gratification, as well as amusement, of the clinic staff. Since then he had rapidly moved on to much higher verbal and occupational achievements.

Janet steered the wheelchair to bring her abreast of a long occasional table, set close to the now sunlit, south-easterly facing main window. Her husband had earlier placed an unopened copy of the *Sunday Times* on the table. It had been delivered with the rest of the papers as usual at eight o'clock, but into the hands of PC Hopkins at the main gate by a delivery boy immediately consumed by curiosity – and the more so when the vigilant constable had stopped him from getting any closer to a crime scene.

Briefly, the woman doctor scanned the front page headlines while listening to her spouse's next observation.

'It's so important the media don't get the wrong impression of the clinic when something like this happens,' he said.

'I agree, my dear,' she murmured, 'especially when they find out that one of the staff was a drug pusher before someone did for him.'

Howell winced inwardly at her last choice of phrase. There was nothing mealy mouthed about Janet, never had been. And he knew well enough that Kevin Rees had not been one of her favourites; in fact quite the opposite. 'Don't remind me,' he responded, while accepting that her sixth sense about gauging people's integrity had scored again.

'He had transparent ears. That's often a give-away,' she observed, turning from the newspaper and moving her conveyance to the side of his chair.

Howell knew better than to challenge his wife's last theory, despite his being sure it had no possible anatomical, physiological or moral justification. Had he done so, she would undoubtedly have offered chapter and verse to prove her point empirically.

'And any idea that Phil Collit was involved in the drugs caper should be expunged from everyone's mind,' she completed, 'which applies to the murder as well, of course.'

'I stressed both points to the police, forcefully. Except...' He paused, his brow knitting.

'Except, as you told me, from the evidence so far, poor Collit is in the soup. Well, we must do our best for him, Edwin. I'm quite positive he didn't kill Rees.' A determined look and her raised, strong chin lent solid emphasis to the words.

'So am I, of course. Incidentally, Eve Oswald is rearranging duties so Rees's work is covered till we can raise a replacement. He was very close to Denis Ingram, of course, both as helper and...and friend, you might say. Denis took to him from the start, and surprisingly, so did Angela.'

'Why surprisingly? She's not at all choosy when it comes to making men-friends. It's most women she treats with disdain.'

Howell grinned. 'I think that's a bit unkind. But Rees certainly contributed to Denis's progress. Thankfully he's almost ready to go home. He was in great form last night, and, you'll be glad to hear, with Angela in attendance rather than control.'

'One of your more significant successes, darling.'

'One of *our* more significant successes,' he corrected.

'No, I've hardly had a look-in on that one. You're suggesting Angela staying away in the middle weeks helped more than us ordinary mortals could possibly have foreseen. Especially after you'd told her at the start to treat the clinic like liberty hall.'

'That was before we'd worked out their...their curious relationship.'

'Before you worked it out, you mean? I'm still bemused by those two.'

'The trick was in persuading him that any guilt he'd felt was as much hers as his, and that it should be discarded by both of them,' he responded seriously. 'Not having her around for a while was essential, of course.'

'And didn't bother Denis either,' his wife put in.

'Mm, that might have been overstating his feelings at the start, perhaps, but, yes, I truly believe it was the winning move that only we could have played. Of course, you've forgotten it was shortly after that Denis started looking more to you than to me.'

'Perhaps.' She gave a reflective smile. 'So what else have we got?'

He opened another file. 'Young Peter Smith isn't responding well enough in speech or mobility. Been here eight days. His walking's improved slightly. We graded him as potentially A for speech recovery and B for mobility.'

'Which seemed about right, except his progress has been nil in both areas.'

'Yes, and he's only twenty-seven. There's a hurdle there that doesn't show in his scans. We can do better, and he needs us to. He's a high flying young banker, or was.'

'I know,' Janet agreed. 'With a first class degree in economics,' she continued without reference to notes. 'More than passable French and some Spanish. Unmarried, used to have a regular girlfriend, but they broke up. Almost daily visits from worried Ma, and sometimes Pa who's an electronics manufacturer. They drive down from Windsor.'

'Mm. Situation's trying for all three of them.' Howell looked up. 'I suggest we second Barbara Edwards to him for a week and do a role reversal.'

'All right.' Janet referred to the file. 'She's back from holiday tomorrow.'

'Good. So intensive French, with no English spoken by Barbara or anyone else involved, including parents. What happened to the abandoned girlfriend?'

'It was she who chucked him I'm afraid, to marry an Australian. Now lives in Sydney. No residual comforts there, I'm afraid.'

'Better and better.'

'You don't think Barbara's French is too good?'

'For a competent and quite glamorous English speech and physio therapist it's outstanding, and she knows the drill. How old is she?'

'Twenty-three and unattached.'

'So, the right age and status. Let's hope she's more desirable than the bird who jilted him. If either or both parents are here today I'll talk to them. If not I'll telephone them tonight.' Howell was already scribbling an entry in the notes.

One of the clinic's intensive methods of restoring speech was to restrict communication to a language or on a subject which the patient knew better than the therapist. In that way the pupil became the tutor, putatively endowed with all the authority, confidence and dignity in one context that a stroke destroys in all of them.

The two doctors continued to apply themselves to the files

for several minutes more. Although at this point they were purposely ignoring the fact that a murder had recently been committed only yards from where they were sitting – their exchanges did have a quite strong bearing on the case.

*

'Good morning, Chief Inspector Parry isn't it? And Sergeant Lloyd? I'm sorry if I've delayed both of you,' Angela Ingram offered, but in a tone that made her apology sound more like an unavoidable obligation. She had been given their names earlier by Dr Howell. Briskly, she walked half way across the room from the open french windows when the two policemen entered. She extended a hand, not for shaking, and only to point the visitors toward easy chairs, before herself sitting on an elegant, straight backed, upholstered mahogany carver.

The room was more than twice the size of the one the policemen had just left and was more in the style of what, in an expensive country hotel, might have been described as a ground floor garden suite. Although there was no permanent division between the sitting and sleeping areas, both those had been ingeniously and comfortably proportioned, while, outside, the room let onto its own hedged-about section of terrace. Parry noted that the beds had already been made up for the day, with russet covers that harmonised with the other autumnal shades in the carpet, the curtains, and in the multi-coloured cushions scattered decorously across the surfaces.

He wondered whether this early labour had been the work of clinic staff or the lady who was greeting them, but concluded quite soon that it would almost certainly have been the former, with only the final creative touches supplied by Mrs Ingram.

'Not at all, ma'am,' he responded to her question. 'We've had plenty of people to see, as you'd imagine. By the way, while it's you we need to talk to right now, we'd hoped to have a word with your husband, too.'

'Ah, well that was the problem, you see? He's made incredible progress in the time he's been here. Quite incredible. We're even firming up tentative engagements for him in July, one very important date in London, as a matter of fact. Dr Howell is a genius, of course.' Mrs Ingram leaned forward slightly, fingering the long gold chain which hung below the ribbed roll neck of a loose fitting, white cashmere sweater. 'As you may not know, the clinic regimen is strict and intensive. On Sundays, when I'm here, I take part in the first hour of his speech therapy session. That starts at nine. The second hour is on mobility, very exhausting as well, and I leave it entirely to the experts. But we all believe it vitally important that anything which might upset the routine should be avoided at all costs. His meeting the police to no purpose might have done just that. A set-back at this stage would be disastrous. I'd have thought Dr Howell would have warned you of that. Also, I'm afraid my husband really has nothing useful or relevant to tell you.'

'But he does know about Mr Rees's death?' Parry questioned quietly, and without voicing the view that it was up to the police to decide what was relevant or otherwise to a murder investigation. Howell had indeed cautioned him against asking to meet patients without permission, but he had conveniently chosen to forget the injunction while testing its seriousness.

'Of course he knows, Mr Parry. Dr Howell came by to tell us the dreadful news when we were having breakfast. My husband was quite distressed enough to learn what had happened without having to have the point laboured unnecessarily. You see he never left this room from after dinner last night until this morning. The doctor stressed that he should not feel involved. I, on the other hand, may have seen, or, more probably, heard Kevin when I walked with Dr Howell from here to the drive.'

'I understand that from the doctor, Mrs Ingram.' Except the chief inspector now wondered perversely why the lady had put up quite such a well-prepared protective statement. 'I gather you both knew Mr Rees pretty well?' he added aloud.

'Yes, we did.' The affirmation was delivered slowly with not so much reluctance as with a hint of doubt as to its accuracy. 'At least we knew and...and valued him as a conscientious clinic employee. But in other ways he was an oddly private young man. One never really got beyond the joshing public persona, d'you understand? But I could never decide whether that stemmed from modesty or secretiveness.'

Gomer Lloyd cleared his throat. 'Either way, you felt he was keeping something back always, ma'am, spoiling the relationship, like?' he asked.

The woman's eyes brightened. 'You know that describes it pretty accurately, sergeant. It was vaguely...irritating, but perhaps that's too strong a word,' she offered to the sergeant with an appreciative smile.

'We were told by Dr Howell that Mr Rees kind of attached himself to Mr Ingram from the start of his time here,' Lloyd continued. 'Would you say that was because your husband was a well-known personality, a celebrity?'

'Partly, perhaps, although he's a successful industrialist not a pop star.' Mrs Ingram sniffed to emphasise the distinction.

'But he's better known than a good many industrialists because of his philanthropic work, ma'am.'

'My husband is chairman of Ingram Developments, one of the biggest house building companies in Britain. It's a company he started from nothing and which the family still controls. We've never gone public, I mean floated it on the stock market, although there's been plenty of encouragement to do so.'

'Might I ask why you've never gone public, Mrs Ingram?' Parry asked.

'Quite simply, because my husband's always valued his commercial freedom. He's never cared to be at the behest of shareholders who might pressure him to put profit before all else. That's not his style at all.'

'But I remember reading somewhere recently that Ingram Developments is one of the most profitable private companies in Britain.'

'So it is, chief inspector, and Denis has always been free to make those profits in the manner he chooses, and to do what he wants with them, after taxes, of course.'

'Turning a lot of them over to the Ingram Housing Trust, ma'am.' It was Lloyd who had supplied the last information.

'That's perfectly correct, sergeant. Profits, as well as shares in the Company. Next to the family, the Trust is actually the largest shareholder in the Company.'

'And one of the biggest provider of housing for the homeless in this country, and in some Third World countries as well,' Lloyd completed.

Mrs Ingram positively beamed at the sergeant. 'Yes, we're not the biggest private provider by any means, but we try to be the most efficient and the most responsible. Up to the time of my husband's illness I never had a lot to do with the day to day running of the company, but I've always been deeply involved in the charitable trust. You obviously know something about us?'

'Oh yes. And all of it praiseworthy. My wife's on the Welsh fund-raising committees of two African charities. Your trust has given them help in money and materials.'

'Good.' There were more mutual smiles exchanged between the lady and the sergeant.

Parry cleared his throat. 'Coming back to the reason why Kevin Rees was so devoted to your husband,' he put in firmly, 'you've implied it may not have been because Mr Ingram is so well-known. Was it perhaps because he gave or lent Mr Rees money?'

Mrs Ingram swallowed slowly before offering almost archly, 'So Detective Sergeant Lloyd is not the only perceptive one.' She smiled and lifted her head. 'Yes. He asked me for two short term loans. Not gifts, loans, for very good causes, and I gave them to him. I'm astonished if the police knew about them. They were handled very discreetly. Neither Dr Howell nor my husband knew about them.'

'We didn't know about them either, ma'am,' Parry admitted, 'but it seems Mr Rees may have needed money recently to meet commitments. You and your husband seemed a likely source. Were the loans repaid?'

'Not yet. They were neither of them due. I have no reason to think they wouldn't have been repaid.'

'Might I ask the size of the sums involved, ma'am?'

'You can certainly ask, but I don't believe I'm obliged to tell you, am I?'

Parry's nose wrinkled. 'We're conducting a murder investigation, ma'am. We're entitled to ask for any information we believe may be relevant to catching the killer. If necessary we can invoke legal sanctions to help us, but I'm sure that won't be necessary, will it?'

'I suppose not.' The woman paused briefly. 'The first loan was for three thousand pounds. That was three weeks ago.

The second, made a week ago, was for five thousand pounds.'

'And you were told what the money was for?'

'Certainly I was. Both were down-payments, deposits on accommodation for what Kevin always described as his deserving clients. The money was to be available through government grants eventually, but the suitable accommodation could have been lost in the meantime.'

'I'm not clear, ma'am, what exactly Kevin meant by his clients?'

'For a short time he worked in a London psychiatric hospital. He kept in touch with a number of discharged patients, helping them to come to terms with...with life outside. Kevin seemed to devote most of his free time to it. Because of the Ingram Trust I was very much in sympathy, of course.'

'And you believed what Kevin told you?'

'I had no reason not to, chief inspector. If you mean did I demand chapter and verse on the clients and their circumstances, no I didn't. I've had my own problems, but I was glad to help with someone else's where I could. The sums were not over large by my standards.'

'And you always paid them to him in cash, I suppose?'

'Yes. That made no difference to me, but it helped Kevin, of course.'

'Of course,' Parry repeated solemnly. 'And you had no security against the loans? No collateral?'

'No I didn't. Speed was of the essence, chief inspector. Kevin assured me shortly after that the accommodations were secured. The loans should have been returned as arranged. I assume in the new and quite unpredictable circumstances there may well be difficulties there, but that's my problem.'

'Thank you for being so forthright, Mrs Ingram. Clearly you trusted Kevin Rees.'

'Yes, but more to the point, I was profoundly grateful to him for what he'd done for my husband. Kevin was devoted to his work, and his healing talent.'

'He was a healer?' asked Parry.

Mrs Ingram decorously crossed her legs under the close fitting, red jersey skirt. 'That may be putting it too strongly, but my husband thought so, not perhaps in a way you could describe specifically. It was just that Kevin had a quietening presence conducive to...to a patient's well-being.'

Parry nodded, but, it seemed, dismissively. He disliked generalised answers to specific questions. 'Oh, one other thing about the loans, you said you never disclosed them to Dr Howell either?'

'That was because Kevin asked me specifically not to. I think this was because he didn't want the doctor to know about his...his 'other job', as he described it, although, of course, what he was doing was voluntary and unpaid. For that reason I respected his wish.'

'Thank you. Could you now tell us if Kevin ever told you or your husband that he was involved in illegal drug dealing?'

'Kevin? A drug dealer? I can't believe it. He never mentioned such a thing to me and I'm sure not to my husband either. Have you proof of this?'

'I'm sorry I'm not at liberty to enlarge on the question, ma'am. And it was only a question of course. But your answer is clear enough. And now if we could just go over your movements when you left this room with Dr Howell last evening at ten-thirty.'

'Certainly. I walked with the doctor from here to the front porch where we chatted for a minute or so. It was a chance to discuss when my husband might sensibly leave here. He wanted to do so tomorrow. I thought it might be better to wait another week. It was easier to discuss it when Denis wasn't present.'

'I understand. The doctor believes he may have heard Mr Rees's voice as you both left the room. Do you remember hearing or seeing him then or later last night?'

The woman looked thoughtful then shook her head slowly. 'I'm afraid I don't. I remember doing most of the talking. For that reason it's possible, I suppose, that Dr Howell heard Kevin's voice in the background and I didn't.'

Chapter Six

'I thought you'd better see this straight off, sir.' The still white-bedecked, earnest Detective Sergeant Glen Wilcox, in charge of the SOCO team, came up behind Parry and Lloyd as they were returning to the room that had been put at police disposal.

The chief inspector moved across to the window to study the handwritten words on the piece of cheap and very wrinkled blue writing paper enclosed in a transparent evidence bag. 'No date or address,' he said. 'Signed by a Megan. Collit's wife is a Megan, of course?'

'That's right, boss,' Lloyd provided.

'And you found it in the victim's room?'

'Yes, sir,' Wilcox replied, looking a touch more pleased with himself than he usually allowed. 'In the breast pocket of a white cotton jacket. The kind male nurses wear on duty. It was hanging on the back of the door. We've checked with matron. Mr Rees's work jackets went to the laundry on Mondays and Thursday mornings. The note was screwed up into a very small ball, sir.'

'I can see that, Glen.'

'Afraid we missed it on our first sweep, sir.' This came as an apology not an excuse. DS Wilcox didn't go along with excuses from himself or anyone else.

'Well, the message is short and pretty pointed,' Parry observed, flattening the bag and its contents on a table-top to make the words more legible. 'It says *"Kev, I'm pregnant. I have to see you. Call me at work Saturday, usual time. Desperate, Megan."'*

'Doesn't leave much to the imagination, does it boss?' said Lloyd. 'And if Mrs Collit wrote it – '

'There are plenty of other Megans in Llandaff, not to mention the rest of Wales,' Parry broke in sharply. 'But if the writing is Megan Collit's, and if the message means what we're all thinking, that Kevin Rees is the father of her child.' He looked from one sergeant to the other before completing. 'Then I'd say her husband had a double motive as well as the opportunity and the means for doing in Rees.'

'DS Norris is interviewing Mrs Collit, boss, at her home. Probably Mr Collit is there by now as well. What d'you want done?'

Parry screwed up his face. 'Call Mary on her mobile. If she's still with them, tell her to move out of range and read her the letter. She can then tell Collit we're coming over to see him, to ask him some more routine questions. Give Mary the letter when we get there. While we're with Collit, she needs to find out from his wife if she wrote it. If she didn't, and she's telling the truth, there's no harm done. If she did, Mary has to get out of her if Collit knows she's pregnant, and why she wrote to Rees about it.'

'Delicate situation, isn't it?' said Lloyd with a frown, while punching in DS Norris's mobile number.

Parry nodded, glanced at the time, then turned to Wilcox. 'Did you find anything else of interest in Rees's room?'

'Quite a few things, sir. But we went back to the pavilion first, like you ordered. There were two cream coloured blankets, folded up and stored out of sight behind the deckchairs on the ground floor. The blankets are extra good quality, the sort they use on the beds in the clinic. Seems they shouldn't have been in the pavilion at all. There was a newish, lilo airbed on top of them, sort of half inflated, like whoever uses it didn't want the trouble of blowing it up again the next time.'

'Rough but ready basis for a love nest, perhaps?' Parry

commented. 'And Rees had the only personal key to the place. Of course, the blankets could have been for patients sitting outside the pavilion in summer, and left there at the end of the season.'

'Definitely not, sir,' the sergeant replied promptly. 'The matron insists they were far too expensive to use for that. She's setting up her own enquiry about how they got there. I wouldn't want to be the person responsible either.' It seemed that Eve Oswald was living up to her stern reputation, Parry construed, as Wilcox continued. 'She says small travelling rugs are provided in all patients' rooms for outdoor use. Oh, and there are stains on the blankets, sir.'

'Semen?'

'Possibly, sir. Anyway, we've bagged-up the blankets and the lilo for sending to forensic. There wasn't anything else of interest in the pavilion, except the ecstasy tablets, of course.'

'So what else was in Rees's room?'

'His bank and credit card statements, sir, that we found in a locked drawer. Amy's had a quick look at them.' Amy was Mrs Amelia Higgs, a civilian employee in charge of logging and filing evidence. She was also the best informed member of the team when it came to accountancy and commerce. 'He had accounts with three banks,' Wilcox continued. 'The Allied, the Border Counties, and the London-Metro. The Allied statement had a balance at the end of last month of thirty-eight pounds. It gets higher at the beginning of each month when his salary cheque's paid in direct, but most of that comes out again pretty quick. It's been the same for the five previous months. The balances at the other two banks are usually a bit higher than the one at the Allied, except they don't get the temporary lift when a salary cheque comes in. He hardly uses them at all.'

'So why did he have them?'

'For the credit cards he got from all three banks, sir,' the sergeant answered with certainty. 'Two Visa and one MasterCard, with a two thousand pound credit limit on two of them, and three thousand on the other. Amy says he's been juggling things so at any time he had between four and five thousand pounds to use, drawn as cash from the cards, and of course without paying interest.'

'By using the free credit period banks allow card customers every month?' Parry questioned. 'But they've stopped doing specifically that with cash withdrawals.'

'Most have, sir, but he found three that hadn't. So, when needed, he's been feeding one account with money he draws from another. The system wasn't perfect. Over the months, his minimum monthly repayments have grown quite a bit.'

'To keep under his credit limits? Presumably he got caught with some interest payments on the card borrowings too.' Parry shook his head. 'Bet it kept him on tenterhooks most of the time.'

'Nearly all his credit card transactions were cash withdrawals, of course, sir. Hardly any retail buys, except for petrol. What he was doing is an old trick and he seems to have over-reached himself at the end of March. That's when his card accounts totted up to nearly seven thousand quid between them, with no way left for him to borrow enough from one card to keep another one happy before April 23rd. That's when the repayment date and free interest period on two of them stopped. So it looks as though he had to find another source of funds then.'

Parry gave a grunt. 'Which he did. I'd guess around the middle of the month to the tune of three thousand pounds, and again next month with five thousand he got hold of at the beginning of May.'

'Well you're right about the three thousand in April, sir.

That's what went in to pay off the whole of the London-Metro Visa card balance. There're no statements for May yet, of course.'

'Congratulate Amy on working his system out, will you?' the chief inspector said. Whatever Rees had used the money for, he mused, housing his 'patients', or, more likely, paying for his wholesale drug deliveries, it was Mrs Ingram who had provided the funding. 'And there was no cash anywhere except in his pocket?'

'Forty pounds in the same drawer as the bank statements and the credit card accounts, sir. That's all, unless he had a statch we haven't found yet. He had two cars, both old bangers. No money or anything worth mentioning in either, so far.'

'I see. Well it's probably unlikely there'll be more significant sums of cash. The nine hundred he had on him was probably an emergency fund. It seems he ran his money affairs right up to the tape, doesn't it? Keep looking though. Anything else of interest?'

'This address book, sir. Looks like he's had it a long time.' The small and worn, black-covered book was also enclosed in an evidence bag.

'It's been finger-printed, has it?'

'Yes, sir. Only his own dabs on it.'

Parry thumbed through the pages, pausing at one place, with a perceptible creasing of his right brow. 'O.K. I'll keep the address book for a bit. And well done so far, especially over the note.'

'Thank you, sir.'

Parry turned expectantly to Lloyd, who had just switched off his mobile.

'DS Norris was about to leave the Collit house, boss, but she'll now be accepting the cup of tea the wife offered. It'll only take us three minutes to get there. The house is in Mary Street, Llandaff North, just over the bridge.'

'Let's go then,' Parry responded, at the same time re-checking an entry on the J page of the address book. It had rated a second look since it comprised the name, London address and telephone number of Perdita Jones, his fiancé.

*

'But the baby's going to be ours. Mine and Phil's. Except he says we can't afford a baby yet. He's going to murder me for letting it happen.' Megan Collit's hand flew to her mouth. 'Oh God, I didn't mean to say that.'

'Of course you didn't. I understand.' DS Mary Norris countered.

The two were seated across from each other at the small, oblong, white plastic table in the kitchen at the rear of the house. They had moved there while Parry and Lloyd went through the motions of putting further questions to Phil Collit in the front room, a ruse solely intended to keep him clear of the other interview. The spaniel dog, who the sergeant had learned was called Waldo, was under the table, damp muzzle resting in its mistress's lap.

'It takes two to make a baby, Megan. Phil is at least half responsible, isn't he?'

'Except he leaves all the precautions to me, like. Only I can't understand how it happened. And he won't either.' Megan was on the brink of tears again.

The woman detective sergeant decided to let the subject of the couple's family planning arrangements drop, much as she privately deplored Phil Collit's attitude – not only for his foisting all the liability onto his wife over something that meant so much to him, but for being the source of the fear and dread the nervous young woman seemed to be suffering now. 'Tell me why you sent that note to Kevin. Was it because you believe the baby could be his?'

Megan caught her breath. 'Of course not. How could it be?'

'Easily if you'd been sleeping with him,' the sergeant answered bluntly.

'But I haven't. Who told you – '

'Nobody's told me anything. It's just that you were obviously very fond of Kevin. Closer to him than Phil was, perhaps? That's what I felt from your reactions at the interview with Phil. You didn't have to admit it in so many words either. It was in your eyes. So when I first saw the letter, from what you wrote it seemed he might have been your lover.'

'Well he wasn't.' There was a long pause before Megan found the words to go on. 'I...I was sort of fond of him, yes.' The sentences were spoken quietly and with hesitation, the speaker's head bowed over her hands which were clasped before her on the table.

'But you weren't in love with him?'

'No.' The denial came slowly, as if it had been well considered first. 'He was nice to be with. Fun to be with. I don't say I wouldn't have...well, fancied him if I hadn't been married.' The speaker's left hand dropped below the table to stroke Waldo's head.

'But you never went to bed with him?'

'Of course I didn't.'

'So long as you're sure. You see, Megan, if you did sleep with him, it'd be better to admit it now. Better for Phil, too.' The sergeant was still in two minds over whether Megan Collit was lying. But if she was lying, she was playing the part convincingly, and it was questionable whether she had that much guile in her.

'Why would it be better for Phil?' Megan had looked up

sharply before putting the question, her movement prompting Waldo to place a supplicant paw heavily on her knee.

'Because if we ever had to prove who the father of your child was, and it turned out not to be Phil –'

'But why would you have to prove that?'

'Possibly because of this letter, Megan. No, listen, now,' the sergeant admonished firmly, leaning forwards and stemming what would clearly have been the other's protesting interruption. 'If, by any chance, Phil is arrested, on suspicion of murdering Kevin, and it could happen, you're going to be asked why you told Kevin and not your husband you're going to have a baby. And if it turned out that Kevin was the father, and that Phil might have known it before he went back to the clinic last night, it'd be a pretty solid reason for him to have assaulted Kevin, not necessarily meaning to kill him, of course. His death could have been an accident. We don't know yet. Not for certain.' She offered the last unlikely possibility in the hope that if Megan had been lying so far it might have prompted her to change her story. Certainly she was suddenly looking more helpless and perplexed than before.

'But how could that help Phil?' she asked.

'It would turn what he'd done into a crime of passion.'

'And that would get him off?' The query seemed more genuine than any of her previous ones.

'Not necessarily, but it does happen sometimes. Juries can be influenced by what's called mitigating circumstances. Do you understand what I mean?'

'That Phil would have had the right to be angry?'

'Yes. That's about it. You see, a genuine crime of passion can lead to a reduced sentence. So do you want to change anything you've said already?'

Megan was shaking her head vigorously. 'Of course I don't. Phil is the father. It couldn't be Kevin, nor anybody else either. And...and Phil didn't kill Kevin, I know he didn't.' The surprise outburst had been vehement enough to prompt a frightened movement from Waldo.

'So tell me why you wrote to Kevin saying you were desperate about being pregnant, and that you had to see him?'

Megan took a deep breath that caught in her throat. 'I was scared to tell Phil, dead scared about what he'd say. Kevin knew a lot of medical people. I thought he'd be able to fix an abortion without Phil knowing. It was a daft idea. But...but I wasn't thinking straight. I panicked, see? And now I've made things worse for Phil. You're going to arrest him, aren't you? Oh God, help me.' She began to sob audibly, which induced the dog to make excited hops from one side of her chair to the other, tail wagging furiously.

Mary Norris produced a clean tissue from her shoulder-bag and put it into Megan's hands. 'I didn't say he was going to be arrested. In the circumstances he's a possible suspect, like a lot of other people. What you've just told me explains well enough why you wrote to Kevin,' she completed, meaning what she had said.

'And I won't have to have the baby...tested?' Megan half pleaded, wiping her eyes and cheeks.

'It's less likely to happen in any case if it's accepted Phil didn't know you were pregnant. And you're sure he didn't?'

'Positive.' Megan was tightly compressing the tissue in her right hand.

'You hadn't told his mother either?'

There was brief but possibly pointed hesitation before the answer came. 'No. I...I might have told her today, and Phil as well, when we were all together. I'd been thinking about it all night.'

'Before you knew Kevin was dead?'

'That's right, when it didn't look as if he was going to help me.'

'Because of the bust-up at the pub?'

'Perhaps. I'm not sure. I thought it'd stop him contacting me, anyway, even if it couldn't have been that yesterday morning, before we knew about the lottery win.' Megan fingered the neck of the tracksuit she still had on. 'I don't want an abortion,' she affirmed, almost to herself. 'That might have been Phil's idea. But when his mother knows I'm pregnant, she'll be ever so pleased. She'll back me, I know. Phil and his mam are close.' There was hope in her tone now, if not a great deal of conviction.

'Good,' the sergeant responded, while wondering how husbands as patently selfish as Phil Collit rated enduring affection from their own mothers, let alone their wives. 'Just a few other things about that letter, Megan. Did you post it to Kevin?'

'No. I put it in the clinic letterbox. That's in their gatepost.'

'When did you do that?'

'Friday night, at five-thirty, on my way home from work. It's not far out of my way. Only five minutes there and back on my moped.'

'Didn't you risk Phil seeing you do it?'

'No, he finishes at four on a Friday. He'd been home ages when I got here. He was making our tea.' She gave a weak smile.

'And you knew the letterbox was emptied regularly?'

'Yes. Twice a day, at eight and six, except Sundays. The matron's strict about that.'

'I see. Now tell me why you had to write to Kevin at all. If you were desperate, as you said, couldn't you have just rung him?'

Megan shook her head. 'I tried twice Saturday morning, when he didn't ring me. When he heard my voice he switched off his mobile both times.'

At least, the sergeant thought, this was something that could be confirmed by the telephone company call sheets the police were officially requesting on the mobiles owned by Kevin Rees and Megan Collit. 'You work every Saturday, do you?' she asked next.

'All day Saturdays, yes, and most Sunday mornings. Not today though. I'm assistant manager at Owen's supermarket, up the road in Bryntaf. I'm there always by quarter past eight. It opens at nine. It's not a proper supermarket. Not big enough really. It's an independent.'

'I know it, yes,' the sergeant nodded. Bryntaf, a wealthy, and still largely rural suburb was three miles north of Llandaff. Its shopping precinct was small.

'In your letter you'd asked Kevin to ring you at work at the usual time. That would be when?'

'Just after I get there. I'm always alone then.'

'So he'd rung you often?' Mary Norris tried to deliver the question in a casual tone.

'Not that often, no.'

'But in the letter you mention a "usual time" for his call?'

'Like I said, he was a lovely man to talk to, about problems, and things.'

'But Phil wouldn't know about the calls? They were secret?'

'Some, not all.'

'I see,' Mary Norris responded, though not entirely sure she did see, unless, and the proposition still persisted in her mind, Megan had been lying some of the time. 'But he didn't ring you yesterday as you asked, even though we know he got the letter?'

Megan shook her head, and the tears began to well in her eyes once more.

'So this time he ignored your cry for help? That wasn't very friendly, was it?' the policewoman pressed.

'No.' The young wife was weeping quietly again as she added in a broken tone. 'And it would have been the last time we ever spoke, as well.' Her sobs were now shaking her shoulders.

'I'm sorry, Megan. You were obviously very fond of him. I think we'd better end this now. But just tell me again that you're sure, absolutely sure, that Kevin didn't ring you yesterday, and that you really don't know the reason why he didn't?' She was giving the witness a last chance to cancel out any mistaken or deliberately misleading answers in what she had said.

Megan blew her nose, then looked up slowly. 'He never rang me. And I don't know why. Except,' she paused for a moment. 'Kev was funny, sometimes.'

There was still a presentiment in the detective sergeant's mind that part of what Megan Collit had been telling her was not accurate, but she couldn't be certain which part. The relationships between this woman and her husband, and between both of them, as individuals and as a couple, with Kevin Rees, their common friend, simply didn't ring true, unless all three were even 'funnier' than they expected the police to believe.

Chapter Seven

Parry tapped on the open door across the clinic hall from Dr Howell's office. 'May I come in, Miss Oswald? My name's Parry, Detective Chief Inspector with the Major Crime Support Unit.'

'Of course, Mr Parry. I'd almost given up hope of meeting you. Met several of your subordinates already. Been wondering why I was left out. Too innocent to rate the time of the boss man, I thought. There's some consolation in that, of course.' Eve Oswald, matron of the Howell Clinic had thumped a key on her computer and risen promptly from the chair behind her desk, set at half-left from the door, and was offering her hand to the visitor with a broad, welcoming smile, the dynamic of her clipped phrases matched by the energy in her movements.

In contrast to the director's room, which had resembled a don's study at one of the older universities, this one was almost starkly businesslike, with steel furniture, state-of-the-art office machines, and adjustable lighting systems. There was also another desk with a computer extension, at present unoccupied, but presumably used by Sheila Radcliffe, the clinic accountant, whose name and title were also displayed on the door.

'I was saving the best till last, Miss Oswald,' the policeman replied with a grin. 'We've been very grateful for the help you gave DS Lloyd and DS Wilcox.'

'Splendid fellows, both of them. I could quite fancy cuddly Mr Lloyd, except he's already suited with a super wife. They go ballroom dancing he told me. Now that's a civilised, down-to-earth activity for a crime-busting detective.' The lady's light colouring and surname did not suggest Welsh antecedents, and her English Home Counties accent confirmed the point. 'So, please sit down, won't you,' she went on, rolling an upright, anodised aluminium chair with black leather cushions closer to the desk, 'and tell me if there's anything more I can do to help with solving this terrible crime. And there must be something or you wouldn't be in here, would you?' She nodded her head approvingly as she returned to her seat. 'We're all devastated, Mr Parry. We want you to catch this madman. To stop him ever striking again. I gather you don't think it was a burglar?' The look that followed this was earnest and concerned.

'At the moment, no, ma'am. We're still gathering evidence. What I'd like is some more background on Mr Rees. I assume it was you who hired him?'

Gomer Lloyd had been accurate in his description of Miss Oswald. Natural blonde hair now probably tinted, Parry thought, but the lady was, he guessed, in her late forties when nature rated help for the deserving. She had certainly kept her figure, and the clinging light blue sweater and wool skirt she had on made the most of the fact. Miss Oswald was not quite as tall as the striking Mrs Ingram, nor as pencil slim, both differences, incidentally, Parry knew would have helped the evident rapport between the matron and Gomer Lloyd. Gracie, Lloyd's wife, also had a well covered and preserved silhouette, though it was several degrees more Junoesque than the matron's. On first encounter Miss Oswald was the embodiment of the well groomed, poised, competent woman manager propelled to greater prominence in British commercial, professional and political life since the mid 1970s when the first woman prime minister had demonstrated that sex discrimination was a challenge not a barrier. Although studiedly non-political, Parry was

100

one policeman who had no hang-ups over feminine advancement.

'Yes, I took on Kevin, seven months ago,' Miss Oswald replied to the question. 'Jack-of-all-trades. Eager and willing. I thought he'd fit in, and he did.'

'You had no misgivings about his performance?'

'No serious ones.' Miss Oswald lifted her head it seemed a touch defiantly at the end of her considered summation. 'He had a natural empathy with stroke victims. That's not so common, even in medical professionals. It's not the same as sympathy. For the most part sympathy tends to be maudlin. Our patients have to do without it. They need practical, often exhausting help, backed by merciless shoving. They have to hit defined, increasingly difficult targets of activity norms, mental and physical. And there are no brownie points for failing. That's the basis of Edwin Howell's philosophy of healing. He's a brilliant man. Unique in my experience. With a wife of the same ilk. Met her, have you?'

'Not yet, no.'

'Treat in store, I can tell you. In his own way Kevin Rees understood our demands. He'll be a loss to us.'

'So as a nursing auxiliary he made a real contribution,' Parry observed quietly, a little overwhelmed by the lady's evangelical vehemence.

'A window-cleaner or dish washer here can do the same, given the acumen, Mr Parry. Rees lacked formal qualifications, but he had a natural understanding.'

'You said you had no serious misgivings about him.'

Miss Oswald raised a hand to touch the string of pearls at her neck. 'He had a second, private self – what you might call a doleful self. He retreated into it from time to time. When he thought no one was looking.'

'Someone else has described him to me as a manic-depressive in the making.'

Miss Oswald gave a knowing nod. 'I think that's fair enough, Mr Parry. Since it was probably Edwin Howell who described him to you in that way, I wouldn't presume to disagree.'

Parry chose not to confirm this accurate supposition except with a good-humoured lift of an eyebrow. 'So what brought on these...these changes in moods?' he asked.

'To give a very personal opinion, I'd say envy. Deep down, when he put his mind to it, I believe he resented success. Or possibly resented his own failure to earn any. It didn't surface often, at least not in company, but it was there. In fairness, he got over his blue moods quickly enough.'

'Of his own volition or with help? I mean might he have used drink or drugs?'

'Illegal drugs, you mean? He might have done, I suppose. Marijuana does the trick. Easy enough to come by, too, these days.'

It was the dismissive comment that led the policeman to assume his present companion took a liberal view on soft drugs but probably not on the other kinds.

'Nothing more serious than marijuana?' he asked.

Miss Oswald frowned at the question. 'Where are we coming from, Mr Parry? Have you discovered he was taking drugs?'

'Not taking drugs, but possibly dealing in them, Miss Oswald.'

'You don't say?' The lady showed more disappointment than surprise. 'Is there proof ?'

'There's circumstantial evidence that he may have been trading in ecstasy.'

'Oh, my God.' Miss Oswald gave a sorrowful sigh. 'I suppose I should have guessed.'

'Any special reason for the guess?'

'Only that his ups and downs had got more frequent. That the intervals between the downs used to be longer. That's a sure sign of an increasing drug habit. Yes, if he was a user I should have twigged it.'

'Would his depressions have accounted for his changing jobs as often as he did?'

'I think so, yes.'

'Incidentally, do you have his c.v. handy?'

'Right here. I ran it off after Sergeant Wilcox was in. I thought someone would want it.' She handed Parry the top sheet from the slim pile of documents in the tray next to her computer.

'I see he "left school at sixteen with three O-levels",' the policeman read aloud.

'The first wrong step, yes,' Miss Oswald provided. 'He should have stayed on. He told me his father needed him to start earning. I think it more likely it was Kevin who wanted that.'

Parry went on studying the sheet. 'Well he doesn't seem to have hit pay dirt for the first two years, not before he joined the army.'

'That's right. Even then he joined the wrong bit of the army. He was three years in catering before deciding he did-n't want to be a cook. He persuaded them to switch him to the medical corp. He was happy enough there, he told me. But that was before he fell out with the powers-that-be in the shape of a difficult staff sergeant.'

'But his five years there couldn't all have been wasted?' Parry was still reading.

'The last few years were, after his record had a blob on it.

Incidentally, a worse blob than he admitted to me. His career must have stood still then, along with his qualifications, which were practically non-existent. He told me he'd done a short term in jankers. In army detention. Six weeks, I think he said. It wouldn't have been longer or he'd have been dismissed from the service. He told me he'd gone absent without leave. It was all over a girl.'

'You didn't press for more details, and you took him on. Was that risky?'

'I was backing my own judgment on a young man I thought deserved a break.' The speaker paused. 'I was an army nurse for eighteen years, Mr Parry. Got all my promotions, and even a minor gong in the Falklands shindig. The Service is a great life while you're still moving onwards and upwards. Hard if you take a fall. I never did, by the way.'

Parry smiled. 'But you...retired early?'

'I left when I was thirty-six. I wanted to specialise in neurological care – in more areas than the army could allow. My father and a long-term boyfriend both died young of strokes, and both were in the army. Father was a brigadier. Happily I answered an ad. Found what I wanted with the Howells. Exactly what I wanted. Edwin Howell is an inspiration. But that's another story. Kevin Rees left the army because he saw no chance of advancement.'

'And he didn't achieve any later, it seems,' commented Parry. 'He switched hospitals pretty often. Was that easy at his level?'

'If you're a sort of permanent trainee with loads of hands-on experience, yes. He'd have been valuable in any hospital or nursing home. Cheap too, because he had no formal qualifications. He was likely to stay that way as well since he switched from NHS to private hospitals and nursing homes, then back again with total abandon. Giving himself fresh chances, he said. Except he kept denying himself a chance to settle on any course of study.'

'His last hospital job was at St Mark's in London.' He looked up. 'My fiancé's there, by the way, doing medicine.'

'Good for her, Mr Parry. When does she qualify?'

'In two months, we hope.'

'Wish her luck from me. Great hospital. As it happens St Mark's is where the Howells met, and got their first qualifications. Yes, Kevin liked St Mark's. Didn't sever his links there either when he joined the Ambulance Service. By the way, that's where he saw his great opportunity.'

'Eighteen months ago?' Parry supplied after checking with the c.v.

'Yes. And about ten years late. Still potentially the best thing he'd ever done. He actually became a qualified technician. Unfortunately it's a qualification you keep only if you stay in ambulances. Takes a year to get as well. At the start you drive the van, and, in his case, assist a paramedic in coping with whatever comes along. Probably nothing in that Kevin hadn't coped with already at some time or another. He was working to become a paramedic himself. That takes longer, but was exactly right for him.'

'What happened?'

'He crashed an ambulance. It was his fault.'

*

'Right, anything new and important not covered by this summary?' asked Parry, in shirt sleeves, waving a yellow report sheet. It was now five p.m. The detective chief inspector was standing in one end of the long police caravan, parked inside the clinic gate which was open and under the control still of a uniformed constable. A board beside the door of the vehicle bore the legend 'DEATH OF KEVIN REES. If you have information please enter'. So far, the few who had done so had been conscripts not volunteers – invited in by the police to give statements, none of which had been seriously useful or even informative.

Eight of the twenty-six members of the investigation team, a mixture of police and civilians, now all squashed inside the relatively narrow space, had been employed here since mid-morning at the computers, the printers, the bank of tele-phones, or around the small interview table or the work-tops hinged to the walls and already over-laden with documents. Altogether it was an ingeniously compact and efficient oper-ational unit, allowing space even for a free drinks machine. Others present had been called in from the routine but neces-sary chore of interviewing on and off duty clinic staff, and as many of the patients as they'd got Dr Howell's approval to approach. There had also been calls on locals thought to have been at the Eight Bells at the same time as Kevin Rees the night before, and any residents, including the cathedral cler-gy, living in the vicinity of the clinic, who might have wit-nessed unusual comings or goings in the area between ten o'clock and midnight. For those policemen and women it had been boring, repetitive and, to this point, a largely unre-warded effort.

Others further afield not taken from what they were doing included DC Lavinia Stotter, who had driven up the valley to Treorchy to talk to Megan Collit's parents, and DC Gowan Ellis who handled liaison work between the Serious Crimes Unit and the Drugs Squad, and who, as yet, had failed to uncover a connection between Rees and any known or sus-pected dealers in illicit substances. Both detectives had phoned in their preliminary reports. Ellis had added to his ruminatively that he might just as well have been playing football all afternoon, which is what he would have been doing if he hadn't been on emergency call.

Although the long white vehicle had become the temporary incident room for the case, it was unsuitable to go on performing that function for much longer. Like most senior detectives, Parry was impelled – or haunted – by the belief that any murder investigation not resolved in the first twenty-four hours (as most 'domestics' were) was at risk of dragging on for twenty-four days or weeks or months, supposing it was ever solved at all. It was why he pressed his teams without let-up over the opening hours of a case, becoming overtly edgy and covertly disconsolate when the end of the first time-lap began to loom with no resolution offering. A probable result had seemed so tantalisingly close since shortly after 8.15 a.m., after DS Mary Norris had first talked to Phil Collit – except the probability had become less promising by the hour almost ever since, despite the temporary fillip provided by the discovery of Megan Collit's note to Rees.

'Right, settle down. Tall ones at the back please, short ones forward. Sorry about the venue,' the chief inspector continued. 'DS Lloyd will give us a fast run through on what's known to date, so we're all singing from the same hymn-sheet.'

The sergeant heaved himself off the collapsible table-top he'd been squatting on and took Parry's place in front of an easel supporting a large paper flip-chart, the prepared top four pages of which he turned over as he spoke at, for him, a rapid pace.

'So, the victim, Kevin Rees, 32, single, nursing auxiliary at the clinic, was last seen on the first floor by Night Sister Ruth Tate at 10.31 p.m. precisely yesterday, as recorded in her log. He'd reported to her after he got back from the Eight Bells public house where he'd allegedly had words with his friend

Phil Collit, the clinic gardener, inside and probably outside the pub. The words were over Mr Collit having failed to pay his half of their joint weekly twenty quid punt on the Saturday lottery the week before. Yesterday they'd won what looks like being two thousand quid or more. Mr Rees was allegedly insisting that when Mr Collit didn't pay for the previous Saturday's stake, he'd reckoned Mr Collit had pulled out of their syndicate. Mr Rees is also alleged to have said he didn't believe Mr Collit would have come to the pub yesterday to pay his stake if he hadn't known they'd had a nice little winner. Mr Collit says he told Mr Rees he'd never intended giving up the lottery, that he hadn't been in to pay up the previous Saturday because he and his wife had been up the Rhondda, visiting her parents. The seven people listed here are believed to be witnesses to the conversation between the two men, or part of it.' The speaker ran his finger down the names writ large on the exhibited page of the flip-chart. 'So far we've only been able to get statements from three of them. None of them could corroborate exactly what either Mr Rees or Mr Collit said, and none of them were witnesses to what, if anything, took place between the two men outside the pub. So it's vital we speak to the other four possible witnesses, and anybody else inside or outside the Eight Bells last evening who could be a relevant witness.' Lloyd took a deep breath and cleared his throat loudly.

'No witnesses so far say they saw blows exchanged between the two men,' he went on. 'But Mr Rees had a bruise on one cheek. Sister Tate didn't notice it when he came in, so he could have copped it after he saw her. Mr Collit had a grazed knuckle this morning which he said he got putting his bike away.'

The speaker turned to the next page which depicted a roughly drawn plan of the clinic and grounds. 'After checking with the night sister, it's assumed Mr Rees left the building and walked in the direction of the cricket pavilion here,' Lloyd was now using a pencil as pointer. 'Mr Collit went to the clinic by bike ten minutes after Mr Rees had got there because, when he got home, in Mary Street, Llandaff North, the weather forecast on the telly had said there'd be an overnight frost, and he had bedding plants that needed protecting.' Lloyd paused. 'Matter of fact, I did the same with mine for the same reason. Mr Collit wasn't seen by anyone at the clinic we know of yet, nor was Mr Rees, except by the night sister, until he was found this morning at 7.35 by Mr Collit. He was face down, dead, stabbed in the back below the pavilion steps. The first report from the pathologist, ten minutes ago, says the time of death was probably between 10.30 – well, that's safe enough, isn't it? – and midnight. As usual, they're not going gospel oath on the last figure.' He looked up and added at speed, 'That's because he didn't die from being run down by a bus in front of ten sober witnesses, two of them nuns, and outside the town hall where the clock was striking the hour at the time of impact.' Lloyd gave a disapproving frown further to evidence his disdain over the reliable disinclinations of pathologists.

'Cause of death was a downward stab-wound with a sharpened steel dibber,' he resumed. 'One new point, he was probably on his knees, or falling forward when the dibber went in. This suggests he'd been knocked over first from behind, which could account for a graze on his forehead. Of course, he could also have been on his knees begging for mercy, but that's not very likely, and puts the wound at the wrong angle anyway.'

'Was he drunk, sarge?' a male voice questioned from the back.

'His blood alcohol level was a good bit over the driving

limit. Not that he'd been driving. We don't know yet whether he'd been drugging. They're still testing for that.'

Lloyd half turned over the next paper sheet, and without revealing what was on it, he continued. 'Mr Rees was a bit of loner, locally at least, and given to moods of depression. The only friends he seems to have made in the six months he'd been here were Phil and Megan Collit. Mrs Collit is two months' pregnant. She said she'd kept it secret from her husband till today, but she'd written to Mr Rees on Friday as follows.' The speaker uncovered a pasted-on, blown-up reproduction of the written message. 'Will you note "I have to see you...call me at work usual time...desperate, Megan." We found the letter in his jacket so we know he got it, but she says he didn't act on it. She also insists the baby isn't his, that she only wanted him to help get her an abortion without her husband knowing. She's so far refused to have a paternity test done on the foetus. She told her husband about the baby at 10.40 this morning in the presence of DS Norris and her widowed mother-in-law. Funny to have the police in for an intimate family announcement, but it was Megan Collit's idea to do it that way. She said it was because her husband was against them having a baby. Except Mr Collit took the news calmly enough, didn't he Sergeant Norris?'

'That's right,' Mary Norris answered from where she was seated on the floor at the front of the gathering. 'Mrs Collit had expected ructions, but they didn't come. Maybe because I was there. She also explained away the letter to Mr Rees, saying he was someone she or her husband would have turned to for help in an emergency. Of course, I don't know what happened at the house after I left. She could have exaggerated her husband's earlier objections about their having a baby.'

'What about his wife having a baby by his best friend?'

110

demanded another male voice with a knowing chuckle. 'And why is she refusing the paternity test?'

'Answer to the first question is we don't know it was by his best friend. To the second, Mrs Collit's objection is reasonable, as it would be to any woman. She thinks it might damage such a young foetus.' Mary Norris had responded much more pugnaciously than defensively.

There was a murmur of disbelief before another male voice questioned. 'Could Collit have known about the baby before today, sarge? Like from before last night?'

It was Parry who chose to break in and answer this with: 'Possibly, but we've no evidence to prove it. We decided to have him in Fairwater nick for further friendly questioning after lunch, but he didn't budge on that or any other part of his story. So we drove him home again without charging him. Carry on Gomer, will you?'

'Right, boss. I'm nearly through.' The speaker turned another page. 'Mr Rees had formed a good professional nurse-patient relationship with a wealthy patient who's in the clinic recovering from a stroke. He'd borrowed money from the patient's wife, eight thousand pounds admitted, for what he called urgent, deserving causes. All well and good, except at 9.20 this morning we found a cache of ecstasy tablets in a locked cupboard in the pavilion. Mr Rees had the key in his pocket, and we've now found another one taped under his mattress. The tablets have a value of between five and nine thousand pounds, depending on whether he was wholesaling or retailing the stuff. It seems the patient and his wife could have been staking a drug dealer without knowing it. It doesn't seem Mr Rees had been borrowing from any other patients, or any we've been allowed to interview so far.'

'Do we know if Collit was in on the drugs, sarge, like he was with the lottery?'

'Good question, Alf. So far we've questioned him on that twice. He steadfastly denies knowing anything about the drugs. Says he's against illegal drugs on principle. His wife has backed him strongly on that as well,' Lloyd replied with a nod to DC Alfred Vaughan, 48 years old, dour, thickset, reliable, and content in his rank without any ambition to improve it.

There was silence for a moment. 'No other questions?' the sergeant asked.

But the silence continued until Vaughan spoke up again, looking at Parry. 'Still Collit by a mile, isn't it, sir? Stands to reason.'

Chapter Eight

'So what have you been doing all day, my favourite woman?' Parry was travelling east in his car on the M4. He was alone, and speaking into the remote control mobile receiver.

'I'm revising. What else, with my finals starting in three weeks? Plenty of time to talk to you though, sweet. Wish you were here. Did you stay in bed till nine this morning, reading the papers? There's sinful.' This was a joke. Parry was a compulsive early riser. 'Oh, but I forgot, you were on call today. Been working then, have you? Anyway, it's lovely to hear your voice.'

Perdita Jones, medical student, accomplished pianist, competent organist, and Merlin Parry's fiancé, glanced at the clock in the living room of her one-bedroom, second floor flat in Guilford Street, Bloomsbury. It was just 6.15 p.m., too early yet to boil an egg for supper. The remnants of a four o'clock cup of tea and biscuits were on the table beside her armchair.

At 29, Perdita was what might reasonably have been described as a mature student, even allowing that medicine is a very long study course. What she was given to calling her 'years off' as a physiotherapist had at least provided her with savings enough to mortgage a place of her own to live in during her time in London.

Although modest in size, it was part of a recent, practical conversion of a well-built terrace house, and close enough to St Mark's Hospital. It had been a sound investment, too, since, over the time she had owned it, the value of property in the Metropolis had increased, while mortgages had become cheaper. Perdita was a shrewd lady.

'As a matter of fact, I've been in Llandaff from just after

eight this morning, running a suspicious death enquiry,' Parry explained, in a stoic tone.

'Then it's even sweeter of you to take time out for me. Poor lamb. A murder, is it?'

'Probably. Do you know a nursing auxiliary called Kevin Rees?'

'Is he the victim?'

'Answer the question.'

'Yes, sir. I've known Kevin since I did my time with Accident and Emergency here. He's Welsh. He'd been staff at St Mark's, but by that time wasn't any more. He'd left hospital nursing to qualify as a technician with the ambulance service. He still came to Mark's a lot. Wangled more than his share of trips for us. That was because he'd made some mates on the staff.'

'A lot of mates?'

'Mm...don't think so. But that's probably why he valued them. He didn't seem to have that many friends generally. He was aiming to be a paramedic. But he left suddenly last autumn, after crashing an ambulance. Left a nasty taste. Is he all right?'

'No, I'm afraid he's dead.'

'Oh dear, I'm sorry.' She paused. 'He...he had a lot of good points.' She paused again. 'How did he die?'

'Stabbed in the back.'

'Oh, God. Poor Kevin. Do you know yet who did it?'

'We're working on it.'

'I'm not a suspect am I?'

'No, how could you be?'

'Gosh, can you hear my sigh of relief?'

'No. But why were you listed in his address book?'

'Was I? Well he wasn't my secret lover, if that's what you mean. I prefer policemen, they're more protective. Well, usually. Is that why you're ringing? Because Kevin Rees had me in a little black book?'

'Yes. And why I'm driving to London. Traffic's light at the moment. I should be with you by seven-thirty. We can have dinner.'

'In or out?'

'Out.'

'Goody, the fridge is empty. Can you stay the night?'

'A short night.'

'But long enough for me to earn the dinner?' She giggled into the phone.

'Yes, by supplying information and contacts. But only if you can spare the time. And I'm serious.'

'So am I. I've swotted for too long already today. And you'll be saving me an egg.'

'That's great. Using the Met would have been cumbersome for what I need.'

'And a lot less satisfying, my darling.' She made a long kissing noise into the telephone.

'I meant information gathering.'

'What sort of information?'

'How well did you know Kevin?'

'Better than I know the milkman, but for the same kind of reason. Kevin provided a service. He was mainly my removal man. Knew somebody with a van. He was always ready to pick up any junk furniture I bought for the flat last year, and bring it here, for a consideration. After that he helped with the decorations and the repairs, too. He wasn't all that cheap, but he was thorough and reliable.'

'Would you say he had enemies?'

'Heaven knows. He had one or two sad male friends.'

'Sad in what way?'

'Mmm...sick, I'd say. Chap he brought here once to help

paint the kitchen was a schizophrenic who'd come out of institutional care. Sort of on rehab. Kevin was good with him. A natural nurse, you could say.'

'At least one other person has said that to me today already, and several others have implied it.'

'It was probably true.' She paused, curling her legs in the chair more tightly under her, while making a little pile of bis-cuit crumbs on her tea plate with her free hand. 'Kevin's partner...or his boss, I suppose, on the ambulance team, she was called Stacey...Stacey Fowler. As it happens, I saw her yesterday afternoon, so she's still around. Paramedic. Jamaican. Pretty girl. I think she had the hots for Kevin, but I'm not sure it was mutual. That wouldn't make her an enemy, would it?'

'It could, but not his killer if she was in London yesterday. It's a coincidence, but St Mark's has come up several times since the case started.'

'Is that surprising? I mean, since the victim spent a lot of time there, one way and another. What was he doing in Llandaff?'

'He'd gone back to being an auxiliary nurse. At the Howell Clinic.'

'Good Lord, I nearly applied for a job there once as a physio, except I didn't have enough specialties. Have you met Dr Edwin Howell?'

'Yes. He was the one who said Kevin was a natural nurse.'

'Then you should respect the opinion. Some neurologists used to say Howell was a charlatan. I always thought he was probably a genius. His wife too. They go in for all kinds of bizarre treatments to bring stroke victims back to life. If they were charlatans they wouldn't have lasted as long as they have.'

'So they're geniuses?' Parry offered.

'I think they're ahead of the competition anyway. They were getting impressive results when I was working around Cardiff. A senior physio at Mark's, she's also from Cardiff, mentioned to me some months back that a lot of private clinics are copying them. Some NHS consultants are too, except free fall methods are hard to apply in an NHS environment.'

'Interesting,' he remarked, although he was more concerned with the murder: a lot more. 'Would you know if Kevin Rees was on drugs?'

'No, I wouldn't.' She paused. 'Possible, I suppose. Soft or hard ?'

'Hard. And if he wasn't a user, we think he may have been trading.'

'Trading, or helping poor people who needed the stuff, and couldn't get it legally because of our antiquated laws?'

Perdita was into an old argument of theirs, and one on which they would never agree. Parry was a liberal in a lot of ways. He was demonstrating as much now by driving at ten-miles-an-hour over the speed limit on a fairly clear road, because he would have supported an uplift to a maximum of 80 mph on motorways. But he was roundly against the legalising of any currently illegal drugs. 'What Kevin might have seen as a public service, you mean?' he asked, careful to avoid any negative inflection.

'What a lot of enlightened people would see as a public service,' she replied bluntly.

'Well, there aren't so many of those in serious trading.'

'But Kevin could have been one if he'd had the money. A Good Samaritan.'

It was a sound point in its way – and the chap did have the money. 'You could be right,' he commented warily, then changed the subject. 'This Stacey...something?'

'Fowler.'

'Yes, the paramedic. Any chance you could get hold of her tonight?'

'Before or after I've had that dinner you've promised?'

'Whatever fits. During, if you like. I'm on duty, and I need to talk to her about who might have done for her boyfriend.'

There came a deep sigh of resignation from the other end of the line. 'I think I know where to reach her if she's not working.'

*

'Daddy, I've told you Phil Collit couldn't kill a rabbit, let alone a human being. It'd be against his convictions. I'd stake my life on it. I'll give you he's dull as ditchwater. I as good as told Megan that before she married him. But murder? Not a possibility. You'll have to pin it on someone else, honestly.' Having delivered this, in her view, unexceptionable sound piece of advice, Lucy Lloyd propelled a heaped forkful of her mother's cheese soufflé, into her mouth. 'Mmm, delicious, Mummy, you haven't lost your touch,' she completed, a trifle patronisingly, beaming at both her parents, including the one whose professional touch she had previously impugned as deigningly as she was now commending the other one's cooking.

It was nearly seven in the evening. Gomer Lloyd had not been long home when Lucy, the eldest of the Lloyd's five children, had arrived unannounced. She had driven over to the newly built bungalow they'd moved to recently in Blackberry Crescent, Pentrebane. This was seven miles closer to central Cardiff than Lucy's much less suburban and decidedly more upmarket home in the small market town of Cowbridge, which was also to the west of the city. The older Lloyds' fresh abode was on raised ground a mile from their previous one in Fairwater which had become too big for their needs. They were all three seated at the round table in the extension to the kitchen, and designed as a dining area. It was still sunny outside, and the rural view from the window was toward St Fagan's, within sight of the open-air Welsh Folk Museum there.

Qualified as an accountant two years before this, Lucy, twenty-six, was a brunette with a rounded, pretty face, and a peaches and cream complexion. Confident, often to the point of bossiness, jolly and, like her mother, given to plumpness, she had done well to be already a non-equity, junior partner in an accountancy firm in Cardiff. She lived with Ifan Ellis, another accountant, who was financial director in a prosperous civil engineering company with headquarters in a nearby industrial estate. That the couple weren't married was a sore point with Lucy's parents, but partly assuaged by the half promise that Lucy and Ifan would wed if she became pregnant – even though this was a remote possibility for the time being. The formidable size of their shared mortgage, their equally impressive pension contributions (something that befitted two responsible accountants), and their taste for exotic vacations, meant that their two substantial incomes were spoken for over the years immediately ahead, without babies throwing the whole discounted-cash-flow for a loop.

Married or not, Lucy had remained the apple of Gomer Lloyd's eye, the more so since she had acquired serious professional qualifications. He had even got over – or almost – a devoted father's natural antipathy to having another male share his daughter's affections. From her childhood up, Lucy had regularly attempted to manipulate her father into humouring her whims – and often with success. Even so, both of them were aware that the purpose of her surprise visit, encapsulated in what she had just said about Phil Collit, while certain to stretch Gomer's indulgence to the limit, was very unlikely to extend it to the point where he would actually alter his opinion to suit her. Detective Sergeant Lloyd was a conscientious policeman in every context.

Since her partner was away for the night, en route to visiting a new factory site in Scotland, when Lucy had presented herself at Blackberry Crescent to assail her father with the error of his ways, she hadn't given the time of day much thought. If she had done she would likely have assumed that the others might not have finished supper by the time she arrived. That her mother was just about to take a soufflé, from the oven at that moment hadn't fazed her welcome visitor. In her normal, take-it-for-granted manner, Lucy had merely remarked engagingly on how clever her timing had been.

Happily her daughter's inviting herself to supper at the last minute hadn't bothered Gracie Lloyd who had cooked for seven for so long. Now that she did the same thing for only two she inevitably provided enough for at least two-and-a-half. So although food served in this house was rarely left unconsumed, the calorie intake of the two senior Lloyds was such that they both benefited for having it curbed. It would be pleasing to believe that Lucy had this in mind all the time – pleasing, but, as it happened, quite wrong, and much too responsible.

Lucy had already reminded her parents that Megan Collit – Megan Thomas before she was married – had been a friend of nearly twenty years from schooldays onwards. 'She's been on the phone to me for over an hour. She's desperate, poor thing. That's why I've come straight over,' she now continued, in a deeply shocked commanding voice, intending that magisterial verbosity should stiffen credibility. 'She's positive Daddy's going to arrest Phil for a crime she knows for certain he hasn't done.'

An awkward silence followed. Since her husband was making no response, Gracie offered neutrally, and a trifle nervously, 'He's a gentle boy, I remember. Haven't seen him for a long time, not to speak to, like. Not since before they got married, come to think. You weren't a bridesmaid or anything, were you Lucy?' She looked hopefully in Gomer's direction both before and after these fairly irrelevant observations.

In truth it hadn't been until Lucy had jogged his memory that Gomer had realised he had known Megan Thomas, that was, until today. It was the change of name that had put him off his guard, that and the fact that even now he truly couldn't remember setting eyes on the girl since she had been about ten years of age, and even then she was just a dim recollection, along with a lot of other little girls Lucy had known at school. He had certainly never met Phil Collit before this morning. Nor did he really accept that Megan and Lucy had been all that close, either, not so close, at least, that Lucy would have been the first person for Megan to have turned to when she was in trouble – or turned to at all if her father hadn't been a copper on the case. Gracie's point about Lucy not being a bridesmaid at the girl's wedding had been more pertinent than he'd first realised.

'Megan said she didn't think to connect you with me, Daddy, not till after you'd been to the Mary Street house for the third time today. It was when you'd taken Phil away to the police station it dawned on her you could possibly be my father.'

'Well, your friend was still way ahead of me, love, because I didn't have the faintest idea I'd ever met her before,' Lloyd responded quietly, putting his fork down deliberately. To this point he had only been playing with what was on his plate, while not wanting to advertise that he had totally lost his appetite. Although usually a keen, even voracious eater, especially of dishes cooked by his own wife, consuming rich food and coping with a mental dilemma for him inevitably led to indigestion.

'Well, Megan really thought she wouldn't see Phil again when you left with him in the car,' Lucy went on, adamantly, before adding, 'Oh, yes, please, Mummy,' at the offer of more soufflé. Lucy's digestive system was seldom upset by cerebral activity.

'I hope she told you her husband came home later, Lucy?' said her father. They had taken Collit to Fairwater police station in the hope that in a more official, not to say more intimidating environment, he might have broken down, confessing to the crime that Lloyd, for one, was pretty sure he had committed. But Collit had made no such admission, which is why he had been allowed to leave – an event about which the young solicitor, whom the suspect had accepted to represent him, had appeared more surprised than his client. Collit had shown little emotion throughout the questioning.

'Yes, Daddy. Of course Megan was relieved when Phil got home. But Phil's a wreck. They both think you still believe he killed the nurse, what's his name? Rees, is it?' When her father made no immediate response she went on. 'I don't want to interfere, but didn't you believe him when he told you he's a...a known, registered conscientious objector? He's against killing in any form, and opposed to every kind of violence? He even joins demonstrations in London. And marches. He's deeply, deeply involved and committed.'

Lloyd looked plaintively at his wife, before turning his gaze on his daughter. 'Lucy, love, since you've been a copper's daughter all your life, I shouldn't have to tell you this, but I will, all the same.' He grasped his hands together in front of him, before going on. 'I'm not allowed to discuss a case in progress with you or anyone else. If you have information you think might be useful about the death of Kevin Rees, that's different, because then it'd be your duty as a citizen to give it to me. But so far all you've done is lecture me for questioning a witness. You have to understand, that's my job. It's what I do, as you all say nowadays. So, do you have information that could help us solve this case, or are you just rooting for a schoolmate's husband?'

Lucy had been smoothing the table with her fingertips, and shaking her head at increasing speed for the last three sentences. 'Well if telling the police a suspect couldn't possibly be a murderer isn't being helpful, I don't know what is,' she expounded, and getting angry.

'It's opinion, love. Well meant, of course, but it's just hearsay, nothing more. I have to deal with facts.'

'So just because Phil was at the Howell Clinic last night, along with about twenty other people, he's your single suspect for a murder. It's not fair, and it's not right either.'

Gomer Lloyd took two deep breaths before he said, looking Lucy firmly in the eye. 'Love, if I tell you something I'm not supposed to tell you, and if you let on to anyone else I have, including Megan, you'll get me into real trouble. D'you understand. Real trouble?'

'I understand, Daddy.' The speaker sounded truthful as well as momentarily subdued.

'Phil Collit was interviewed today at his home, and later at the station, because he'd had a row over money with Kevin Rees last night, because we thought he might have found out that Rees was the father of Megan's baby, and finally because he could have been involved with Rees in trading in illegal drugs, which is a classic situation where men can and do fall-out with each other in a big way. And, yes, Phil Collit was in the clinic grounds at the time of the murder. If even half of that is true, we'd have to have been pretty green young plods not to have him in for questioning about Rees's death, wouldn't you say?'

'No, I wouldn't say. Because it's not true, Daddy. None of it. It wasn't a real row they had. Rees hasn't been sleeping with Megan, and Phil is as much against drugs as he is against killing.'

'So he's told us. So we've let him go. Isn't that enough?'

The two were now sniping at each other hard and sharply across the table.

'But do you believe him, Daddy? Do you really believe him?' Lucy cried. She had lit a cigarette, the third since her arrival, and was choking her father with smoke as well as invective.

'Oh, calm down the two of you, I don't – ' Gracie Lloyd tried to put in.

'Keep out of this, Mummy,' her daughter interrupted without taking her eyes off her father. 'Tell me you don't believe him when he's telling you the truth?'

'I believe him to a point. The rest depends on what fresh information we get. And you haven't given me any for a start, despite the bluster.'

'You mean you'll believe her if Megan lets the bloody barbarian police ravage her womb cutting bits from her foetus?'

'Don't dramatise, Lucy. The sample won't be from the foetus itself. There's no cutting involved and no danger either.'

'Try telling Megan that. Why don't you believe her that the baby can't be Rees's? If she says so, it can't be, you dolt,' she exclaimed loudly, leaning forwards, her upper half stretching across the table. Lloyd was hurt by the insult and was breathing heavily from the exchange.

'The fact remains, Lucy,' he responded with steely emphasis, his temper just under control, 'Phil Collit was in the grounds, at the site of the murder, at the time of the murder.'

'Except he wasn't.' Lucy had begun her triumphant rejoinder on the instant, and now at the top of her voice. But whatever it was she had intended to add was never uttered. Dramatically she had fallen back into her chair with a capitulating kind of groan, her frightened eyes bulging, hands pulling at her chest, the still burning cigarette dropped onto her empty plate.

Her father bolted from his seat to her side. 'It's all right, love. Just try to relax. Breath as deep as you can. Gracie, phone for an ambulance. Say it's a heart attack. We need a defibrilator fast.'

Chapter Nine

The languid River Wye, famous for its salmon, wraps a shimmering, protective arm around three sides of the ancient town of Chepstow. Three miles onward it flows into the wider, and, at this point, less dreamy River Severn. The convergence happens close to the most recent of the two 20th Century bridges that soar above the beginning of the Severn Estuary – the waterway that further west graduates to the title of Bristol Channel.

Chepstow lies within Wales, but only just. It has retained its rural nobility because the area was never sullied (nor its inhabitants enriched) by the mining or shipping of coal. Chepstow castle, built by the Normans, on limestone cliffs, was deemed impregnable until Oliver Cromwell proved it wasn't by blowing holes in its walls. Today, the castle, like the old West Gate, the six foot wide Portwall stone wall (intended to protect the only approach from land), and the enclosed warren of medieval streets within, make the place a much visited attraction for tourists – and, incidentally, for policemen since the South Wales Police Forensic Science Laboratory is housed there.

Two miles inland from the town, in ravishing, rolling green country, Blycot Manor, a well-preserved, early Georgian country house of manageable size, nestles in the heart of its own remaining hundred acres. The equally picturesque hamlet of Blycot Mawr, in turn, kneels dutifully nearby, lending the present house a proprietary provenance as it had done for its Jacobean and Tudor predecessors. In former times, the manor acreage had been tenfold what it is now, whilst the present owner of the estate, Denis Ingram, leases most of his land for pasture to a local sheep and dairy farmer. When he bought the place, Ingram was indulging his taste for Welsh antiquity not for farming. His wife too had always savoured the role of squire's lady – and coveted a more genuine title to go with it.

On this Sunday late afternoon, at roughly the time that Chief Inspector Parry had been starting his journey to London, Angela Ingram had completed the short drive from Llandaff to Chepstow, and had already gone over the monthly report that Oliver Grant had brought for her to see. For the Director of the Ingram Housing Trust to have driven from London on a Sunday to do this when he, and its senior trustee, could have done it on any subsequent weekday at the trust's London office was of no consequence to either of them. That they had actually examined the figures and other data before getting down to the more pleasurable purpose of their encounter was to the credit of them both – though mostly to the lady. Mrs Ingram's conscientious application to the execution of her corporate and charitable responsibilities was becoming the stuff of legend with her business associates, even though that legend had been originally, purposely, and assiduously inspired by the lady herself.

Oliver Percival Grant was not at all inspired, nor even conspicuously conscientious, but he was extremely handsome as well as amusing. Flaxen haired, tall, and languid in speech and manner, he was an ex-regular army officer with a strong jaw, and a bewitching smile – when he was not sporting a practised, earnest expression that suggested serious thought. Now aged thirty-two, and still single, he had been at one of the more expensive public schools before going to Sandhurst. His subsequent army career had later been cut short at the pressing suggestion of those in authority over him. He had not been a total failure, just a misfit, with no prospect of promotion when service cutbacks had become the order of the day.

After a false re-start as a trainee stockbroker, and another as an insurance salesman, Oliver had been showing definite promise as an executive in a public relations agency where the earnest expression, coupled with his dashing appearance, his plummy accent, and the smile when appropriate, had gone down well with enough of the clients, especially those whose public affairs' executives had been female.

He might easily have reached greater heights in his new milieu had he not been poached by the most appreciative of the clients, the Ingram Housing Trust, whose guiding light had been Angela Ingram. This had taken place when the trust had been in its infancy. It had grown enormously in the subsequent four years, not least because Oliver, its salaried chief executive, had, with the sense of obedience inculcated through military training, steadfastly implemented everything that Mrs Ingram had directed – to the greater satisfaction of all the trust's swelling numbers of deserving beneficiaries. She was a leader, and in this context a brilliant one, who never needed her creative concepts either to be improved or questioned, and her chosen implementer at the trust was both too well-paid and too canny to attempt to do either of those things.

The Ingram Housing Trust had been the joint invention of both the Ingrams. Denis Ingram had scarcely been involved in its further day-to-day development, and he had seen to it that his wife was acknowledged as its most publicly visible trustee. From the beginning Ingram had viewed the enterprise as a sound exercise in effective public relations for his company, which was the trust's sole source of finance.

The function of the trust was to provide living accommodation for low income but worthy tenants. This it did by acquiring derelict housing for refurbishing, or land for re-development, in run-down, mostly urban areas. 'The Ingram' was popular with cash-strapped local authorities from whom it regularly bought awkward, unsaleable structures or sites for its benefactoring, thus reducing the waiting lists for 'council' housing.

The Ingram Housing Trust openly brought in Ingram Developments executives as visible advisors on its activities. This was encouraged by the company management because it served to expose its senior personnel to local authority housing planners in a lily-white context. It was hardly incidental but wholly felicitous that those planners were the same influential officials who needed to be approached when the company sought permission to develop building sites in highly desirable areas for impressive profits.

Denis Ingram had been an inspired executive chairman of his company, effectively guiding the enterprise single-handed – the way in which most successful property companies are managed. He had made his wife a non-executive director primarily for tax reasons, but also to give her an adequate sense of involvement in the company, though, he had assumed at the time, not on a day-to-day basis. Although he credited her with a high degree of business acumen, in his view, an active top role in the Ingram Trust was best suited to her capacities and charitable nature, the commercial building industry being a harder, cut-throat world. He also arranged that the Ingram Developments accounts department kept a watchful eye on the trust's finances. Ingram House, an imposing glass-walled, six-storey edifice in Hammersmith, West London, served as headquarters for both enterprises, though the Ingram Trust and its small full-time staff took up very little space there.

So it was all the more surprising that, following her

husband's illness, Angela Ingram proved more capable and unstoppable as his temporary successor at the head of the company than he or any of their colleagues on the board might have imagined possible. Meantime, the trust had perforce become more of an agreeable, less frequent out-of-hours interest for her – just as its Director, Oliver Grant, had been from the day she had appointed him.

'But you and Denis must have known this assistant nurse, or whatever he was?' Oliver grunted into the flattened bed clothes. 'Oh, that's the very spot...just there...gorgeous, total heaven.'

He was lying relaxed, and face downwards, on rumpled sheets and disarranged pillows, in Blycot Manor's master bedroom. The double bed on which he and Angela Ingram were disporting themselves the lady hadn't occupied with her husband in all the seven years they had owned the property – and had no intention of ever doing so in the future either. She had gone through the motions of sometimes spending the night in his room at the clinic because it suited them both to give the impression to others that their marital relationship was a normal one. Even so, such demonstrations had been limited to the occasional Saturday night, after which, like today, she left on Sunday to meet her paramour at Blycot Manor. Nor had it truly bothered her when Dr Howell had tactfully requested that, after all, she should cease visiting her husband for the middle weeks of his stay at the clinic, though she had shown a proper degree of disappointment at the time.

Maintaining the, for them, outwardly minor deceit in their relationship suited both Ingrams. They were deeply fond of each other, and neither would have enjoyed co-habiting with anyone else. Together, they had made a perfectly agreeable design for living. Angela took pleasure enough from time to time in bedding her decorous but always intellectually wanting lovers, but the prospect of enduring any of them every day for breakfast and dinner, plus lunch at weekends for the rest of her life, had no appeal at all when compared to the stimulating company her husband provided.

For Denis Ingram, the sensuous imperative of his sexuality, while a necessary indulgence, was controllable and containable within rational bounds. In all other contexts life with his accomplished and much admired wife at his side took precedence.

It had been very early in the marriage when Angela had produced the heir, now a student at Cambridge, to whom both parents were devoted and deeply proud, and who had ever afterwards given reason enough for the endurance of their union.

Neither partner being given to unbridled promiscuity, if it had not been for Denis's homosexuality they would most probably have been entirely faithful to each other. Of the two, Angela had the keenest sexual appetite. As it was, not one of her, over the years, three extra-marital partners had been aware that the husband she affected to be cheating on was gay. It was simply, she would explain to them a touch bitterly, that he was too devoted to his business to have time for carnal indulgence. This was also quite close to the real truth.

Denis Ingram had been bisexual at the time of their wedding – a fact known at the time to both participants. Instead of his married status helping him to overcome his homosexual inclinations as, somewhat naively, they had hoped it might, it had done the opposite. While he and his wife became resigned to the situation, he was unready even to consider the possibility that it should ever become known to anyone besides Angela herself, and to his own discreet, infrequently visited, ungreedy and faithful lover of many years standing, a man Ingram maintained in a style deemed more than adequate by both of them.

The current relaxed acceptance of homosexuality by society in general had done nothing to alter Denis Ingram's attitude to the subject. Curiously his conviction, even prejudice in this, was as solid and fixed as any that was likely to be encountered in the most homophobic of men. What it did colour was his enduring fear that his orientation might be exposed, uncovered, 'outed' or whatever the appropriate phrase might become. This was his single besetting anxiety.

'Oliver, I sometimes think you only bed me for the afters,' said Angela, feigning irritation, then added in answer to his earlier question. 'Kevin Rees? Of course we knew him.'

She was sitting astride him, methodically massaging his neck and upper back with firm, searching fingers. Her long, loosened hair was cascading over her shoulders, the ends lightly brushing his bare flesh as she followed her task with ardour.

The two had spent the previous hour in boisterous love making. Oliver was now affecting a heavy weariness because he so enjoyed what she was doing to him.

Angela was inexhaustible in this, as in all things that she was good at. It was also important to her self esteem to show that the difference in their ages had no bearing on the extent of her energies when compared to his.

'We knew Kevin quite well, as it happens. Or rather Denis did,' she continued. 'Kevin was very fond of him.'

'Good nurse, was he?'

'Yes, he helped enormously with the treatments. Especially with Denis's walking.'

'And the poor sod's ended up stabbed to death in the clinic garden.' Oliver punctuated the words with continued expressions of contentment. 'Mmm...what you're doing now is fantastic.'

'We aim to please.' Angela concentrated her hands on the declivity between his shoulderblades. It was the area that usually gave him the most relief. This had nothing directly to do with sex. He was a regular squash player given frequently to dislocating the muscles in his upper spine.

Oliver turned his head to look in the opposite direction. 'And no one knows who killed him?'

'They didn't before I left. The police have been hard at it all day. It's possible it was a burglar.'

'Burglars don't usually kill people.' He was, in turn, voicing what seemed to be a generally held opinion, if one that purportedly might have been put about by the burglars' union, had there been one. 'Was he popular with his mates?'

'I've no idea. I only saw him at weekends. Same thing with you darling.'

'But with me simply because you've deserted the trust.' His voice affected hurt and regret.

'Not so, and you know it,' she responded quickly. 'But you know I can't give the trust the same attention I give the company. Not any more. Anyway, you're doing very well without me.'

'Thank you, ma'am.' He was genuinely pleased at the confidence, then added with an enquiring frown, 'Was Rees the person at the clinic you needed that Ingram Trust money for? The one who looked after discharged schizophrenics?'

There was a moment's hesitation before she answered. 'He was, as a matter of fact.' She now regretted that she had involved Oliver at all. Sourcing the money quickly through the trust had seemed a clever move at the time. It had given credence to the stated purpose of what she had styled as the loans.

'That was on the up and up, was it? He wasn't kidding you? Did you get receipts eventually?'

'Of course it was on the up and up,' she lied. 'We'd have got receipts eventually, except we may not now, I suppose.' She paused in her movements as if contemplating the possibility for the first time. 'Well, that's life. And it was a perfectly legitimate involvement for the trust. Anyway, what's that got to do with Kevin Rees being murdered?' she completed.

'Schizophrenic – '

'He told me they were patients well into rehabilitation,' she interrupted. He could feel her irritation building through her fingers. 'And they were in London, not Cardiff. It wasn't one of them who stabbed him. The money went to good use, I'm sure, but don't mention the Ingram Trust involvement to anyone else, please.'

'Of course, Angela. Like you said, I've entered it as a temporary working advance,' he offered promptly, aware that he'd been close to upsetting her.

Temporary cash advances did not come to the attention of the Ingram Developments accountants until the financial year-end in October.

'Good. I'd better cover it with a personal cheque tomorrow. We don't want the trust mixed up in a murder enquiry, however tenuously. And don't bring it up with Denis when you see him either. I don't want him bothered with trivia at a crucial time in his treatment.' She had stopped the massage.

'Right.' His brow wrinkled. 'So Denis doesn't know about your helping Rees?'

'No. I thought it better not.'

Her last words had come from the heart. She had vowed to herself from the time of the stroke that there was nothing within her capability, and anything even assumed to be beyond it, that she would have hesitated to do if it promised to secure her husband's recovery. There was no reason now why anyone other than herself and her one unavoidable confidant should ever know that she and Denis had been black-mailed.

There was no danger either that the knighthood would be put in question. Everyone, especially the Howells, had built up Denis's going to the Palace. They had succeeded in making it the first major attainable goal in his return to normal living, something he had come to accept as positive fact.

Now her resolve had been put to the test, Angela regretted nothing that she had done.

'I understand, Angela. Anything you say.' Oliver turned his body around under her, his smile in place while he looked for an approving expression in her eyes.

'Of course you understand, my sweet. You know you have such a gorgeous body,' she exclaimed softly.

Chapter Ten

'So, you were at the Eight Bells from around eight last night, Mrs Radcliffe?' said Mary Norris, making a note.

'That's right, love. And you can call me Sheila. You're Mary, are you? I don't stand on ceremony. That's why I left my husband. Assistant bank manager, he was. Small branch. Stickler for rules and regulations. Gets you down after a bit, I can tell you. Anyway, your Detective Sergeant Lloyd sounded a bit the same on the phone, so I'm glad you're here instead. Ready for more tea?'

'No, this is fine, thank you. Gomer Lloyd is a super person, really. I'm taking his place tonight because his daughter's been taken seriously ill. Heart attack.'

'Go on? Oh, sorry to hear that.' Sheila Radcliffe was a jolly, robust, and garrulous fifty-two-year-old brunette with well-shaped wavy hair, cut to medium length, and a strong contralto speaking voice which she exercised with gusto. Dressed in a white, loose fitting, roll-necked sweater over tailored black trousers, she used a good deal of carefully applied make-up which highlighted her full lips, and the good-humoured, eager dark eyes. Her heavy costume jewellery responded audibly to her body movements which also made her pendant earrings shimmer in the light.

'Well, help yourself to the sandwiches,' she urged. 'Those are egg and the others are ham. Sure you won't have some of this white wine? It's not bad. From Chile. Four pounds-odd a bottle in Tesco. Now, you can't complain at that, can you, even if you got it for making trifle, or giving to a church fete?' The speaker swallowed a mouthful of the golden liquid to justify the commendation, replaced the glass on a side table, and pushed back both sleeves of the sweater, producing more tinklings from the bracelets at her wrists. The de-crusted sandwiches had been produced from Mrs Radcliffe's refrigerator on the detective sergeant's arrival. They had been made early in the morning, enough for two, the provider had explained, since the friend she had been with all day had been expecting to join her for drinks and a snack, but was having to baby-sit for her daughter at short notice instead.

'Thanks, the sandwiches are delicious,' Mary Norris responded to the invitation. She had needed to cancel her evening date, and with it supper at Gio's in Cardiff, her favourite Italian restaurant, when someone had called from the Kevin Rees incident van at the clinic to say Gomer Lloyd was at the University Hospital with his daughter. It was Gomer who had said she should take his place in seeing Mrs Radcliffe. She was relieved that they had made contact at last with the accountant of the Howell Clinic – and despite the disappointment, the overtime money was always welcome.

Mrs Radcliffe had been out since seven a.m., until twenty minutes before this. She had returned to find DS Lloyd's message on her answering machine and had responded to it immediately, except her call had been diverted to the incident van. The two women were now seated in easy chairs in the cosy living-room of the older one's four-roomed, first floor flat. It was part of a house in Bridge Street, just beyond Llandaff Cathedral Green. There was a modern, teak-encased piano filling one corner of the room, the heavy load of well fingered music on the instrument's stand suggesting it was in regular use. But what the visitor had first noticed about the comfortably furnished room were the flourishing house plants in it, plus what looked like several hundred CDs of serious music neatly stacked on a bookshelf.

'Iris Hewitt,' Mrs Radcliffe continued, 'that's the friend I was with today, widowed she is. Now she had a lovely husband. Except he dropped dead at fifty, poor soul. Heart it was with him, as well. She and I often go to the Bells on Saturday nights for a bit of supper in the bar.' Her ringed left hand went to smooth the two gold chains around her neck. 'The food's good. Most of it home-made by the landlord's wife, and they usually have a nice little group playing on Saturdays. Piano, guitar, and clarinet, not too noisy.'

'You play the piano yourself,' said the sergeant.

'After a fashion, love, yes. Don't practise enough though these days, that's the trouble. Never the time, is there? Last night the pub group wasn't playing. There was just a young woman pianist. Music student she is. Lovely touch. Played what's called popular classics. Well, that's all right, with bits of Noel Coward and George Gershwin worked in, like. We enjoyed her. It's why we stayed later than usual.' She drank some more wine. 'Anyway, sorry I was out all day, and for once I didn't have my mobile with me. Iris had hers, but the clinic wouldn't have known the number.'

'You were saying you'd been in the Rhondda Valley?

'Yes, stewarding for a one day motor rally. Well Iris was. I went to keep her company. She's mad about motor sports. We entered a charity Monte Carlo Rally together four years ago. Not the real thing, of course, but a great experience it was. The rally today was only regional. For charity again. It'd been cancelled last year because of the foot and mouth. We went up in Iris's MG. Lovely day for it, but it cooled later. I was glad I took this thick sweater, I can tell you.' She flicked imaginary crumbs from the garment, before going on. 'But I'm wasting time, aren't I? You want to know about Kevin Rees. I can't get over his being murdered. Crazy burglar was it?' She caught the look of caution in the policewoman's eye.

'Oh, I suppose you can't say? We heard about it on the car radio coming back. The announcer did say it was suspected murder though. I can't think of anyone who'd want to kill Kevin. Anyone who knew him, I mean. To think that at ten last night I was standing as close to him as I am to you now.' This was followed by some tut-tutting.

'He arrived before Mr Collit, did he?'

'Yes. About quarter-past nine. Pleased as punch about his winnings on the lottery. Buying drinks for his buddies.'

'With friends was he?'

'Not that he came in with, no. I meant just some of the Saturday regulars at the Bells. Acquaintances, they were, rather than buddies, I suppose. You get to know pub regulars, don't you, without always knowing their names.' She sniffed. 'As a matter of fact, I don't believe Kevin had made many proper friends in the time he'd been here.'

'What about Phil and Megan Collit?'

'I was coming to them. They were pretty close to Kevin, yes. Phil and he had been doing the lottery together up to a few weeks ago.'

'You mean they'd stopped doing it?'

'Kevin hadn't, no. Before Phil came in someone had asked him how much they'd each hoped to get from yesterday's win. He said Phil wouldn't expect anything because he'd dropped out of the arrangement for two Saturdays, including yesterday. That was the same as – '

'Sorry, were you there when Mr Collit arrived?' the visitor interrupted while making a note.

'Oh, yes. He was a bit later than on the other Saturdays we've been there. Must have been after quarter-to-ten, and Megan, his wife, wasn't with him. Nice girl, she is. Not very sociable. Bit reserved, but that's shyness probably. I gathered later she was home looking after his mother. He was more lively than usual until after he started talking to Kevin. They were standing at the end of the bar very near our table in the corner. It wasn't our usual table. Too close to the gents, if you follow, but it was the only one free when we got there. The group Kevin was with was the same as before Phil arrived. Phil probably knew most of them better than Kevin did.'

'Did the question of the lottery winnings come up?'

'You bet it did. I saw Phil take some money from his pocket. It looked like two ten-pound notes. He offered it to Kevin who just stared at him blankly, shaking his head. I didn't actually hear what either of them said because of the piano and the general chatter. It was Iris who'd heard Kevin explaining it all at the bar. That was earlier when she was getting our drinks. He was saying how Phil and his joint punt on the lottery had ended the Saturday before.'

'Did you get the impression Phil Collit was upset by Kevin's attitude?'

'Upset wasn't the word, love. You could see he was bowled over at first. Then he started arguing the toss, embarrassing the other people they were with. After a bit Phil seemed to calm down though. He drew Kevin aside, into the corner away from the others. The two of them went on talking by themselves after that, quietly like, Phil very intense-looking, Kevin mostly shrugging and shaking his head. At one point Phil got a pocket diary out and was pointing to things in it, dates I suppose. Anyway, it looked as if he was trying to persuade Kevin to change his mind.'

'Did that have any effect on Kevin?'

'On Kevin? Not a scrap. Boot-faced he was about the whole thing. Then he turned round suddenly and went back to the group. Instead of going with him, Phil went into the gents. This young clergyman who was at our table by then looked quite relieved when he did. He could see as well as anybody there'd been an awkward argument going on, and I think he was wondering if he should try to...well, make the peace, like. In fact he said so after Phil disappeared. I'm not sure how much he meant it.'

'A clergyman had joined you and Mrs Hewitt?'

'That's right. Didn't I say? Oh, he was lovely. Big strong fellow, but gentle with it. Late twenties or perhaps early thirties, with a mop of blond curly hair and a cuddly beard. Australian. His name was Derek. He said his surname but it's gone out of my head for the moment. Iris will remember, I expect.'

'Dressed like a clergyman, was he?'

'Yes, but not formal. Not in a suit. Just an anorak and a grey sweater over his black, what do they call it?... er...stock, clerical stock, the thing they wear below their dog collars. He'd looked a bit lonely at the bar earlier.' The speaker sniffed. 'Funny, people can be stand-offish with strange parsons in pubs. I've noticed it before. Like they don't want them intruding. As if they expect them to start preaching against the evils of drink, and taking a collection. Derek told us later he'd meant to change into an ordinary shirt. But he'd come straight off the bus, and hadn't eaten. Been up to Brecon for the day. Anyway, when he'd got his food, there was nowhere for him to sit, except a spare chair at our table. So we told him to join us.'

'That was charitable of you,' said the sergeant with a smirk.

'Well, it's a matter of anything good-looking in trousers, isn't it? And Iris is quite religious. I am too, come to that, when I've got the time. Anyway, he was so grateful. Told us he's been over here for two weeks already, at the start of a sabbatical. Finishing a university thesis, For his doctorate.' Mrs Radcliffe gave knowing, nodded abeyance to the importance of the heavily emphasised last word, before pouring herself another half glass of the Chilean nectar.

Her guest looked suitably impressed. 'And is he attached to Llandaff cathedral in some way?'

'You know we never asked him? He didn't say he was. His thesis is about the influence of Christianity in New South Wales in the Nineteenth Century, or something along those lines. I didn't really take it in. But I know the real South Wales came into it too. Well, you'd expect that, wouldn't you? He was staying at a local B&B for the weekend. Moving on to Bristol after a service this morning.'

'Was he officiating at the service, did he say?'

'Well, there again, we didn't ask him. He might have been, I suppose. Generally I got the impression he was sight-seeing more than anything else at the weekends. Don't blame him really. Mark you, that wouldn't have stopped him helping at a service. You could ask the cathedral Dean, lovely man, and very approachable, or Dr Janet Howell. She usually goes to the eleven o'clock there on Sundays.'

'Thank you.' Mary Norris bit into another sandwich while making a brief note. Like most police officers, she would have welcomed the bonus of clerical corroboration on some of the things Mrs Radcliffe had mentioned.

'Oh, Derek did say he'd been trying to get hold of a cheap car to buy,' Mrs Radcliffe put in as an afterthought. 'To use while he was here. He was finding bus travel a lot cheaper than rail, but what he really wanted was his own transport. He thought buying a banger was going to be cheaper than hiring over a long period. That's why I introduced him to Kevin.'

'Kevin Rees?'

'Yes. I knew Kevin was trying to get rid of his old Fiat UNO. It's reliable enough, but he'd just bought something a bit bigger, and newer. He'd asked me in the week if I knew of anyone who might like to buy the Fiat. When Phil left the group I took Derek over to meet Kevin. I told him Derek might be interested in buying a car.'

'And did they arrange for Derek to see the Fiat?'

'I don't think so. When Derek came back to the table he said Kevin's price was much higher than he could afford, but he might think about it overnight.'

'I see.' The sergeant was looking thoughtful as she continued. 'But Kevin did keep both cars at the clinic. I know because we fingerprinted the two of them this morning. So if Derek had changed his mind, he might have gone back with him there to see the car.'

'Possible but not probable, Mary.' Mrs Radcliffe paused a moment before adding. 'Derek's B&B was somewhere in Ely Road, so they wouldn't have been heading in the same direction. Anyway, I got the feeling Derek wasn't really a buyer.'

The policewoman nodded slowly, while inwardly determining to interview the cleric who conceivably could have been the last person to have been with Kevin Rees before he was murdered. 'Do you have the address of the B&B?'

'Well I'm pretty sure Derek said it was in Ely Road, but I don't remember him mentioning the number. Iris did offer to give him a lift back, when we were all getting ready to leave. But when she admitted it wasn't exactly in her direction, he said tactfully like that he'd just as soon walk. Lovely manners he had.'

And now he was in Bristol, thought the sergeant with an inward sigh. Well there wouldn't be that many residents offering bed and breakfast in Ely Road, and once she had found which house the paragon Derek had slept in, there was a chance he might have told the owner where he was planning to stay next. 'And what did Phil do when he came back from the loo?' she asked.

'Well, for a start, he'd stayed there quite a long time,' Mrs Radcliffe offered. 'He had a mobile with him, and we thought he might have been making a call home to Megan, because when he did come back he had the phone in his hand, and we could see he wanted Kevin to take it and talk to whoever was on the line.'

'Did anyone hear him say Megan Collit was on the phone, do you know?' None of the other people so far interviewed had mentioned the possibility – including the woman's husband.

'I don't know. As I said, Iris and I drew that conclusion. When Phil came back in, Kevin was talking to the barmaid, and like before, Phil had drawn him away from the bar, into the corner. So probably no one else really heard what they said to each other. Kevin had just finished the last of his pint, his second or third, I think, since he'd arrived, and he was about to leave.'

'And did he leave straight away?'

'Yes, with Phil following behind him. We left a minute or so after as well.'

'And did Derek go with you?'

'No, a bit before Kevin, it must have been. We said good-bye to Derek in the bar, because Iris had seen someone she wanted a word with.'

'But you saw Kevin and Phil again outside?'

'Yes, having a real barney they were too.'

'Did it come to blows?'

'I think it may have done, just before we emerged onto the pavement.'

'You mean you didn't actually see either of them hit the other?'

'No. But Kevin fell back into us as we left the doorway, and we'd heard Phil shouting. At least, I think it was Phil. It looked as if he might have elbowed Kevin, so he tripped, most likely. We both thought that. I don't believe he'd hit Kevin, but he'd nearly gone down, and might have done if we hadn't been there to stop him. I said something like "can we all join in the scrum then, boys", making a joke of it, see? Trying to reduce the tension, I was.'

'And did it?'

'A bit, yes. Phil just turned round, unlocked his bike where he'd chained it to the railings, and rode off home without another word. Kevin wasn't in the mood for chatting either. He just said "thanks, Mrs Radcliffe," wished us good-night, and walked away.'

'In the direction of the clinic?'

'Yes. I suppose he was going home too.' Mrs Radcliffe was examining her guest's cup. 'More tea, Mary?'

'No thanks. So there couldn't be any doubt the two men parted on bad terms?'

The other woman smiled. 'I know what you're getting at. You mean is it likely that Phil turned back, followed Kevin to the clinic, and murdered him. In his room was it?'

'No outside. On the steps of the pavilion.'

'I didn't know. On the radio they didn't say where it happened.' Mrs Radcliffe paused. 'I'd bet my bottom dollar Phil never did any such thing. That boy wouldn't harm a soul. Especially not someone as close to him and his wife, and, in my view, with no real grounds for him to be at all upset with Kevin.' Then she paused again, as if she was choosing her next words with care. 'You see, Mary, it really shouldn't have been any surprise to Phil that he wasn't going to get a share of the lottery winnings. He might have hoped Kevin would give him a small share for old times' sake, perhaps. And that may have been what he'd been asking him to do all evening.'

'You didn't hear him doing that?'

'No. Like I said, we weren't really near enough to hear what was said.'

'So what makes you think Phil could have had no real expectancy?'

'Not having grounds for any?' The speaker took a deep breath through her nose, and leaned forward in a confidential way. 'Well, because last Monday he popped into the office during the morning. I was alone at the time. Eve Oswald was with a patient. I knew the Collits had been away for the weekend, and I thought I knew what he wanted. Other times, usually when they'd been staying with her parents on the Saturday, always taking his mother with them, of course, he'd leave me with ten pounds on the following Monday to give Kevin who knew where he could pick it up.'

'The lottery stake?'

'That's right. Some weeks those two boys never saw each other from one Saturday to another, and Phil was meticulous about those dues being paid – or he knew Kevin was, which amounts to the same, doesn't it? So, as I started to tell you just now, I said to Phil, "Hand me your tenner, then". Except this time he shook his head at me. "Not any more, Sheila," he said. "Megan and I have given up the lottery. It's a fool's game".'

Chapter Eleven

'I love watching the river, darling. It was sweet of you to come here,' said Perdita Jones, stretching a hand out to squeeze Parry's arm. They had just been shown to their table, and were looking out across the water through the giant window wall of the People's Palace Restaurant in London's Festival Hall.

'Yes. Remember it used to be called the Review? Since it's the grandest of the places to eat in the building, I'll never understand why they gave it such a naff name the last time it was made over,' Parry replied.

'Not naff. Egalitarian perhaps?'

'Exactly. No style. Very USSR. The name People's Palace can't have much appeal to the carriage trade, and I doubt many of the other sort want to pay the prices.'

'Food's good though. D'you remember when we ate here before a concert three years ago?'

He smiled. 'That snatched London weekend? Of course I remember it. And the reason. It was the day you decided to go back to medicine.'

'And you ordered champagne. Oh look, that's a pretty boat.'

Although it was still early in the season, the fast flowing Thames was busy already with tourist traffic.

'Pity the water's such an unromantic brown,' Perdita complained.

'Same colour as the so called blue Danube at Budapest and Vienna?'

She shrugged. 'Suppose so.'

Spruce pleasure craft, recently dolled-up for a hopefully

prosperous summer, all with cabin as well as navigation lights ablaze, were emerging from or heading under the graceful, low arches of Waterloo Bridge in the burgeoning twilight. Most had already disgorged their passengers, or perhaps had never attracted any, and were making toward their homing berths for the night. All were overtaking working barges which, unexpectedly for a Sunday evening, were busy delivering produce off-loaded from larger vessels downstream to points higher up the river.

'Clever sticks for getting a window table, anyway.' Perdita was enthusing again, as she brushed the fringe of her corn-coloured hair away from her face.

'That was just timing, not influence or bribery,' Parry answered almost primly. He was not an avid tipper, and definitely not before any service had been earned – though in this instance the choice situation of the table was filling their happy, hovering waiter with hopes of tangible reward in due time. The policeman had made the reservation from his car only half an hour before this while he had been waiting in traffic on the way to Perdita's flat. He looked at his watch. 'The main concert started at seven-thirty,' he said. 'Since we couldn't have made it for that anyway, I figured at least there'd be a choice of empty tables around now.'

'And all set wide enough apart to stop conversation becoming common knowledge. I like that,' Perdita observed, her gaze taking in the high ceiling, the generally cavernous ambiance of the place, and the slimness of the furniture and fittings. 'In 1951, the year the Festival Hall was built, I suppose this was London's first minimalist restaurant. It took another half century for the principle to catch on, not that I really care for the style as such.' She paused. 'Anyway, your interrogation of Stacey Fowler won't be overheard.'

'Well, since you've persuaded Kevin Rees's girlfriend to

join us at no notice, I'd rather she didn't feel she was slumming it. But I shan't be interrogating her. This is supper for three friends, nothing more.' It was supper on him, too, which he didn't begrudge if talking to Stacey Fowler cleared up some problems about the murdered Rees – and conceivably led to the cause of the crime. Although he was in London at his own expense and mostly on his own time, he had come solely on a hunch to do with the Rees case. The rest, meaning the presence of his fiancé, was a bonus.

Perdita would certainly have preferred having Parry to herself for the short time he would be in London. But when she had reached Miss Fowler on the telephone and learned that she would only be free for two hours this evening, and not at all in the morning, she had dutifully followed instructions by arranging that they all ate together. She had called Parry back in his car to say so, certain, as well as content, in the knowledge that the paramedic would have to leave them before ten.

'You said she was unemotional about Rees's murder?' Parry questioned after tasting and approving the two-year-old Pouilly-Fumé, he had ordered – a decidedly superior wine to the one Sheila Radcliffe had offered Mary Norris, though at four times the price so it should have been, even allowing for a restaurant mark-up.

'She'd known about his death for several hours,' Perdita responded. 'Seems it was the talking point with the ambulance crews from lunchtime. Even so, I'd certainly expected her to be more upset than she sounded. Tearful, even. I mean they were pretty close last summer.' She paused, before starting to add, 'Except...'

'Except what?' he pressed after her hesitation.

'Difficult to explain, really.' She was watching a police launch moving very fast down river. 'I never thought they were made for each other, and I don't believe Stacey thought so either, not deep down. I met her through him, but I warmed to her much more, and got to know her better, too. I told you she was born Jamaican? Mother and father came here twenty-five years ago.'

'And she was brought up in London?'

Perdita nodded. 'She's twenty-six. Educated in South London, but didn't get enough good A-levels for university. She wanted to be a doctor, but lack of A's kept her out of med school too, that and the fact her father died when she was sixteen, her younger brother's a waster, and her mother needed financial support. Nothing daunted, Stacey went for nursing, then transferred to ambulances, basically because the job sounded exciting, with chances for using her initiative unsupervised. She got the para-med qualification in no time.'

'Does she still want to be a doctor?'

'I expect so. And it's not too late, any more than it was for me, except I had better basic qualifications. Last year I was encouraging her to try, without much support from Kevin Rees. After he left for South Wales, I'm sorry I rather lost touch with Stacey, though mostly because I've had to work so hard. Pity, because she's a worthwhile lady.' Suddenly she looked across the room to the door and waved, before completing: 'Anyway, here she comes.'

Parry got up to greet the hurrying, head up, blue uniformed figure who was stepping quickly toward them between the tables. Stacey Fowler was short and upright, with a well rounded not over-full figure, straight black hair, a tip-tilted nose, big smiling brown eyes, and gleaming teeth behind a full lipped, resolute mouth. 'Hi, Perdita,' she exclaimed. The two women embraced warmly, before the newcomer turned and firmly shook the policeman's hand.

'So this is the celebrated Detective Chief Inspector Merlin Parry? I'm very honoured.' Her comments were followed by a richly musical chuckle as she took the seat he was holding for her.

'I'm glad you could join us,' said Parry. 'Will you have a glass of this wine or something else? And may I call you Stacey?'

The chuckle was repeated. 'No thanks twice, and please do, in that order. Merlin, I'm on duty at ten, which is why I'm in uniform, to save time.'

'The uniform's very becoming.'

'Well thank you, gallant sir. It doesn't do to have an on-duty ambulance paramedic reeking of alcohol, even if she isn't doing the driving, and especially after dining with a top policeman. I lay off the booze well before I go on duty. I may not be that hot as a healer, but I'm always a stone cold sober one.' Her contagious laughter erupted again. 'That fizzy water will do me fine. But, hey, you two love birds, I feel like the third wheel of the chariot here.'

'Well you mustn't,' said Parry, pouring her some water. 'Perdita must have told you, I need your help. Incidentally, you know we both sympathise over your loss of a dear friend.'

Stacey thought a moment before answering. 'I'll miss Kevin for sure. Dear friend? Yes, I suppose so, and will now always stay that way in my memory. But he and I had kind of drifted apart emotionally, I'm afraid.'

'I had the feeling you might have done?' offered Perdita.

'Mm, he was an strange mix. A classic odd-ball, really. St Francis of Assisi most of the time, but Osama bin Laden for the rest of it.' Stacey took a sip of the water. 'I mean there was real good and real bad in him, and because I'm an optimist, I'd hoped the good was driving out the bad. That was until the last two times I saw him.'

'Could I ask when they were?' Parry put in.

'Sure, Merlin – '

'OK, but choose some food first or you won't have time to enjoy it,' the practical Perdita interrupted, beckoning the waiter.

When they had all ordered, it was Stacey who returned to Parry's last question. 'The last time I saw Kev, he stayed the night with my ma and me. It was three...no, four Wednesdays back. No hanky-panky either,' she laughed aloud. 'My ma's strict Baptist and don't approve of what she calls free loving under her roof, which was convenient because at the time I didn't either, at least not with Kev any more.' She shook her head slowly.

'Had something happened to – '

'To bring about a rift? Yes. I hadn't heard from him in ages when back in...in early April it must have been, I found him waiting for me when I came off duty one Tuesday evening. He had to be back in Llandaff the same night so he came straight to the point over an espresso in a Paddington caff he took me to. Didn't think to offer me a bite to eat, of course, and I was starving, but that was Kev's style. Single-minded. He asked me if I'd help with raising what he called a charitable contribution.' She gave a derisory kind of grunt. 'Some charity. He was aiming to buy a parcel of hash he'd been offered, and by hash, man, I don't mean potatoes, I mean cannabis,' she completed in a convincingly strong and contrasting real Jamaican accent.

'That's what I assumed you meant,' Parry put in quietly.

'O.K. It didn't impress me the dope was part of his Robin Hood act, taking from the rich to hand out to his poor schizo-phrenic rehab patients. You know about them, do you?' She looked from Parry to Perdita, and back again.

'Yes. From what I've gathered so far his basic impulses over them seemed praiseworthy,' said the policeman.

'To an extent, Merlin. Meaning, provided they always existed, and that wasn't all.' Stacey replied in a doubtful tone. 'Granted he was a good nurse, even though he was theoretically unqualified. But a doctor he wasn't, and it was as a doctor he fancied himself, and not just an ordinary doctor, either. He liked to behave as if he was some kind of whizz-kid neuro consultant, know what I mean, dispensing all kinds of serious goodies to the deserving? Doing that with mentally disturbed patients, even ones well on the way to having their problems under control, that was crazy.'

'Even if he was only dispensing cannabis?' This was Perdita, with a hooded glance at her fiancé.

Stacey gave a doubtful look, rocking her head one way and then the other.

'Well, I guess I'm a liberal like you, honey, when it comes to hash.'

'Merlin isn't. That's right isn't it, darling?' the other woman questioned, opening her eyes wider.

'Fine. It's a point of view I respect, Merlin,' Stacey cut in before he could answer, although he had made no indication of being inclined to do so. 'Smoking hash can lead to taking hard drugs,' she continued. 'Not always, but sometimes. If I was a detective chief inspector I'd have to have problems over that too. Thank you.'

She looked up and smiled at the waiter who had brought the paté, and toast she had ordered.

When the others had also been served, Parry asked. 'Was it a lot of money Kevin wanted from you?'

'Oh, he didn't want money. Not from me, anyway. Not that time. He wanted me to help get it from someone else. I just had to consent to back up what you might call his irresistible sales pitch.'

'By irresistible, do you mean the customer had no option but to buy?'

Stacey paused while holding a piece of paté-laden toast between her plate and her mouth. 'You could describe it that way, yes. Except he claimed he didn't think he'd need to use it except as an emergency measure.'

'Did it strike you he was trying to involve you in blackmail?'

'That's what I thought it might have been, yes.' She chewed and swallowed the mouthful. 'He wanted me to sign a...a confirmation, that's what he called it. It was typed. Said that on September third last year, the two of us had been involved in collecting a patient, who'd suffered an incapacitating stroke, at a location that could have been compromising for the patient in certain circumstances. Except our official report of the call-out said something different about the actual location of the pick up.'

'Because it was in a less compromising place?'

'You've got the point, Merlin, yes. Not compromising at all. This is delicious paté.' She was scooping more of it onto the toast as she went on. 'Can we leave it that I told Kev he could stuff it? That I wasn't going to sign anything, and that what his paper said wasn't true anyway. Well, not strictly true.'

'Could you enlarge on that, Stacey?'

She gave a droll smile. 'I could, but I'm not going to, unless you put thumb-screws on me. And I don't believe you're going to since this is just a chat between friends. Anyway, people might hear my screams.' She closed the comment with a high pitched peal of laughter.

Parry nodded understandingly. 'Agreed. But from what

you say, would I be right in believing the report sheet you completed that day was a charitable act on your part? That while it wasn't strictly accurate it'd be difficult to prove the inaccuracy, since it listed the location you'd actually reported to in the first place?'

'The bit about where we reported in the first place is dead right, Merlin, and it was specified by the ambulance service despatcher. We went where we were told to go. End of story. You see, I was the one who signed the pick-up report, not Kev, and I'll stand by what I wrote on it. Splitting hairs over the description of the location wasn't going to make a blind bit of difference to what happened to the patient.'

'Except it made a difference to Kevin Rees collecting some money?'

'Possibly. The thing is, Merlin, old Kev enjoyed playing God by getting round or ignoring regulations.'

'Handing illegal drugs out free to his grateful ex-patients, and in the Paddington caff, arranging to scrounge the money to pay for them with your help?' interrupted Perdita, who was following the conversation with increasing interest.

'That's right. I just gave him a piece of his own medicine by playing the Archangel Gabriel myself to help someone else, not Kev. I figured he was up to no good.'

'Because he wanted you to help him pressure that someone else into shelling out a lot of money.' Parry stated rather than questioned.

'Exactly that, Merlin, as I saw it.'

'You understand my prime motive is not to expose wrongdoing by Kevin? It's to find his killer.'

'I understand, sure. What you mean is the patient involved in what I've told you isn't going to be hurt now by what Kev was planning, because poor Kev is dead?'

'I'd say that's also exactly right, yes.'

'But you can't guarantee it?'

Parry, who had chosen leek soup, not as a patriotic gesture involving a Welsh national emblem, but because he enjoyed leek soup, nudged his now empty plate away from him. 'I'm not sure,' he answered, wiping his mouth with his napkin. 'But perhaps I can guarantee it. It's a question of how many witnesses there were to that ambulance pick-up you described, or partly described.' He was looking Stacey straight in the eyes as he continued. 'If it was just you and Kevin Rees, it seems from what you've said that you personally never did intend the patient to risk harassment in any way. Quite the opposite, in fact.'

'That's right, and Kev was the same, except he may have got money out of someone else involved strictly for good ole Kev's personal benefit. He was alone with the other witness while I was injecting the patient inside the ambulance before we started back to the hospital.'

'Can you tell me who that other witness was?'

'Not unless it becomes totally necessary. And I don't see why it ever should, especially since it might mean two people could get hurt for no reason.'

'I understand.'

'Anyway, Kev changed his mind later, much later. It was when he found out the patient was someone important. He never would tell me who, and frankly I didn't give a damn. Still don't. It was none of my business, or Kev's either for that matter.'

'The patient didn't have any identification on him?' asked Perdita.

'No. He had money, gold watch and cuff-links, but nothing to say who he was. And he couldn't tell us because he couldn't speak or communicate in any other way.'

'Presumably he was identified eventually?'

Stacey's expression clouded for a moment. 'Yes. By his wife, someone told me.'

'But how did she know where he was?'

The paramedic grinned. 'Spouses, especially wives, don't usually take long to call the police and the hospitals about their missing nearest and dearest.'

Parry nodded. Except he had a better idea about how Angela Ingram had been alerted to her husband's plight.

'The problem is I don't know if Kev involved anyone else in his caper,' Stacey added.

'He could have done,' Parry put in. 'But the only people who can hurt the patient have to be witnesses to what happened. If you're the only one left from the ambulance crew, you're not only against harassing the patient, you're denying what Kevin wanted you to say against that person.'

'True, I suppose,' Stacey agreed.

The policeman rubbed his forehead. 'Can we move to the night Kevin spent at your mother's flat four Wednesdays ago?' he asked.

'Sure.'

Except it was at that moment that the waiter with a laden tray arrived at his serving station with everyone's main course, and it was several minutes before the exchanges could be resumed.

'You said earlier,' Parry eventually returned to the point, while eagerly dissecting lamb and roast potatoes cooked the way he liked both, 'that Kevin didn't ask you for money that time in the café. Did he do so this time?'

'Yes. He wanted me to give him what he called a bridging loan. Five thousand pounds in cash for five days, delivered next morning. He was desperate. Well, he had to be to ask me for that kind of money, especially at the interest he was offering.'

'Which was?'

'Five hundred pounds for the five days, also in cash.'

'Drugs again?'

'You have to believe it, Merlin.' Stacey, like Perdita, had chosen roast halibut on a bed of spinach, which both appeared to be enjoying.

'And you refused to help him?'

It was Perdita who said, 'Of course, he knew you'd been saving to go to med school. Are you still?'

'You bet he knew it. He also thought I'd be stupid and greedy enough to take the offer. Well I couldn't, even if I'd been tempted. My savings are in a deposit account with three months' withdrawal notice and expensive penalties for breaking the rules.'

'So you sent him away empty-handed,' said Parry.

'Too right I did. He admitted it was a drugs deal, with the usual spin about his helping his needy friends. When I said it sounded like too much for the amount of hash he usually bought, he avoided answering directly, so I pressed him. Asked if he was into hard drugs now. He never admitted that either, but I figured I was right by his reaction and...and when he let slip later he was seeing someone we both knew next day.'

'Someone you knew was a dealer in hard drugs? In ecstasy for instance?'

'Not necessarily. And anyway it doesn't signify,' she responded, avoiding the issue, though this time it was she who was looking Parry straight in the eyes. There was a break in the conversation hardly accounted for simply by the relish with which the three diners were attacking their food.

'I'm glad you're still aiming to become a doctor, Stacey.' It was Perdita who eventually broke the silence.

'Haven't been accepted by a medical school yet. But I got

all three of the A-levels at Christmas at the right grades. I could get lucky soon. The government's screaming so hard for more medics they may even have to accept little old me.'

'I'm sure you'll make it,' Parry offered, except his mind was on a much more pressing subject.

Chapter Twelve

Nantwich Court was a back-street off the busy, shop-lined Earls Court Road, on the opposite side to the nearby underground station. The first door on the left firmly bore the number 3 in the centre of a narrow fanlight. The single bay, but fairly wide two storey house was part of a Victorian terrace, and was joined to the back wall of the green-painted Antico Restaurant that fronted onto the main street. After a cursory look at the brickwork leading up to the common wall, Parry deduced that at some point in the probably more recent history of the area, the owner of what was now the premises occupied by the restaurant had acquired number 1, Nantwich Court and had incorporated it with the bigger property. The first house in the terrace on the other side of the narrow road was number 2, which, in the common order of such things had been predictable.

Number 3 had evidently been converted into two flats. He studied the name cards under both bell-pushes beside the door, and debated for a moment before pressing the one marked 'GROUND FLOOR – G. ROSPER'. Then he waited. Stacey had not provided him with a name because she claimed that she had never noted one. She had only been able to tell him that the house was the first on the left in Nantwich Court and that she couldn't remember seeing a number.

It was 7.10 in the morning. Parry and Perdita had breakfasted together at her flat before he had dropped her off at the hospital. She was due to do ward rounds with Dr Marian Reynald-Kane, the consultant gynaecologist who had, the year before, persuaded Perdita to try for the same specialty after she had qualified. Except, to Parry's great relief, Perdita had dropped the idea after she had become pregnant because specialising would have meant staying in London for several more years. She had reverted to their original plan that she would find a GP post in the Cardiff area and make their married home there with the baby.

It was doubly galling for her future husband that the miscarriage had now set Perdita hankering after the specialising plan again. They had discussed it on their Spanish holiday without resolving anything, but the night before, after they had delivered Stacey Fowler to the ambulance depot, Perdita had raised it again, emphasising how keen she was to go for it after all. This had been their sole topic of conversation into the early hours, marring Parry's brief London visit. The atmosphere at breakfast had been distinctly strained. While neither had wanted to part from the other on a discordant note, there had been no time to do much else except, at Parry's suggestion in the car, Perdita had agreed that they would put all further discussion of her future career on hold until after she had finished her finals.

Parry's personal problem with his fiancé apart, he could hardly complain about the amount of progress the short trip had produced on the Rees case. It was Perdita who had finally got Stacey Fowler to yield up one extra and vital piece of information, only a minute before she had left them. Perdita had persuaded the reluctant paramedic that any admission on her part should be a swap. In return for her telling Parry the location of the pick-up their despatcher had given the ambulance crew on that early afternoon in September, he would have to agree never to disclose the source of his information. The trade had done the trick. While the resulting intelligence had been only marginally useful to Parry – it would eventually have been available, if slowly, through

161

official channels in any case – collected this way it saved precious time.

For her part, Stacey had accepted that her disclosure to Parry would reduce or eliminate the need for the police to look up the despatcher's instructions to her. She remembered that the directive had been to pick up a casualty 'on the pavement at the corner of Earl's Court Road and Nantwich Court'. Her failure to amend the instruction stating accurately where the patient had actually been when the ambulance arrived was hardly a massive one. Even so, following the murder of the technician who had been with her on the call-out, and the interest the police might be taking in his ensuing involvement with that particular patient, she preferred to have the call-sheet stay buried deep in the London Ambulance Service computer.

Anything that prompted the authorities to suspect that Stacey might have colluded with Rees, even unknowingly, in anything irregular would be bad news for the paramedic. She was very close to having her ambition to study medicine accepted. For her to be caught up in a murder investigation might be disastrous for her prospects. The bitter part was that, as she told Parry, she still didn't know, or want to know, the name of the patient.

After pressing the bell a second time with no result, Parry next tried the one for the upper floor flat. The name under the button was JACKSON.

'What do you want?' The question had been levelled from directly above Parry, by a seemingly bald-headed man, and possibly naked as well, who was leaning, bare from the waist upwards, out of an upstairs window. Half of the individual's lower face was covered in shaving foam.

'Mr Jackson, is it?'

'Yes.'

162

'Sorry to trouble you so early, sir – '

'I should think so too. Are you selling something?' the man interrupted in the same mildly irritated tone as before.

'No, I'm not.' Parry was aware that by calling his interlocutor 'sir' he had posed the possibility that he might have been an obsequious salesman, not a well-mannered police officer. Even so, that he was a copper might have suggested itself to a dishonest citizen summoned to the door so early in the morning – so in a convoluted way the attitude of the wooden-faced occupier of the upstairs flat could indicate the existence of an honest character beneath the lather. Parry produced his warrant card and held it up at arm's length in the hope the man could read what was on it. 'I'd appreciate a word with you, sir,' he added.

'Well, you're getting one. Tell me what you want?' The fellow was either short-sighted or plain cussed. In fairness, most doorstep salesmen carried identity cards these days as a selling prop, though often as not this proved nothing more than that the holder photographed badly.

'Detective Chief Inspector Parry, sir, South Wales Police,' the policeman announced with resignation – and intendedly in a tone loud enough to reach the ears of the other man, and hopefully not those of his close neighbours, and assuming that he was not hard of hearing as well as caught without his glasses.

'Why didn't you say so?' The head disappeared from the window, and a few moments later the door was opened by its frowning owner who was both taller and younger than his caller had first judged, his hairless head close-shaven not bald. Also he was now wearing an expensive, well-pressed, blue silk dressing gown and wiping his face with the ends of a thick white hand towel that was wrapped about his neck. 'But God knows what I can do for the South Wales Police,' he said. 'Better come in, and mind the stack of mail. The downstair tenant's away and he gets a lot of it. Seems to collect computer catalogues. I keep meaning to drop it all inside his door.'

Parry nodded with a smile. 'Might I have your full name, Mr Jackson?'

'Yes, Jeremy Blair Jackson. But let's go upstairs to my flat shall we? I'll lead the way. Slam the door, could you?' Jackson moved energetically along the narrow hall that contained only a small table burdened with what seemed to be almost exclusively junk mail in large transparent covers that threatened to cascade to the floor if disturbed. The only illumination now was coming from the fanlight. A few steps along, past a Yale locked door on the right, identified with another card as G. Rosper's abode, the passage ended abruptly with a natural wood-panelled partition with a door set into its left side. The door was standing open below a steep, straight staircase, close-carpeted in black which was in stark contrast to the dead white of the wall. Parry closed the staircase door behind him too.

Upstairs was more expansive and ritzy than the policeman had expected, and gave the impression of an interior whose single-minded creator had spent a great deal of effort to realise a colour scheme as simple as it was consistent – not to say determined.

The staircase ended in a landing that led onto a starkly white-walled corridor with one closed door to the far left and three open ones to the right, all of them painted a gleaming black. The continuing, unremitting black and white contrast recalled for Parry's the set of a ballet called *Checkmate* which had impressed him deeply as a student at the Cardiff Theatre Royal many years before.

The door that ended the passage to the far right, beyond

the white-painted ballustrading running back above the stairwell, gave onto the bedroom from which Jackson must have called down. The wall running up to this room held a massive unframed painting, a landscape-shaped, arresting conception of black and white oblongs. The black carpet that continued into the bedroom, only partially discernable, was over-laid with, so far as Parry could see, a circular white rug set below another white wall dominated by more abstract paintings, but this time smaller works.

The second door let on to a bathroom with, predictably, a white tiled floor and black tiled walls, and enough exposure of white fittings to demonstrate that there was no deviation from the overall colour scheme here either.

The third opening, across from the stairhead, was into a sitting room, from whose depths came the smell and noise of coffee percolating – indicating that the kitchen was through there, with the remaining and presently closed door to the left giving direct access to it.

'Coffee, or orange juice, or both?' Jackson asked in a matter-of-fact tone, while moving through the unexpectedly large sitting room.

'That's kind of you. Just coffee, if it's no trouble, thank you. I'm sorry again to be crashing in on your breakfast,' Parry responded, genuinely contrite.

'Never eat breakfast,' said Jackson, his bare feet still leading through the furnished space – sofa and small armchairs at one end, with scatter rugs on the carpet, and small bronzed sculptures of mostly undraped male figures on occasional tables and the brackets above the slim radiators, plus a great many multi-coloured oil paintings from different periods and artists well hung in close but dramatic juxta position on three of the walls. Parry found it relieving that the black and white fixation, though persisting in this room

165

in the walls, floor, and some of the furniture coverings, did not dominate here in the unremitting manner it had done elsewhere. Before this pleasing disclosure, it had gone through his mind that his host might even be the perverse possessor of a television set that received only black and white pictures. In fact, there was no sign of a TV receiver of any kind.

Almost the whole of the wall to the left of the door was taken up with open bookshelves neatly arranged from floor to nearly ceiling with volumes of varying size and age, all with the appearance of regular usage and serious scholarship about them.

At the end of the room, under the window which looked out over the next door restaurant patio, was a small dining area with four round-backed, raffia bound, black metal framed chairs and a matching table. To the left of this, through an open archway, was a small, neatly arranged and well equipped kitchen.

'Attractive set-up you have here, Mr Jackson. You're clearly of...of one mind when it comes to colour schemes,' Parry commented with a grin from where he was standing on the sitting room side of the archway. Jackson was busy beyond with the percolator.

'Being single-minded, as you suggest, saves making big decisions, don't you think?' the other man responded. 'Everything tones in with a chess set after all.' There was a handsome black and white ivory set Parry had noticed set up on a low table behind the sofa. 'Anyway, I'm far too busy making small decisions to have time for any big ones,' Jackson added, running a hand over his shining head. 'Gave up having hair to comb for a similar reason.'

'For no reason other than being a nosy copper, I'm trying to deduce what you do for a living, Mr Jackson.' Parry had moved across to the books which included an impressive variety of reference volumes on fine art and architecture, old and modern, as well as tomes on the decorative arts generally, including quite a large African, Japanese and Far Eastern section, again covering ancient and modern work.

'What do I do? Oh, that's easy. A little of this, a little of that. I'm a searcher. I find things for people. Information for businessmen. Facts for writers. Houses and pictures for people. That's people with money and usually no taste, but who know it, even boast about it by claiming they only want pictures that'll appreciate. First editions of rare books ditto.'

The speaker glanced at Parry through the archway before he continued. 'Kant, the German philosopher, said our sense-impressions are ripe for converting into intelligible unities. In most people that has nothing to do with aesthetics, but everything to do with converting an aesthetic perception into an assessment of what a picture will fetch in twenty years time.'

He paused to take two coffee cups very carefully from a shelf. 'A searcher on behalf of the rich and pliant, that's me. And I have a natural aptitude for not using the internet. Finding things in other ways is more practical, and quicker, if you know the right people.' He shrugged. 'And what does it all give me? Money, no obligation to take a dreary nine-to-five job, and time for my own work which is compiling a definitive study of avarice through the ages.'

'That should be a life's work.'

Jackson looked up sharply. 'I sincerely hope not. I'm thirty-five already and I'm scarcely a quarter of the way. Mark you, I've got some hot ideas. I expect the final opus to run into at least eight hundred pages.' He chuckled as he moved back into the sitting room. 'But, enough of me. Tell me, do detective chief inspectors from South Wales often make dawn raids around the Earls Court area?' He placed a white tray bearing the bone china coffee cups and saucers, with matching coffee pot, cream jug and sugar basin on the table and motioned Parry to sit.

'The answer to that question is no. I'm way off my beat,' the policeman answered. 'But I happened to be in London last evening, and it made sense unofficially to tie up some aspects of an on-going inquiry while I was here.'

'And the tying up involves me?' Jackson's eyes lit up with coy amusement.

'Possibly, yes. Can you remember if you were here around 2.30 in the afternoon of Friday, September 3rd last year?'

'Only with difficulty, unless of course I go and get my last year's diary, which I will now. This is intriguing. Like being in a gangster movie. My work-station is in the bedroom.'

'You have a work-station?'

'Just for trivial things. Takes up far too much space, but it's quite a big bedroom. Hang on,' the speaker called as he left the room. He re-appeared a minute later with a formidable but neat looking calf bound organiser. 'I was here on September 3rd. Well, in and out.' He closed the book.

'I see.' Parry sipped his coffee. 'So do you recall something upsetting happening?'

Jackson, who had reseated himself at the table, spread his long hands, palms outward in a punctuating kind of gesture. 'Could it have been the day I came back from lunch and found a poor chap collapsing outside the front door? He was sort of wobbling in a dreadfully worrying way.'

'I'm sure that fits, Mr Jackson. Was it you who sent for an ambulance?'

'Not before I'd brought him inside. It'd started to rain. Only a shower, but I reckoned the poor fellow could do with-out getting wet.'

'You got him up here?'

'With difficulty. As usual Garry Rosper from downstairs was away in a hot climate. Has been all winter, lucky bunny. The spare key he leaves in case there's a fire was up here. The poor chap at the door was more or less collapsing, but he managed to stagger to the bedroom. He had trouble forming words, then couldn't form them at all. Yet he obviously wasn't drunk. Then his right arm and leg seem to give out on him. I twigged then that he was probably having a stroke.'

'You'd told the emergency services he was on the pavement outside?'

'Did I? Yes, well he was when I found him, and I didn't want to get involved with paperwork.'

'And you gave a false name and address on the telephone?' Parry was guessing, but he had guessed right.

'Probably. Yes, Dick Tearle, which isn't a false name, it just doesn't happen to be mine. Dick is a friend who visits London often. I think I gave his parents' address in Scotland, except they've since moved to New Zealand to join their daughter. Anyway, I was sure no one would ever want to check.'

'The casualty had no identification on him.'

'Didn't he? No, that's right. The ambulance got here in double quick time. I remember they told me they had to take him to St Mark's. There was a fire or something at the Charing Cross which would have been closer.'

'You didn't know him?'

Jackson looked puzzled. 'Total stranger to me. I was just doing the decent thing by a human being in distress. He was well dressed. Obviously a gent.'

'Later someone rang his wife to tell her what had happened, and where he was. Was that you?'

'How could it have been when I didn't have the first idea who he was or where he lived?'

'That's right, of course, sir.' Parry paused. 'By the way, his name was Ingram. Denis Ingram.'

'What, of Ingram Developments?'

Parry swallowed some coffee. 'That's right. A very well-known businessman, of course, but not one of the businessmen you've done searches for?'

'No, he isn't.' Jackson shook his head. 'Well, I never. I know the name, of course. Their offices are in Hammersmith.'

'And neither he nor his wife has ever been in touch to thank you for your trouble that day?'

Jackson shrugged. 'They may have tried to, but I'm out a lot.' Then his eyes lit up as he added, 'But they didn't know my name either, of course. Nor the address.'

'You mean because it wasn't entered on the record by the ambulance crew?'

'Wasn't it? I don't know. They just turned into Nantwich Court from Earls Court Road.'

'Which is what you'd told them to do?'

'Yes. Whoever took my 999 call. Is that what this is all about?'

'Mostly, Mr Jackson, yes.'

'How unexciting not to say deflating.'

'Most police work is, sir. Better to stick to finding pictures or rare first editions. Aesthetically pleasing and no doubt pays better as well. So what did you do after you'd made the call to emergency services?'

'I watched for the ambulance, then called to the driver from the window.'

'And told them your name was Jackson did you?'

The other man swallowed. 'I don't remember having to give them my name. They weren't here long.'

Parry nodded. 'Purely as a matter of interest, did you...did you tip them not to enter your name or this address on their call-sheet?'

'Tip an ambulance crew? Like a taxi? What a bizarre idea.'

'Might have been worth a try, sir. That's if you didn't want to be involved any further. I mean you'd done your bit, coming to the aid of a fellow human being, as you said.'

Jackson's eyebrows lifted a fraction. 'You know, come to think of it,' he offered slowly, 'I may well have given them a small contribution...in thanks for the swift, efficient service, as it were. One likes to show appreciation when it's earned.'

'Quite so. And did you perhaps mention you didn't want any follow-up calls?'

'Honestly, it's so long ago anything's possible. I may have been resenting the time I'd already devoted to my act of mercy, and offered those good people a...a small reward to make sure I didn't have to waste any more. Really, I don't remember. Is it important?'

'Not at the moment, Mr Jackson.' Parry smiled. Stacey had suggested money could have changed hands when Rees had been briefly alone with Jackson. 'And now I'll let you get back to your busy day,' he added. 'Thank you again for your help, and for the coffee.' He made as if to rise from his chair. 'Oh, a final and much less difficult question. Can you tell me where you were between ten and eleven last Saturday night?'

Jackson raised his hands and clapped them together. 'You know I've been hoping you'd ask me something like that from the very start.' His face was alight with pleasure. 'Oh, I wish I could say I can't remember, or that I was alone all evening with no witnesses to prove it. Tell me, was that the time a crime was committed?'

Chapter Thirteen

'It'll be better now he's with her, Gomer. They're so much in love, aren't they? You could see it in both their eyes. Ifan must have got such an early plane from Edinburgh. What a really good, caring boy he is.' Gracie Lloyd sighed, hesitating to add aloud that she hoped Lucy and Ifan would decide to marry and have children when Lucy got better. She was thinking as much all the same as they drove away from University Hospital, known locally as The Heath, at the start of the normal Monday rush-hour – or, as it seemed to Gracie, a lot more normal for everyone else in sight than it was for Gomer and herself.

'Well, perhaps all this'll bring them closer together, love. Yes, it might even make them want to get hitched. You never know,' said Gomer, who was less inhibited than his wife about speaking his thoughts. He had mentioned marriage because he knew it would cheer up Gracie after all they had been through during the night. Even so, like her, he was wondering if a weak heart would prove more of a deterrent than a commendation in a future wife from the viewpoint of Lucy's partner. On the other hand, Gomer also felt it could prove a gritty test of true affection and loyalty.

'Oh, I do hope you're right, love,' Gracie responded gratefully. 'They're so perfect for each other.' She paused, still watching droves of healthy people on foot or in cars going about their normal business, and probably with equally healthy dear ones doing the same. 'I still can't get over what's happened to Lucy. Well, to all of us. She's so young still.'

It was 7.55 on a gloriously sunny Monday morning in Cardiff. Up to this point, Gracie had said very little since they had left the cardiac intensive care unit. It was the second time that the two had made the three mile round trip since the previous evening. The first time, she had been in the ambulance with Lucy, while Gomer had driven behind in their car. Then, despite the assurances of the ambulance crew, they had expected that their oldest daughter might die, and sensing instinctively that their guess in the matter was probably as good as that of the young, upbeat paramedics who were tending her. Gracie had been so distracted it had scarcely bothered her that she hadn't changed out of the oldest if most comfortable pair of slacks she owned, and that she'd left home without her lipstick.

They had stayed in the hospital until just before midnight, most of the time sitting in the waiting space outside the unit. It was then that the tall, gangling, seriously bespectacled and, to them, incredibly youthful-looking cardiologist had come out to reassure them, saying that Lucy was no longer in any immediate danger, that she was comfortable and sedated. He had also suggested that they should go home and get some sleep – which they had done, except that the sleeping for both of them had been fitful.

By unspoken, joint consent they had driven back to the hospital at seven to be rewarded thirty minutes later when the same, now incredibly wide awake consultant had made his early ward rounds. At the time he had been accompanied by the unit's senior staff nurse who had just come on duty, and a bevy of keen, if not quite so lively medical students. He had later returned alone to tell the anxious Lloyds that their Lucy was out of danger, that the scans and observations made so far were encouraging, but that she would need to go through more investigative procedures in the following two days. If his prognosis proved accurate, he had continued in a careful but confident tone, the myocardial attack would turn out to have been relatively minor, its effects controllable and reversible. Rest, medication and changes in lifestyle, he had concluded, and not invasive surgery, would probably be the outcome of what had been a serious but ultimately manageable event.

Ifan Ellis had arrived shortly after this, hot-foot from Edinburgh. The Lloyds had left him sitting at the bedside of the oxygen-masked, piped and wired-up Lucy. He had been holding her hand, or the small bit of it that was clear of attachments.

'The consultant said Lucy's blood pressure, her smoking, being overweight, and on the pill for so long, and...and having a diabetic mother was a perfect prescription for a heart attack,' Gracie detailed with another, longer sigh after a further period of silence that had lasted until her husband was turning the car into Blackberry Crescent. 'So it was my fault. My diabetes,' she completed with Judas guilt sounding in her every syllable.

'Don't be daft. It was nothing of the sort,' he responded with a forced chuckle. 'Well, your little touch of diabetes could only have been a minor contributory factor, if that. Lucy's not diabetic. Anyway, everybody inherits good and bad things from their parents or grandparents. That's how I got my gout. From my grandmother, that was. Funny because she wasn't a drinker, and they say – '

'You can't die from gout,' Gracie interrupted, still disconsolate.

'Nor from mild, controlled diabetes once removed,' he answered her forcefully, being fairly sure of his facts. 'I might as well say it was the row she and I were having that must have brought the thing on. But if she had all those problems, and high blood pressure as well, she must have been at risk for ages for this to have happened. What it amounts to is she's had a gypsy's warning. She's an intelligent girl and let's hope she'll do as she's told. Like giving up smoking, and going on a strict diet. That's what the doctor said.' He wished he was certain that stubborn Lucy would follow the advice faithfully.

'Let's hope,' Gracie put in with feeling, searching for the house-key in her opened handbag and finding a spare lipstick there too. She sighed again, but not because of the lipstick. 'Perhaps Ifan will be a good influence.' Her eyes narrowed slightly before she added. 'Of course, if they were planning on a baby she wouldn't need the pill any more, would she?'

Gomer grinned silently at Gracie's silver-lining sort of optimism, while he turned the car into their short drive. Passing the small area of recently mown grass on one side, with its circular bed of pruned and budding rose bushes in the centre, he stopped the car in front of the garage. The door was electrically operated at the touch of a button from a hand-held control box, except there was no point in his doing this since the garage interior was full of excess furniture from their previous, larger house, and none of which they were prepared to part with – well, not yet. Gracie was not so much a hoarder as a compulsive provider, certain in her mind that one or more of their children would be glad of all or some of the items if they moved to bigger abodes than the ones they were occupying now. So her husband's precious, nearly new Rover 25 had to live outside, though he had painstakingly put a plastic cover over it each night in the winter.

Five minutes later the two were sipping tea at the round kitchen table which Gracie had cleared of the sparse breakfast things before they had left for the hospital. She had done the same with the abandoned supper plates before they had gone to bed in the early hours.

'Suppose I'd better shave and shower,' said Gomer, checking the time.

'Going to work, are you?' But there was not much surprise in his wife's tone.

'Well, it's not me who's had the heart attack, is it?'

'I just thought you might take the morning off at least. Still, better to be occupied I expect.'

'Yes. And anyway, there's too much on. You'll be all right will you?'

'Me? Of course. Plenty to do. First I have to ring the others now we've got some solid news.' They had been on the telephone from the hospital to their other daughter and three sons the night before, all of whom lived some distance from Cardiff – one of the sons in Perth, Australia. 'And I'll need to do more shopping, of course. There'll be Ifan to cook for as well, while Lucy's in hospital.' This was notwithstanding that there was always enough food in the house for 'emergencies', not that they'd had anything of the kind since a then three-year-old grandson had swallowed a gold charm from a cracker at Christmas lunch two years before, and when it had taken the whole distraught assembled family, an overworked hospital intern, several nurses, and a radiologist to divine late in the evening that the charm had been a lemon jelly baby. 'Ifan's welcome to have supper with us every night. Breakfast and lunch too, if he wants,' Gracie added, compensating relish in her voice. 'And before all this happened I'd been meaning to plant out those geraniums from the cold frame. I'll do that after the ironing this afternoon, before I go back to the hospital.'

'It's not too early for geraniums?' Gomer left most of the scientific part of their gardening to Gracie, while doing the heavy work himself. The planting of geraniums had always qualified as light work in the previous house where their garden had been a touch smaller than the one in Blackberry Crescent. Even so, there weren't many plants to put in.

'No, no, love. People cosset geraniums too much. If they don't get out in the air they won't acclimatise,' Gracie stated with expert assurance.

Her husband finished his tea. 'Phil Collit wouldn't agree. He's still got half a big greenhouse full of them up at the clinic.'

'Professional gardeners don't know everything;' she responded.

Gomer frowned. 'I'd give anything to know what Lucy was going to say about him when she collapsed.'

'I don't remember. Talking about him was she?'

'That's the point, love. She wasn't, but she was going to. You won't remember because of what happened.'

'Well I can do without being reminded, I can tell you.'

'It's not as if I can ask her,' Gomer mused, half to himself.

'I should think not,' Gracie bridled.

'Well not yet, of course. But it was important. I know it was from the triumphal look on her face. In fact, I'll never forget it.'

*

Dr Edwin Howell replaced the telephone receiver. He and his wife were in the living room of their cottage, preparing for the morning staff meeting across the drive in the clinic.

'That was Angela Ingram,' he said in a ruminative tone.

'So I gathered,' his wife replied. 'She's one of the few women who bring out the grovel in you. Your mother was another, except she had better justification.' She gave him an unctuous smile, and returned to sorting through her patient notes.

He grinned back, the fingers of one hand toying with a silver miniature of Pooh Bear on the table beside his chair. 'Oh, I don't know. I'd be the same with the Queen. Women in authority have always unnerved me.'

'Nonsense. Anyway you've never met the Queen. And stop being so...so defenceless, it doesn't become you, not unless you're preoccupied with something important. I gathered Angela wants to take Denis home.'

'Mm. She didn't go back to London last night. Slept at their Chepstow house.'

'Who with, I wonder?'

'Now that's unkind.'

'I agree. Sorry, but I'm sure that woman's uppishness is simply a barrier to put people off daring to pry into her weaknesses. Is she whisking Denis away to avoid his having a confrontation with the police?'

'I've...I've been wondering that. On the face of it there's no reason I know of likely to precipitate such a thing. Denis hasn't been interviewed yet because, as Angela explained to them, with my corroboration, he was in his room all Saturday evening.'

Janet Howell affected surprise. 'So you don't think the very switched-on Chief Inspector Parry has twigged that Denis is a dedicated, terrified closet gay?' she questioned. 'With a very supportive wife, in that context at least, who'll go to any lengths to keep the fact a secret for his sake? A double-headed conclusion, incidentally, it took my perceptive husband all of two hours to fathom. Yes, I'd say a good copper might do it in two days. He doesn't have a psychiatric degree, after all.'

'So?' But his one word question begged too heavily.

'So, Kevin Rees, overly devoted nurse to Denis Ingram, and now exposed as a drug dealer, had been acquiring quite large sums of money from someone to pay for his dirty trading.'

'That's only supposition, because of the bank accounts and credit cards the sergeant asked us about yesterday afternoon.'

'Closet gays are often the victims of blackmailers –'

'In fiction, my dear,' he interrupted.

'In fact as well, still. And if, as it were, a decent man chooses not to come out for what he believes are good reasons, he's entitled to his secret. It means he has to run risks, of course, and the chance that someone he trusted will prove unworthy. Kevin Rees was despicable.'

Her husband raised both hands in mock surrender. 'Of course, you never cared for him from the start.'

'Too ingratiating by far.'

'Which didn't make him a criminal.'

'Except we now know he was one. We can only assume that Mr Parry takes that view after what's been disclosed since the murder, and that he may believe Rees's connection with the Ingrams rates further enquiry.'

'I think you're building on quicksand.'

'Mr Parry's been to London where the ground may have been firmer,' Janet responded, tight-lipped.

'How d'you know that?'

'Eve Oswald mentioned it just now when she dropped some more notes in. You were on the phone to Angela Ingram. Eve had just bumped into Sergeant Lloyd. She also told me that Angela had telephoned earlier to ask if you were out. She couldn't get an answer on our number at eight this morning.'

His eyebrows lifted. 'When we were here having breakfast. She didn't mention that to me. She must have misdialled.'

'Or dialled your consulting room number by mistake, Eve

thought. Anyway, Angela told her that she was pretty keen on taking Denis home today if you approved. She didn't say whether to Chepstow or London.'

Edwin Howell thought for moment. 'Mm. She has London in mind,' he said. 'But honestly I can't believe Parry is that interested in the Ingrams.'

'And I can't believe he isn't if he's put two and two together over Rees's involvement with them. And if you think about it, you'll see that too.'

'Perhaps you're right.' He sat up much straighter, his mask of diffidence melted. 'Well, although I've said they can interview A.J. Claverhouse, if they must – '

'Because it will do A.J. the world of good, and bore the police to distraction,' his wife put in.

'Quite.' He smiled. 'But under no circumstances am I going to let Denis Ingram be questioned by any policeman at this vital stage in his recovery.'

'I'm so glad you said that, my dear,' she offered quietly.

'I mean it, too. But of course it's still more likely to happen if he leaves here than if he stays under our protection.'

'I'm sure that's right,' Janet agreed.

'Did you hear me say to Angela I'd see her at noon, and that I wanted you there too. Moral support, really. Is the time all right for you?'

She frowned. 'Not really. But no time would be today, I'm afraid. Such a lot to fit in. But I'll do my best.'

'Of course, it's Monday. I'd forgotten, you have your other hospital sessions late this afternoon, don't you?'

'Afraid so.' The answer was regretful but resigned.

'Then please forget about the confrontation with Angela. I'll manage well enough.'

'We'll see, darling,' she replied, but was still intending to be there to head off any grovelling.

180

Chapter Fourteen

'Jocelyn Jackson had supper Sunday night with two friends, at the flat of one of them, across the river in Battersea. Posh address overlooking the park,' said Parry, standing shirt-sleeved at the open window and doing deep breathing and arm exercises. He had been too long driving the car.

'Male friends, boss?' asked Gomer Lloyd, but as if he knew the answer already. He was seated in front of Parry's desk.

The two men were in the chief inspector's office on the first floor of the headquarters of the Eastern Division, South Wales Major Crime Support Unit. The unit shared the site and the converted buildings of the old Fairwater Brewery with the state-of-the-art City Police Communications Centre which, since its recent inception, had put street crime prevention and detection in Cardiff ahead of most other forces in Britain.

It was 9.50 a.m. Parry had arrived ten minutes before this. He'd had a fast drive from London, even without exceeding the speed limit in Gwent Police territory – the county constabulary to the east of his own, and noted for its fiercely strict observance of speed regulations, with no leniency given to police officers of any rank and from any force. Gomer Lloyd had been waiting for him by arrangement, but they'd had a lengthy telephone conversation before this, so Parry knew about Lucy Lloyd's heart attack, and the circumstances that had brought it on. During the same call, he had given the sergeant a summary of what he had done in London.

'Yes, they were both men.' said Parry. 'Jackson gave me the names and phone numbers. Seemed genuine.'

'Too genuine to cross-check, like?'

Parry grinned. 'Not that genuine, no, but well-briefed ahead of any call from us. The friend with the flat gave me the right answers on the phone almost before I'd asked the questions. He's some kind of assistant in a section of the British Museum. I haven't rung the other friend yet.'

'No point, is there?' Lloyd worried the edge his moustache with one finger. 'Being coppers makes us cynical. Like tax inspectors, I should think.' He examined a peppermint as though for contamination by foreign bodies, then blew on it before putting it in his mouth. 'It's a sin to believe evil of others, but seldom a mistake. Have I told you that before?' he completed, apologetically.

'Not recently, Gomer,' Parry grinned, while taking a last glance at what was happening in the yard below. The transformation of the brewery buildings into an important police domain was still considered a moral triumph, a victory for the forces of good over evil, by total abstainers from alcohol, which properly included the Salvation Army. The imbibers of real ale took a different view, and there were many honest policemen amongst them. Aesthetically they had a case as well.

The wide, still partly cobbled area that Parry was regarding while imbibing lung-fulls of not especially clean, exhaust-filled city air, was at the moment occupied by mostly unmarked police vehicles and equally nondescript, plain clothes police personnel. It was not difficult to imagine the same area's colourful appearance half a century before, and more, when it would have been commanded by richly decorated brewers' drays, with sparkling painted and lacquered wheels, being loaded with great copper-bound barrels by brawny, capped and aproned labourers, and ready to be clattered away by obedient, draught shire-horses, white 'feathering' hairs draping over their hooves, and burnished brasses adorning their stout leather equipage. Nor had Parry needed to make his own mind's picture either. There had been a painting depicting the scene in the boardroom of the old brewery which he had once caught a glimpse of as a child.

This was mostly why the chief inspector looked out of that window as often as he did. His paternal grandfather had been a drayman here, and a traditional ten pints a day man – normal, in those days, for his calling – who had lived to be ninety-seven. So according to common legend it should have been Parry not poor Gomer Lloyd who had inherited boozer's gout. The sergeant's maternal grandmother, the one who had purportedly passed on the affliction to him had irritatingly been teetotal, as well as a member of the Primitive Methodist Church in Llandoch.

'So you reckon the London trip was worth it, boss?'

'We'll see,' said Parry, but here was hope in the sharp reply. He turned about, still taking deep breaths, and moving with energy, sank straight-backed into his desk chair. He put aside the new reports on the Rees case he'd scanned on arrival, and began leafing through some earlier ones. Although the police caravan was still at the Howell Clinic, the incident room function had been moved to Fairwater, to a section of the large general office beyond Parry's office door. He looked up. 'Stacey Fowler's off-the-record input could be pivotal. She'd make a good witness, if not a specially willing one.'

'Because she wants to stay out of the case, boss?'

'Yes, and because I think Rees was buying drugs from her brother. Her estranged brother.'

'She admitted that, did she?'

'She didn't mention him by name, no, but he fitted as the dealer she said Rees and she both knew. Perdita says it almost had to be her brother who's done time for drug dealing. Anyway, the ambulance episode definitely featured Denis Ingram, but we still need to prove it involves Rees's murder.'

'At least Miss Fowler's corroboration confirms Rees was into drugs, boss. Seems she's given us a better picture of the real Kevin Rees than anyone here,' the sergeant offered encouragingly. 'Miss Fowler's brother could fit as the murderer, could he?'

'Nelson Harvey Fowler,' Parry recited without reference to notes. 'Answers to the nickname Rabbit. Well known to the Met. They even knew exactly where to find him at six-thirty this morning when I called for an urgent assist. They found out where he was Saturday night and rang me back in the car. He was playing in a calypso band at a Brixton club till one a.m., no doubt with an army of witnesses. The Met is e-mailing the details, but I'd guess he's a non-starter as our killer. No point in wasting precious time on him.'

It was now past thirty-six hours since the estimated time of the murder. Earlier promising trails were petering out, and, in the absence of attractive new ones, the divisional chief superintendent would soon be looking to re-assign some of the personnel on the case. But that was the way in times of economic stringency, though not everyone involved understood the fact. The moving of the incident room to the Unit's headquarters was the beginning of the scale down. But Parry was sure the fresh leads would alter attitudes positively, which was why he was anxious to follow them up quickly.

'And Rees was blackmailing Mr Ingram through his wife like you figured?'

'Seems so. That's as much from what Jackson didn't tell me as from what Stacey Fowler did. If Ingram is one of those closet gays who choose to open themselves to blackmail,

Jackson fits well in the scenario as a colluding friend. He could have pocketed all identifying material that Ingram had on him at the flat. And it must have been him who alerted Mrs Ingram to what had happened, anonymously or otherwise.

'But not as a blackmailer?' the sergeant questioned.

Parry shook his head vigorously. 'No, I wouldn't think so. He possibly rang her saying he was a well-wisher. On the other hand, they could very probably know each other – or of each other at least. I'd say Denis Ingram is paying Jackson's rent and living expenses.' The chief inspector hadn't been impressed with the income potential of the effete, if intelligent and informed, young dilettante's purported job as a 'searcher'.

'And you reckon Mr Ingram had his stroke while they were...behaving like consenting adults at the Earls Court flat, boss?'

'Well, that's a hell of lot more likely than Jackson coming across a well-dressed total stranger pegging out on his street corner, whom he says he carried upstairs to bed with some difficulty. That was his embroidering, I thought, to make it sound convincing. And all before he called an ambulance.' The speaker shook his head. 'No, the real picture there is clear enough. Including Jackson bribing Rees to stop Stacey Fowler altering the details of the pick-up point on their call sheet.'

'Ah, and that could have suggested to Rees that he was onto something potentially profitable, boss.'

'Possibly, yes. Except he couldn't do much with the information at that point because he had no idea who Ingram was.'

'Right.' The sergeant started searching through his own notebook as he added. 'And he didn't have for another eight months until he ran into Mr Ingram again at the clinic.'

'Sure, but that was carelessness, or indolence on his part. If he'd been that interested I imagine he could have found out what happened to the patient after he was transferred from St Mark's to the specialised hospital in Bloomsbury.'

'And got his name into the bargain,' the sergeant agreed.

Parry sniffed. 'Stacey Fowler didn't actually admit that Jackson paid Rees, but she got close to it, and I'm pretty sure it's what happened. But for heaven's sake, it's not an offence to be gay, and being a closet gay isn't a good enough reason for murder. Not this murder, anyway.'

'It might just be if Mr Ingram is that keen to stay inside the closet, boss. I mean deadly keen. No pun intended. Of course, we still have to get Mrs Ingram to admit they were being blackmailed.'

'Except we now have good reason to accept they were,' Parry commented firmly. 'And I'm also ready to accept the important London public engagement coming up in July – '

'The one that mustn't be upset between now and then by police interviews, like Mrs Ingram said,' Lloyd broke in.

'Yes. I've given that some thought. It was Perdita who reminded me last night that July's the time of year for Buckingham Palace investitures.'

'You mean he could be in for a gong like our last Chief Constable, boss?'

'Oh, very possibly a better one. If he is, it isn't the engagement that's so important, it's the honour. Or the honour he might not have got if he was mixed up in some kind of scandal. That's if the bad news had been leaked before the list was announced on the Queen's Birthday in June.'

'You mean the gong could be stopped?'

'It's possible, I suppose, since it's supposed to be dead secret till it's actually announced. It'd depend on the size of the scandal probably. Ingram's a pretty important bloke.'

'That's right, boss. The matron said he and his missus had been to a garden party at Buckingham Palace last summer. Mrs Ingram told her that was because of the Ingram Trust. Fine work it does, of course. It'd be for that he'd be getting an honour now, I expect.'

'If he's getting one. It's still guessing on our part, Gomer, but it fits well enough.' Parry thought for a moment. 'The tabloids could have made a pretty juicy story out of his having a stroke in his boyfriend's pad in Earl's Court, if they'd had chapter and verse on it from one of the ambulance crew sent to pick him up.'

'Do you think Rees could have known Mr Ingram was about to get a gong, boss?'

'Well he certainly could if Ingram or his wife had told him, because they trusted him, and they seem to have been on close enough terms for that. Assuming Rees did know and was prepared to trade on it for some reason, the risk of the boyfriend story coming out could have been pretty devastating for someone in Ingram's still dicey state of health.'

'Bad enough to bring on another stroke?'

Parry shrugged. 'You and I can't know, but there'd be plenty of people in the clinic who would.'

'And ready to chop Rees to stop him blabbing if they knew he was trying to blackmail Mr Ingram?'

'One of them might. Question is, which of them knew the whole story of Ingram's secret?'

'Mrs Ingram for certain,' Lloyd offered. 'By the way, boss, she's here again this morning. Changed her mind about going back to London last night. Decided to stay at their Chepstow house instead. Seems she wants to take Mr Ingram away with her today. Could be to keep them both out of a murder investigation.'

'Who told you she wants to take him home, Gomer?'

'The matron, Eve Oswald, so it's gospel. I went to the clinic before I came here. Met her in the drive.' The sergeant gave a complacent grin. 'Mrs Ingram's seeing Dr Edwin Howell and possibly his wife too, at noon.'

'Well, I'd like to see her first. Do we have her Chepstow number?' Parry asked, checking the time.

'Yes, boss. You're not thinking Mrs Ingram could have killed Rees?'

Parry blew out his cheeks. 'Feasible from what we know of her movements on the night. Psychologically possible as well, but would a jury agree, I wonder? She's a pretty persuasive lady.'

'Like she could have got someone else to kill him?' Lloyd sucked on his mint, before completing. 'Dr Howell?'

'Bit fanciful, Gomer. It's true Ingram's been a star patient. His...his recovery will be a fresh feather in Edwin Howell's cap, a big feather too, considering the importance of the patient.'

'He had the opportunity,' Lloyd put in thoughtfully.

Parry shifted in his seat. 'No. Too much at stake.'

'She could have got an outsider.'

'What outsider? No one saw any strangers in the clinic Saturday night.' He paused for a moment. 'Come to that, nobody there seems to have seen anyone late Saturday night, and the place is pretty secure after six.' But the chief inspector had finished the point with less assurance than he'd been showing at the start. 'Of course, there's that visiting Australian clergyman in Mary Norris's report on Sheila Radcliffe,' he added, pulling out one of the sheets he'd been reading earlier. 'We don't know what happened to him from the time he left the pub, and he did have a reason for seeing Rees.'

'Buying the car, you mean, boss? He sounded genuine, but we haven't found him yet. The Dean wasn't available this morning, but the verger who was on duty at the eight o'clock service on Sunday said the Dean ran the service by himself. There were two clergymen in the congregation, both elderly, and neither had a beard.'

'But we know he was staying at a B&B in Ely Road.'

'Except there's only two regular B&Bs there, boss, and he hadn't been at either of them. We're doing a house-to-house on the area now. He may have got the street wrong.'

'Or he may be an imposter and a murderer, Gomer. We've got to find him. If he's genuine, and if he's gone to Bristol – '

'We've got Bristol CID on it, boss, checking the cathedral and the tourist bureau at the old docks.'

'OK. And you've sent DS Norris to follow up on Megan Collit?'

'Over what Lucy started to say to me before she had the heart attack last night,' Lloyd confirmed with a nod. 'Mary Norris left for Bryntaf just before you got here. Mrs Collit works in the supermarket there. I'll check on how Mary's doing.' He was reaching in his pocket for his mobile when it began ringing. 'DS Lloyd here,' he said, then listened to the caller, his brow furrowing more deeply with every passing second. 'OK, Mary. Keep after it. Nearly two-and-a-half hours is too long. I'll start a search from here.' He ended the call and looked up at Parry. 'Mrs Collit's mother-in-law says Megan left home on her moped for Bryntaf as usual at 7.45 this morning. She hasn't shown up at the shop which she was supposed to open at nine.'

Chapter Fifteen

Detective Constable Alison Pope had returned late on Sunday night from a cheap 'away weekend' in Bruges. It was the first time that she and her flatmate, Siriol Hughes, had been to Belgium. Siriol was also a policewoman, but in the uniformed branch. The two had enjoyed themselves enormously. Both intelligent young women, they had been enchanted with the atmosphere of the ancient city, the expansive main square, the entrancing architecture, the pretty canals, and the horse-drawn carriages, although they had never actually hired one of those because of the cost. Their charter flight back to Bristol had been two hours late. This had marred the proceedings a bit, but, for Alison, not nearly so much as the drudge of knocking on doors in the good deal less-entrancing Ely Road, and surrounding streets, the householders in which she was charged to question when she came on duty next morning – although it was really the same morning, since she and Siriol hadn't arrived home in their Cardiff flat until two. It was now 10.15.

The Kevin Rees murder was intriguing, or what Alison had gleaned about it, which, as yet, wasn't all that much. Someone who was deeply attached to her work, she wished she had been involved when the crime had been discovered, but you couldn't have everything – Bruges as well as a challenging murder on the same day. At least most of her colleagues seemed to believe the slaying was not run-of-the-mill 'domestic', which made a change from the nine out of ten murders that were usually just that.

On the face of it, Derek, the disappearing Australian clergyman, seemed only to be an interested bystander, but his testimony could be important. DCI Parry clearly thought as much, which was good enough for Alison. It had been Mr Parry who, not so long ago, had backed her transfer from the uniformed branch to the CID. Not all her superiors had been ready to do that at the time, and she was still making every effort to justify Mr Parry's faith in her.

Alison and six other police officers were today urgently charged with finding where Derek had slept on Saturday night. They were trying every house because clergymen were often put up by members of church congregations who didn't normally do B&B.

Alison rang the bell on the front door of the next mock-Tudor dwelling (after Bruges, nothing much here seemed genuine to her), the street number of which was missing, or else it had simply been replaced by the nameboard that bore the title 'Raleigh House' in Gothic script. For a semi-detached, with flaking paintwork, in a row of look-alikes, most of which, in fairness, were in better repair than this one, the dedication seemed not so much uppish as comic – though the artistically informed Alison allowed that the lettering, at least, was broadly in period.

There had been no answer at two of the last four houses, and no help from occupants of the previous fifteen, only questions from several over-inquisitive housewives about why the police were after a cleric – with thoughts of naughty vicars not far from the enquirers' minds if the looks in their eyes were anything to go by.

The woman detective and her team had been made very aware that the witness they had dubbed the 'Rev Derek' might have been the last person to see the victim alive, except for the murderer – unless of course the Rev Derek was himself the murderer, which added more point to the search for him. However, Alison was not minded to believe that he would be the villain. She had been brought up to respect clergymen, and six years in the police force hadn't much altered her attitude – despite the recent scandals about paedophile priests. In any case, none of those had been murderers. But since she was aiming for promotion to detective sergeant it would help if an important witness was traced through her dogged application.

Ungainly but earnest, Alison made up in initiative and effort what the superior officers who hadn't backed her transfer had defined as a lack of inventiveness. It has to be added also that in the opinion of male colleagues in general she was a touch lacking in overly feminine allure – although this would have been hotly disputed by her boyfriend, a regular soldier at present serving in Iraq and deeply anxious to see her again. As she waited impatiently on the doorstep, she shifted her weight somewhat woodenly from one foot to the other, the rest of her lanky body swaying in concert. It was a habit she had developed playing in goal for her school hockey team.

'Yes?' The green front door had opened suddenly with a jarring noise that suggested its surrounds urgently needed easing. The human instigator of what, in the circumstances, must have been an effortful accomplishment, turned out to be a plump, curly-headed girl aged about seven, dressed in an oversized yellow tracksuit and blue trainers, and sucking a large red lollipop. The confection was clutched in one hand while the other trailed a dilapidated teddy bear, the appearance of which wasn't enhanced through its being carried upside down.

'Hello. Is that your favourite bear? What he's called? Teddy?' Alison enquired with an engaging smile. She wasn't very good with small children, but she always tried her best.

'No.'

'Oh, a secret, is it?'

'Yes.'

'My name's Alison. Is your name secret like your teddy's, or are you going to tell me what it is?'

'No.'

'Does that mean no your name's not secret, or no you're not telling me what it is?'

This time the only response was an unaccompanied scowl.

'I see. Well I think your name's Priscilla and you don't like it.'

'No it isn't. It's Jessica.'

'Oh, Jessica's a lovely name,' Alison tried not to show pride in victory. 'So you're having a day off school, are you, Jessica?'

'I'm at the dentist.' The threatening look that went with this palpable untruth defied challenge. Jessica gave the lollipop a long slow lick.

'Well I hope the tooth's not painful.' Alison felt that there was hardly any purpose in her delivering a homily about the dental perils induced by sugar confectionary. 'Is your mummy in?'

The girl gave an energetic sniff that exercised every muscle in her face, including those below her ears. 'What are you then?' she demanded, demonstrating that a grasp of the premise about the best means of defence being attack might possibly be as much inborn as the result of sophisticated tutelage.

'I'm a police detective.' It was an admission that usually impressed the young. The infant, who had treated the caller's earlier stooping movement with suspicion, drew backwards a little into the hall before demanding: 'So where's your ID then?'

Alison gave an approving smile unmatched by her inward

feeling. 'It's here, and you're quite right to ask for it. Well done.' Her warrant card had been ready in her hand, except she hadn't expected to be asked for it by an unlettered innocent.

'From Fairwater nick, are you?' the innocent enquired, eyeing the card with a deep frown but without registering that she actually understood anything printed on it, which might well have included the decidedly unflattering likeness of its owner.

'That's right. Now, you were going to tell me if Mummy's in?'

'Don't know,' was the guarded reply.

'I see. Well I think she'll want to see me.'

'Why?'

'We're wondering if she does bed and breakfast.'

'You want to stay the night?' The question came so quickly it would have been reasonable to suppose that the child made a commission on bookings.

'I don't want to stay, no.' Alison was finding the interview tiresome and the slight strengthening of her tone showed as much. 'We're trying to find a gentleman who stayed around here on Saturday night.'

'Why?'

'Because, Jessica, he may be able to help us with some enquiries.'

'About the murder Saturday?'

'Possibly. Now if you'd just ask Mummy to come and speak to me.'

The child pondered for a few moments, taking several, behind schedule, quick licks on her lollipop. 'What's his name, then?' Her uplifted gaze had become strangely earnest – and, it seemed, perfectly guiltless.

Alison had been on the verge of ending the encounter, but

her devotion to duty was now paying off. 'We believe his first name's Derek, and he's probably a clergyman. You know what a clergyman is?'

Jessica either treated the question with the contempt she thought it deserved by ignoring it, or else she had no idea what a clergyman was. 'I think he's upstairs with our Phoebe,' she vouchsafed quietly.

'Is Phoebe your sister?' Alison whispered back.

'That's right. They've gone up to sweep the chimney in her bedroom. That's what she said.' Hurt was reflected in the childish eyes.

A frisson of excitement swept through Alison's long frame. Her enduring trust of clergymen took a sudden knock, until the probability that Derek wasn't a real Rev repaired the damage. 'Jessica, how old is Phoebe?'

The small eyes widened. 'Fourteen.' The small mouth remained open, showing at once, with the rest of the little face, doubt and awakening sisterly concern.

'Is Derek a big man, Jessica, with curly hair like yours, and a beard?'

The answer came swiftly. 'I think so.'

'Right, Jessica. Mummy's in the kitchen, is she?' Alison demanded, throwing regulations to the wind, and stepping over a private threshold without invitation or a legal warrant. She had also produced her mobile.

'My mam's shopping,' Jessica replied with a sudden burst of candour, hurrying behind Alison and adding: 'Phoebe's looking after me,' in a despairing voice, which could also have harboured malice. Then without warning, she hollered at the top of her voice: 'It's police! The police! The police!' But it wasn't an alarm she was sounding, so much as a gleeful declaration, though hearers might have chosen to interpret it either way.

What followed was to remain imprinted in the mind of DC Pope.

The response to the child's outburst was instant. The sounds of frightened voices and hurried movements emanated immediately from upstairs. A door was opened there, then closed again with a bang with a male voice shouting : 'Window'.

Alison pushed the child into the nearest downstairs' room. 'Stay in there Jessica till I come back,' she ordered, closing the door, mistaking her charge's grimace for one of obedience, not massive satisfaction. Then she made for the stairs.

While calling for back-up on her mobile, she was aware she should be waiting for it to materialise before taking further action. But she was torn between the dictats of her training and the probability that delay could lose her a wanted criminal – not to mention marks for promotion. Before she had reached the landing a high-pitched female scream emanated from behind the door immediately ahead of her, and there was a muffled crash of glass and snapping timber, she gauged from outside the house.

Turning about, she raced down the stairs again, through the hall and the kitchen beyond. Wrenching open the door into the yard, she was in time to witness a partly clothed and half-soaked man picking himself out of what was left of a wooden rainwater butt and a small garden cold frame beside it. He had evidently tried to shin down the drainwater pipe above the butt and both had collapsed under him. When he saw her, his expression of pain turned to one of fury. Staggering from the frame and brandishing a ragged piece of wood, with a roar, he started a blind advance on her.

*

'It's good of you to see me at such short notice, Mrs Ingram,' said Parry, stepping into the imposing, oblong hall of Blycot Manor.

'From what you told me on the telephone, Chief Inspector, it seemed I had no option. Naturally, my husband's well-being has priority over everything.'

'I assumed that, and how important you'd think it was to keep his recovery on-going.'

'And how desolate I'd be if anything happened to set it back.' The prompt response had been sharp. She led her visitor briskly across the polished tile floor toward the second door on the left. Her progress was trailed by an agreeable musk scent that was penetrating without being brashly obtrusive. Parry found himself pondering to no purpose on whether the purveyors might ever have considered describing its properties that way in their advertising. He enjoyed the scents that women wore provided they weren't unsubtly invasive, which meant that he sometimes missed noticing the least invasive because they were altogether too subtle – or perhaps because the wearers had always been too far down-wind of him.

'We'll use the little morning-room,' said Mrs Ingram, over her shoulder, subtle fragrance still wafting Parry's way since she was inventing her own draughts. 'As I told you, I've had a housing trust meeting this morning in my husband's study. We've only just finished, otherwise we could have gone in there, but there's a lot of clearing up to do – hordes of site plans, that sort of thing. The trust chief executive arrived earlier from London. We've been going over the programme for the next quarter. It's a question always of my finding the extra time to fit things in while my husband's still...indisposed.'

'I'm sure,' the chief inspector responded politely, though the explanation had seemed to him unnecessarily elaborate.

'Your Sergeant Lloyd isn't with you?' she added in an almost injured voice as he followed her into the morning-room. 'He and his wife know the trust very well.'

'That's right, ma'am. But in the circumstances I think it's best that what we have to discuss stays between the two of us, for the time being at least.' Parry had parked in the drive alongside a new, red Aston Martin. If this belonged to the chief executive of the trust, he or she must have arrived very early indeed because the car bonnet had been stone cold, and there had been unevaporated dew on the rear fender, the only part of the vehicle still shaded from the eleven o'clock sun. He knew that Mrs Ingram drove a Mercedes. Since he had called her from the outskirts of Chepstow only a minute or so before this, pressing for an immediate audience, there had scarcely been time for any previous caller to have quit the house. Saying that he was virtually on her doorstep with a very urgent need to talk to her had been a ploy to make it hard for the lady to refuse him. 'If my being here broke up your other meeting, ma'am, you and I needn't be long. That's if your trust colleague has the time to hang on?'

'No, he needs to be getting back to London anyway,' Mrs Ingram broke in dismissively – consciously or un-conscious-ly out-maneouvering Parry's hope of meeting the individual now defined as male without his seeming suspiciously eager to do so. 'Do sit down, won't you? These chairs facing the window are more comfortable than they look, and the view is quite special.'

'It's a very pretty room. Unexpectedly modern,' he commented.

'Yes, my husband chose all the decoration. He actually prefers it to the drawing-room, or says he does. The drawing-room's arranged in keeping with the period of the house. It's much...much grander than this room, perhaps.'

Parry felt she might also say that the elegant corner room was grand enough for an itinerant copper. It was lit by two windows that gave the space both an eastern and a southern aspect onto Capability Brown inspired rural vistas. The preponderant colour of the interior was white, with some blending of blacks – in the leather of the chair covers and even more in the dramatic, dominating darks of the easily identifiable Mondrian painting over the fireplace, and which not so much commanded the place as lent it a stylish imprimatur. The room was also strikingly reminiscent of the Earls Court flat the chief inspector had been in a few hours before. Although here the cost of the accoutrements was in an altogether more expensive league, it was highly probable that the two interiors had been concocted by the same person.

'You said you'd been to London?' Mrs Ingram remarked almost as if she had been party to his thoughts. She was seated in a reclining armchair like the one to which she had motioned her visitor. Crossing her legs as she had spoken, her left hand was now arranging the skirt of her light woollen dress. She was wearing her hair with its normal high folds looser than before over her ears. Only her lightly made-up eyes seemed a touch less commanding to Parry than they had been at their previous meeting.

'Yes. I've been back to Cardiff since then. Been trying to confirm some theories about Kevin Rees.'

'And you've succeeded?'

'To my own satisfaction, but on the face of it possibly not to yours, which would be understandable.' Her response was merely a look of mildly heightening interest as he went on. 'It's why I needed to see you. I want you to hear me out while I tell you what I've pieced together. By extension it involves your husband as an innocent party in the Rees case. And innocent though he may be, if the circumstances got out it could be detrimental to his reputation in...in another context, as well as possibly to his health. I wish you'd accept that I'm genuinely concerned to avoid either of those things happening unnecessarily.' His left cheek had twitched as it sometimes did when he was either mentally uncomfortable or undecided.

'A noble sentiment, Mr Parry, which I could only applaud if I accepted your extraordinary premise. My husband couldn't possibly be involved in Kevin Rees's murder. All right, you've said as much, or nearly as much. What do you mean by "another context"?'

Involuntarily, Parry took a deep breath. 'I believe your husband may be gay, Mrs Ingram. If he is, it's a fact that bothers him more, it seems a lot more, than one would expect these days, and which he's gone to extreme lengths to hide, to date very successfully.'

The speaker had paused, momentarily expecting an interruption, but since there was none, only a lift of his companion's firm chin, he continued. 'When he suffered his stroke, he was possibly in the flat of a gay man who may have been a close friend for...for some time. I believe this man did his best to cover up the circumstances surrounding the episode, removing any identification your husband had with him. I also believe that he later alerted you to what had happened, telling you where the ambulance had taken Mr Ingram. The name of the man is Jocelyn Blair Jackson. In his youth he was a gay activist involved in several public demonstrations, one of which cost him a fine and a night in jail, and in consequence a police record. Nowadays he's a very sober citizen.

'The house is Number 3, Nantwich Court, Earls Court. It's leased by a firm of solicitors, perhaps on behalf of your husband? It contains two flats. There's no active tenant on the ground floor, though the name Rosper is over the bell push.

The accounts for the whole house for gas, electricity, and, I expect, water, though we have no report on water yet, are billed to Mr Jackson and paid by him. My belief is that the lower flat is used by Mr Ingram perhaps as...as a *pied-à-terre*, or more probably as a bolt-hole when he's visiting Mr Jackson upstairs and doesn't want to run into other, but unexpected callers. All of this would demonstrate his super sensitivity to the...the gay question. Of course, he could hardly have used the lower flat in the way I've suggested when he suffered his stroke upstairs. It could easily have complicated things, of course. And can I emphasize that my conclusions about the status of 3 Nantwich Court are quite incidental in terms of our catching Mr Rees's killer.'

At that moment, outside, an antlered, stag-deer moved slowly across the main lawn and disappeared into some bushes. The event caught the attention of both Mrs Ingram and the more surprised policemen.

'He's after the early bush roses down there, but it's really too early yet. They adore eating the flowers, but cleverly it seems not the thorns. The males are such proud and bold creatures, don't you think? But sensitive too, just like so many gifted men,' the lady commented, returning her gaze back to Parry. 'I'm listening,' she completed.

'Thank you.' He was encouraged that she had made no further protest about his fresh assertions, only what he took to be an opportune, oblique reference to her gifted husband. 'The junior member that day of the ambulance crew of two was Kevin Rees,' he went on. 'I talked to his paramedic partner last night. Rees was...persuaded by Mr Jackson to make sure the ambulance call-sheet stated your husband was picked up on the street outside the house, not upstairs inside it. Mr Jackson was only taking the protective actions he knew your husband would want. That might have been the end of the matter from Rees's viewpoint. It seems he'd never thought to try finding out who your husband was, but he recognised him when he turned up as a patient at the Howell Clinic. Subsequently he made himself indispensable to Mr Ingram, while at the same time blackmailing him through you.' The speaker raised a hand to stem what was threateningly to be Mrs Ingram's first interruption. 'That was after you'd twigged his claim about finding homes for rehabilitated schizophrenic patients was a charade, or worse, a deception he pulled on others which eventually became one he believed himself,' he completed. The woman's dropped gaze seemed to affirm his assumption.

'The money he extorted from you was actually used to trade in drugs. I can only imagine the kind of threat he used to get it. I don't believe you're easily moved by threats, but the circumstances at this particular instance were very special. For your husband to be revealed as a practising homosexual would have been a disaster in his eyes at any time. For it to happen now could be more so. I'm assuming he's about to receive an honour, a knighthood perhaps? For services to industry and charity?'

This time Mrs Ingram was not to be gainsaid. 'Who told you that. Was it Dr Howell?'

'No. It was a matter of deduction, which incidentally, you've now confirmed. Mrs Ingram breathed out slowly. 'It's a knighthood,' she said.

'Well, like a lot of other things, ma'am, I shall keep that in the strictest confidence.'

'It's all I've confirmed, of course, Mr Parry. In one other respect however you're perfectly correct. If all the scuttlebutt apparently being...deduced about my husband and myself is wrong, deeply wrong, cruelly wrong, if any part of it became public – '

202

'No matter how wrong it is, once your husband became aware it was in the public domain it could wound him severely. And it could easily do just that during the course of this investigation,' the policeman had interjected.

'Not just severely wounded, but perhaps fatally,' Mrs Ingram stated bluntly. 'I've been advised it's unlikely he'd survive another stroke as bad as the one he had last year. Now that he's back in the real world, reading the papers, following events on the radio and television, he desperately needs protection against harmful comment. The stroke has made him unbelievably sensitive. Really you can't imagine how deeply. I mean anything to the detriment of the company, or the trust or more than that of himself could upset him deeply. I'm not suggesting there is anything that could possibly be brewing, scandalous or otherwise. But it's precisely why I intend bringing him home today so I can look out for him, protect him.'

As Mrs Ingram finished speaking, they both heard the sound of a supercharged motor car leaving the drive. 'I understand, ma'am. You don't think he's better off under the...the professional protection of the clinic – '

'No I don't,' she broke in. 'Now regarding anything approaching the seriousness of the things you've been suggesting, at this point I give credence to none of it.' But although this choice of words was firm, the tone of her voice as she went on became measurably less hostile. 'Before we go any further, Mr Parry, I need to know why you've told me so much of what you think you've uncovered. You're an intelligent man and I accept it's not merely for your own satisfaction. Is it because you truly believe that neither I nor my husband could have been involved with Rees's murder? That the crime had nothing to do with our private lives, but that for some reason you believe my...my co-operation will establish who was really responsible for it?'

Parry leaned forward. 'That's almost precisely what I believe at the moment, Mrs Ingram,' he volunteered. 'If you and your husband are involved I believe it's without your knowledge, something it's always difficult for someone in the circumstances you're in to credit. For a quite different set of reasons it can also be impossible for outsiders to credit. In any event, it's why I'm here, and why I'm by myself.'

And in his mind he hoped sincerely that he was right.

Chapter Sixteen

'My name, young man, is...is...' It was at this point that the speaker broke into song and warbled to the opening bars of Annie Laurie, *'Algernon Justinian Claverhouse the Third.'*

The sprightly, balding American had drawn himself up to his full height, which was five-foot-five, and stamped his left foot hard before delivering all four constituent parts of his title in a pleasing tenor voice. He had carefully notated the syllables to fit the music, pitching his rendering to begin on middle E, or close to it, and to conclude with an extended A which gave a nice emphasis to his family provenance. He beamed at the tall, ginger-haired Detective Sergeant Glen Wilcox with considerable affability over the top of his gold-framed bifocals before adding: 'I apologise for my unconventional way of answering your first question. The fact is, I've been taught to overcome a stroke-induced, nearly total inability to speak by singing my words instead of saying them wherever necessary. For some time after my arrival at the clinic three months ago, virtually everything I managed to utter was sung, if you follow me, which was bad luck on the people listening. My recovery took longer than that of many of the Howells's other successful patients, but I've made it in the end.'

'If it did the trick, sir, I wouldn't complain about the timing. You have a fine voice, as well.'

'Ah, at Princeton I belonged to several choirs, and I guess I've always kept my singing voice in shape. That was the reason the brilliant Dr Janet Howell hit on the regimen. The therapist she allocated to me is tone deaf. We began by singing well-known tunes together. Since I proved so much more adept at this than she did, after a while I established an ascendancy which eventually produced the degree of self confidence essential to my recovery.' He paused. 'You know there's a young banker here who, like me, had lost his speech almost entirely after a stroke. He's British but he knows the French language tolerably well. His therapists here are all people who have a lesser...facility in French than he has, with orders to conduct all spoken...*communication* with him in that language.' Mr Claverhouse had delivered the key word on a single gathering note but with musical gusto. 'The ruse is working for him too,' he added. 'Not as well yet as the singing has for me, but he's getting there. In both our cases the root problem was largely self confidence. Dr Janet tells me that not every case is as easy to solve as mine. Easy, she says! Well I can tell you, I attended five top clinics in the USA who found no solution at all for what ailed me. This is a very wonderful centre of healing Mr...?'

'*D.S. Glen Wilcox, sir,*' the normally unbending policemen supplied in a rich baritone on a beautifully pitched middle C, and with a broad grin afterwards. 'My father belonged to the famous Treorchy Male Voice Choir, sir. My brothers and I were brought up to sing. Most Welsh people are, of course.'

'Well, join the club, Mr Wilcox.' The American shook the other man warmly by the hand. 'Except I hope you never have to sing for the same reason I did. Happily I now have recourse to rhapsodizing my words less often. It's usually when for some reason I'm nervous.'

'When interviewed by strange policemen, sir.'

'I fear that may have been the reason this time, though it's not always the case. Memory lapse is another cause. On the good doctor's strict instructions I must still resort to the musical ploy whenever need arises. I've been a reasonably successful court attorney for nearly forty years, and I've used most every trick in the book, and a lot that aren't in the book, but I've yet to sing in court. Maybe I'll find an opportunity yet.' He rubbed his hands together. 'Of course, my full name is...is... *ludicrously* pompous.' He had contrived a musical *glissando* with the sung word, gliding it down from middle F to C, again after the same introductory beat with his foot. He next continued: 'But by golly I was proud when I could pronounce all of that name again. My friends call me Algy, by the way. Take a pew, won't you?' The last two sentences were delivered at speed with evident confidence.

Wilcox observed that the sung words or phrases had so far been prefaced not only by a stamping foot but also by a small facial contortion, as though the always open mouthed performer had been about to take a bite from a very large apple.

'Thank you, sir,' he said, occupying a seat across from the one his host was moving toward. 'Nice room they've given you,' he completed, gazing about him, with his glance lingering on the cut glass vase of gracefully arranged spring flowers.

'I'm glad you like it. You've noticed the bouquet? My mentor Dr Janet is also a great gardener, did you know? She brings me flowers from her private plot. What a bonus.' He too looked around his well-furnished accommodation. 'I'm told many patients have turned down this room because there's no view to speak of, but I like it well enough. The rooms on either side are empty at night, so I've never disturbed others with my obligatory sessions of singing to myself. I'm able to watch people, as well, coming and going, day and night. As you can see, the window is above and just to the side of the front door, which is well lit at night. My home is in New...New...New York City. ' He had been on the verge of another choral outburst, but overcame the need. 'My wife and I have an apartment on Park Avenue. Our view there is similar to the one from this window, of traffic, and people going about their business. That's interesting to contemplate, don't you think?'

'I'm sure it is, sir.'

'Especially if folk don't know they're being watched.' The speaker gave an impish grin. 'They're more natural that way. Not that I'm a snooper. Just an interested observer of the human scene. Even so, I've never mentioned my window watching habit to anyone here. It might serve to spoil the spontaneity of my subjects.'

For his part the sergeant would have chosen a room overlooking the long lawn. He doubted that the traffic, human and motorised, on the clinic drive was all that heavy or diverting, but he was professionally delighted to have found a witness who sometimes had it under observation. He opened his notebook. 'As I expect you've guessed, sir, I'm here about the events of Saturday night.'

'The dreadful murder of Kevin Rees. Such a helpful nurse. I'm very...very... *grieved* over his death. Who could have done such a terrible thing?' His appropriate minor key chanting of 'grieved' matched the pathos of his sentiment as well as its depth.

'That's what we're trying to find out, sir. Dr Edwin Howell gave permission for you to be interviewed.'

The American beamed. 'Because he knows I won't be upset. They've repaired me well enough to stand a police grilling. The ever resourceful Dr Janet has even provided me with a tool to clear the linings of my hearing aids, so I've no excuse for mishearing your questions,' he added with a chuckle. 'So you see, you're actually a remedial activity for me. So fire away, Mr Interrogator.'

'Oh, it won't be an interrogation, sir, I assure you. Just a few simple questions for the record, like. We'd hoped to talk to you earlier, but I gather you'd left on Sunday morning before the body was discovered.'

'That's right, Mr Wilcox. My son-in-law was here to fetch me at seven. He's British. He and my daughter live in Marlborough town.' He wagged a finger in the air. 'And I know that's spelled differently from the cigarette brand, if most of my countrymen wouldn't. It's only an hour's drive from here. I spent the day and last night with the family. Another remedial activity, except my young grandson is pretty well an activity on his own. My daughter brought me back only a few minutes ago. My wife is flying over again next week. I'm due to go home then.'

'That's good news, sir. Could you tell me, were you here in this room Saturday night after dinner?'

'You bet, from nine, watching baseball on the television. I do a lot of reading as well, but my eyes get tired of that at the end of the day. Dr Edwin Howell looked in. He usually does.'

'At what time would that have been, sir?'

'Let's see...around ten after nine. Strangely for an educated man, American baseball doesn't interest him that much.' His eyes twinkled before he completed, 'but we chatted a while.'

'Did you also watch from the window at all, sir?'

The aquiline Claverhouse nose wrinkled. 'Yes I did. Not for long, and it was later on.'

'How much later, sir?'

'Well, I was in my dressing gown ahead of turning in. I usually switch the lights off after that, except for the bed lamp. Then I open the drapes.' He hesitated for a moment. 'I'd say it was around ten-thirty.'

'And did you see anyone arrive or leave?'

'Yes I did. I saw Dr Edwin cross from the clinic to his

house. That was after a short conversation with Mrs Ingram on the clinic steps. Mrs Ingram is the wife of Denis Ingram another patient who's done well here. They said goodnight in the drive and Mrs Ingram went back to the clinic. A while later, poor Kevin Rees walked up, I guess from the main gate. He told me a while back he usually took a drink in the High Street on Saturday nights. He stepped into the clinic but left again soon after.'

'Where did he go then, sir?'

'Can't tell you exactly, but he was heading toward the greenhouse area.'

'And the pavilion, sir?'

'Sure. The pavilion's beyond the greenhouse, of course. Is the pavilion significant, Mr Wilcox?'

'Yes, sir. He was found dead on the steps.'

'You don't say? Oh my. But that was on Sunday morning?'

'Yes, sir. But we have reason to believe he died on Saturday night.'

'You mean I could have been the last person to see him alive?'

'It's possible, sir. Were Dr Edwin, Mrs Ingram and Mr Rees the only people you saw, sir?'

'Er...not quite. Oh, and I saw the doctor again. I went back to the window a while later to star gaze. I was looking for Algol, what they call the Demon Star. That's because it lies in the head of the Gorgon in the...the...*Perseus Constellation*.' This fresh choral offering was set to the first line of Onward Christian Soldiers. Mr Claverhouse was an Episcopalian. 'And do you know why Algol appears to wink at you?' he went on. 'It's because it's frequently eclipsed by a close, dimmer companion that keeps blocking its light. Saturday was a very clear night.'

'And you saw – '

'Algol? No. Don't know why.' The speaker appeared puzzled.

'I meant about you saying you saw Dr Edwin Howell again, sir.' DS Wilcox was unversed in astronomy.

'Yes. He went back to the clinic. Expect he'd forgotten something.'

'At what time was that, sir?'

'Oh...10.35, or thereabouts.'

'Thank you.' The sergeant made a note. 'Did you, by any chance, also see Mr Collit, the gardener, sir?'

'Phil? No, I didn't, but a little later I did see a woman, young I think. No one I knew. At least I didn't think so at the time.'

'Could she have been a member of the staff, sir, medical or domestic?'

'Possible. As I said, I don't believe I'd ever seen her before.'

'Did she arrive on foot?'

'So far as I could see, yes. She might have parked a car short of the building, of course. Come to think, when I was leaving my bathroom a minute or so earlier, I thought I heard the crunch of a car drive up. Except when I got to the window there was no new car parked outside. Of course I'd taken my hearing aids out by then.'

'I understand, sir. This young woman you saw, was she tall or short, slim or fat, sir?'

'Medium height, and slim...yes, definitely slim...as I recollect now.' It was the last phrase that suggested the American was indefinite about the sighting.

'What about the clothes she was wearing?'

'Oh...a raincoat, dark blue probably, I seem to remember that. And...and *trousers*,' he sang the word, less boisterously than some others earlier and his spoken words had developed a nervous edge. 'I...I couldn't see the colour of her hair. Her head was covered, you see. By...by a scarf, I think.'

'Did you see her face, sir?'

'No, not really. As I said, she came by later than the other people. It was after I'd gone to bed. That would be around ten-forty. Although I like to sleep with the drapes and the window open, the moon was giving a mite too much illumination. I'd got up again to rearrange the drapes. I'd already taken off my glasses. Like my hearing aids earlier. Hm, happily I have all my own teeth, you may be surprised to hear.' This was accompanied by a soulful grin. 'But I saw her going past the front door in the direction, as you'd say, of the pavilion.' He took in a slow breath. 'I doubt she could have got that far though because she was back again very soon.'

'Was she moving quickly, sir.'

'Yes, when she arrived. Quicker still when she was leaving. Pity she had her head down then. And when I'd first seen her she was already moving away from me. Sorry I can't do better than that, Mr Wilcox.'

*

'I didn't see Megan here at the store. She came straight to my home at eight this morning, after she phoned to ask if I'd see her. She sounded upset. I said of course I'd see her. One of my most valued employees.' The fifty-six-year-old Mrs Agnes Craig-Owen was a large and commanding figure, and imperious with it. The way she was voicing her decision to DS Mary Norris about her encounter with Megan Collit early that morning served strongly to convey the regal degree of condescension that had been necessary on her part.

Mrs Craig-Owen was the owner, by inheritance from her father, of the only grocery store in Bryntaf, as well as, by determined aggrandisement, the freeholds of seven of the remaining ten retail establishments in the village's shopping parade. The parade was just short of the railway station and there was ample free parking for shoppers and travellers.

The other shops in the Craig-Owen near monopoly had been bought over the years from the profits on groceries. Mrs Craig-Owen was not enamoured with stock exchange investment, nor the puny return on bank deposit accounts either. But she understood retailing, and she had watched the development of Bryntaf from the time it had been a small working class community, long before it had blossomed into one of Cardiff's most prestigious, convenient, and expensive rural suburbs. Her determination from the start to plough her business gains into local shops, as proprietor or landlord, had paid handsomely.

The home she referred to, a sizeable mansion, had been acquired well before the price of such establishments had reached their current dizzy heights. As an only child, she had lived with her parents in the flat over the shop. This now served as the office and part of the stockroom for a retail business many times the size it had been then, particularly since her recent amalgamation of the original premises with the two shops she had bought up on either side, extending all three units at the back. She now termed the enterprise a select, as opposed to a small, independent supermarket. Certainly it had proved large enough to deter any supermarket chain from opening a branch in the vicinity, a situation strengthened over the years by Mrs Craig-Owen's vociferous opposition to any such encroachment on her territory, first through her presence on the parish council, later by her election to a seat on the local authority, and, later still, by her appointment to that authority's planning committee.

It was in the upper floor office, a small glass-partitioned

area with unrestricted views of the stock shelves beyond, that Mrs Craig-Owen had agreed to see the detective sergeant. Mary Norris was seated across from her on the other side of an elaborate L-shaped work-station, which included a computer, screen, and printer, cable management conduits, two telephones, a fax machine, a copier – and a modesty panel. The desk surface was adjustable for height since Roland Craig-Owen, the owner's husband, a weedy but fairly contented man and the nominal manager of the store, was considerably smaller than his consort. The modesty panel was hardly needed to shield Mrs Craig-Owen's substantial legs from being exhibited to the vulgar gaze since she invariably wore trousers when working at the store. It did, however, at the moment prevent the policewoman from crossing her own legs while resting her notebook on her side of the desktop.

'Did Mrs Collit say why she was upset, ma'am?'

'I'd have thought that was obvious, wouldn't you?' Mrs Craig-Owen's nostrils flared as she rearranged the closure of the grey cardigan she was wearing over a matching grey sweater and her ample bosom. 'She and her husband have been harried unmercifully by the newspapers and the police,' she continued, 'about the death of that...that male nurse at the Howell Clinic where the husband works.' She had diffidently emphasised the gender of the nurse as though there might be something intrinsically undesirable in such an occupation for a man. 'Neither of the Collits had anything to do with that person's death, of course. I know both of them well,' she completed, as if the last comment made her view on the issue incontestable.

'So her upset was to do with the murder, ma'am,' the sergeant persisted. She'd had dealings with Mrs Craig-Owen some years before this, and was less susceptible to being browbeaten now than she had been then.

'Well that's what I've said, haven't I, dear? No reason to think anything else is there?' This was delivered with a tolerant beam.

'Not if Mrs Collit didn't give you one, ma'am, no.' If there was anything that irritated Mary Norris more than being addressed as 'dear' by a man, it was being addressed in the same way by an older woman. 'And did she come to tell you she wouldn't be working today? I mean, we were told on the phone earlier that she wasn't in yet, and later that she wouldn't be in at all today or tomorrow. We were also told she'd been to see you.'

'Yes, it was my husband you spoke to both times.' The speaker's tone left no doubt that the related fact accounted for the inefficiencies in communication. 'He came down to open the store instead of her. He was...mistaken in saying she definitely wouldn't be in tomorrow. We don't know that for sure.'

'I see. Funny Mrs Collit didn't tell her husband she wouldn't be working today before he left home this morning. And she didn't tell his mother either. She lives with them.'

Mrs Craig-Owen gave a short sniff. 'Perhaps she forgot. When people are upset – '

'She left their house at ten-to-eight.' The sergeant interrupted, glancing at the time. 'It's now nearly midday. Don't you think she'd have told her close family by now where she was going? They're worried about her.'

'Well I expect she'll be in touch with her husband soon. She's usually very thoughtful over things like that.'

'She came to your house on her moped, did she, ma'am?'

'I think so, yes. I didn't see it, but that's usually the way she gets about.'

'Thank you. Is there nothing else you want to tell me about her visit? For instance, did she say where she was going

215

next?' The sergeant was fast deciding that the term reluctant witness wasn't in it where Mrs Craig-Owen was concerned.

It was at that moment that Roland Craig-Owen entered the office, dressed in a long white cotton coat. He gave a gentle tap on the nearest glass partition, there was no door, before moving deferentially halfway across the short distance to the work-station. He smiled, but almost covertly, at the sergeant whom he had greeted on her arrival. 'Anything I can do, love?' he asked his wife. 'You said you'd see that wholesaler's rep at noon.'

'So I did.' Mrs Craig-Owen seemed pleased by the interruption – possibly because she'd arranged it in advance, the sergeant suspected. She also figured that Mr Craig-Owen had been carpeted by his wife for admitting to the police that she had seen Megan Collit. 'No, Megan didn't say where she was going, sergeant.'

DC Norris closed her notebook. 'Well, if you remember anything else that Mrs Collit said, please call us on this number day or night.' She pushed a card across to Mrs Craig-Owen. 'We have to face the fact that there's a murderer at large. Mrs Collit may be innocently involved with the crime, so she could be in danger. Grave danger. I'm sure you understand that withholding information about her could have serious consequences, not just for her, but the person withholding it as well.' She waited to see if the scarcely veiled threat had any effect on Mrs Craig-Owen. All it had elicited was a not very solemn nod, and while the woman's husband had seemed more moved by the words, he made no utterance.

A minute later, while Roland Craig-Owen was showing the sergeant out, his wife was congratulating herself on the interview. She had dismissed the policewoman's homily as irrelevant. Mrs Craig-Owen knew well enough where Megan

Collit had gone, and why Megan hadn't told Phil Collit about her intentions.

The young woman was in no danger, and Mrs Craig-Owen had been graciously pleased to lend her the money she needed, against future salary of course, for a purpose that in the long run suited the profit-conscious employer quite as well as it did Megan, if for different reasons.

Chapter Seventeen

'You think I was wrong, Eve, to tell her Phil said he'd given up the lottery?' asked Sheila Radcliffe.

She and Eve Oswald were in their shared office consuming prawns in aspic, and other bite-size party pieces, concluding with fresh fruit and coffee, around the matron's desk. This was instead of lunching in the clinic refectory. It was part of their regular Monday routine, the day of the week when they had the extra task of consolidating the previous seven day's clinic accounts. Lunching with the rest of the staff and patients, an agreeable but carefully structured activity, was in many ways more nourishing for everyone – in mind as well as body – but more costly in terms of staff time. It involved the clinic employees in purposefully encouraging the patients, allocated to them according to their stages of recuperation, to be more outgoing in company – all part of accelerating their recovery. The food and wine were of Michelin star calibre, to use Dr Edwin Howell's own description and firm requirement of the clinic chef. By comparison, what the two ladies had for their fifteen minute Monday lunch break was bought for them by a part-time staff member who came in at mid-morning and lived close to a high-class Cardiff delicatessen.

'Anyway, given it up is exactly what Phil said,' Mrs Radcliffe continued unhappily. 'A week ago today, in this very room, and almost to the minute. I think you must have been in the loo.'

'Well it was the truth, wasn't it, Sheila? What you mean is you volunteered it when you needn't have. So now, as things have turned out, you feel awkward about it.' Miss Oswald, essentially a realist, hesitated with a spoonful of sugar poised over her Royal Doulton coffee cup before shaking some of the granules back into the matching basin. She appeared for the moment to be more concerned about her calorie intake than her colleague's exchange with the police.

Despite the utilitarian, modernist design of their office, and the catalogue of up-to-the-minute computer hardware and software housed in it, the two women regularly used a cherished set of fine bone china when they lunched in-situ. Plastic cups and plates had no appeal for either of them.

'It's difficult,' the matron added, 'but what you said was still important.'

'Well that's why I said it, of course. But it makes Phil sound like a liar, whereas all I meant was he'd forgotten what he'd decided if he was claiming Kevin owed him half those winnings, or else he'd changed his mind. It didn't sound convincing.' She breathed in hard with feeling. 'The sergeant, her name's Mary Norris, nice kid, bright as a button too, she told me straight away what Phil had said to the police, and it didn't fit. I couldn't have known that, but if I had I'd have been less...well, forthcoming, like. Perhaps I'd had too much wine. Makes me garrulous – or more so than usual.' She gave a self-deprecating pout which served as an admission that she was hardly taciturn by nature. 'What I said puts Kevin in a better light, of course. Except he's dead, so there's no change coming for him out of that, is there?' She shook her head, which made the gold-coloured earrings she was wearing sparkle.

'Seems poor Kevin's reputation has taken quite a few knocks since his death,' the other responded with evident regret.

'You liked him, of course, Eve. Well, so did I, in many ways.'

Miss Oswald sat quite still for several seconds, before she answered the comment in a thoughtful voice: 'Yes, I once had a soft spot for him. I think it was out of sympathy more than respect, though. He really did get a raw deal in the army. And those...good works of his, some of them I know were genuine enough. But what's come out about his drug dealing doesn't exactly cover him in glory.' She also harboured another reason for disdaining Rees – one that she hadn't been able to share with her colleague, any more than she had with Merlin Parry earlier.

'At least it widens the field of possible murderers,' said the clinic accountant, sugaring her own second cup of coffee with less scruple than Eve Oswald had shown, which helped to explain the just discernible difference in their waist measurements. They were both mature, attractive women who cared greatly about health and appearance, and who had worn well in consequence. 'I mean, if he was selling and buying drugs he was in a different world to ours, wasn't he? Thugs they are, those drug dealers. You're always reading reports of London gang killings. Fights over territories and so on. And it's all to do with drugs, isn't it?'

'Except I really can't believe Kevin was in that deep, Sheila.'

'Perhaps you don't have to be to get killed, love. In a way, I hope the crime was committed by mobsters, just so long as they didn't hurt Kevin more than anyone else would have done. Well, that's a silly thing to say, of course, but you know what I mean. Just so long as it wasn't done by someone connected with the clinic.' She eyed the smoked salmon ring with a cheese spread filling which she was holding in her fingers before devouring it with evident pleasure – and no sense of guilt since the spread was low-fat with an anti-cholestoral ingredient. Dabbing her mouth with a good quality, pink paper napkin she then added: 'Phil's normally such a very gentle chap. He really couldn't be...' she hesitated, then changed tack. 'So what can have happened to Megan Collit? You said Phil was pleased about the pregnancy?'

'He seemed so, yes, for both of them, but you can never be sure with him, he's such an undemonstrative type. I'd guess she's probably gone home to her parents, for a bit of solace.'

'But surely she'd have told him and the people she works for if she'd had that in mind?'

'Not if it was on the spur of the moment, after Phil had left the house this morning. As for her employers, he told me she works all hours at that supermarket for a big title and a small wage, so I don't suppose they're going to fire her for one oversight. According to Phil, she's a bit unpredictable, though from what I've seen of her she's never struck me as venturesome. Anyway, when he came in here this morning, I told him to take as much time as he needed to find her, and make sure she's all right. I said I'd square it for him with Dr Janet. What a pity his wife's causing him worry in a period that ought to be one of great joy for the two of them.'

Phil Collit had come into the office soon after the police had asked him if he knew why his wife wasn't at the supermarket. This was before Mrs Craig-Owen had unwillingly volunteered that she had seen her. Sheila Radcliffe had not been present when the encounter between Eve Oswald and the gardener had taken place. It was then that he had told the matron that Megan was pregnant.

'You don't believe the police could think he's spirited her away somewhere?' Sheila questioned.

'Why should he?'

The other woman shrugged. 'No idea. Perhaps because she knows more than she's telling about the murder and he wanted her off the scene. No, that's too far-fetched.'

'A lot too far-fetched,' the matron replied responsibly. 'You'll be saying next he's done away with her because she knew he killed Kevin.' She spurned the last tasty fish-ball and helped herself to a modest sized sprig of grapes instead. 'Strange thing to do, all the same, disappearing without a word to anyone,' she completed.

'Probably doesn't realise what a fuss she'll be causing. Anyway, I'll bet Phil's traced her by now.' Mrs Radcliffe also reached across for some grapes. 'Oh, I didn't finish telling you about Algernon J.Claverhouse the Third.' She had run into him in the corridor at noon. 'As you know, he got back quite late this morning, after spending last night at his daughter's in Marlborough. Well, he was interviewed by the police almost on arrival. He told me at length – and he does go on, doesn't he? – how very interested another detective sergeant had been by the people our Algy had seen from his window Saturday night. Well, he would, wouldn't he?' She took some more grapes. 'Did you know Algy window-watches quite a lot, day and night?'

'No, but it fits. He's an inquisitive chap. So, as they say, he was able to assist the police with their enquiries? Who did he say he'd seen?' Eve Oswald seemed almost as interested as the detective had been.

'Well, he told them exactly what time he saw Kevin get back from the pub, and when he left the building again heading for the pavilion.'

'The pavilion?'

'In that direction, anyway. It was where his body was found,'

'Of course. Who else did he see?'

'A woman who came and went, apparently, on her way to and from the...the pavilion, or the tool shed, I suppose.'

'Anyone else?'

'Dr Edwin. Twice. When he left here for the cottage at half-ten escorted to the clinic steps by Mrs Ingram, and when he came back a few minutes later. But he went into the clinic again, not round the building.'

The matron's lips had tightened. 'Algy Claverhouse was a busy little spotter, wasn't he?'

'Mm.' Sheila Radcliffe checked the time and finished her coffee. 'I wonder who the woman was?' she queried, picking up the tray for the used crockery the matron was passing to her.

'Annie from the kitchen, probably, after she'd finished the hot drinks round. She does it on Saturdays instead of Kevin. I'd better tell Chef to see she does it every night till he's replaced.'

'No, Eve, this woman wasn't leaving the building. She came from the direction of the gate.'

Miss Oswald shook her head. 'Could still have been Annie. She has orders from Chef to see the covers are on the garbage bins when she's on late duty. Ever since that patient said he'd seen a rat. If Annie forgot, she might have come back. She's very conscientious. I'll ask her. If it could have been her, we ought to tell Sergeant Lloyd. Otherwise we don't want the poor girl involved with the police unnecessarily.' Annie was a willing, young, 'evenings only' kitchen-hand and occasional waitress – literally a 'moonlighter'.

'Well she's certainly no murderer.' Mrs Radcliffe carefully put one cup on top of the other on the tray. 'I wonder if the police will be asking Dr Edwin why he came back?' She gave her companion an expectant rather than an enquiring look. This was acknowledged not with words but with a gentle lift of the eyebrows and a widening of Eve Oswald's eyes.

*

223

'Excuse me, I think you left this in the cathedral. Where you were sitting in the Lady Chapel.' The bearded young priest, in an anorak over his dog collar, had hurried after Megan Collit who had already left the building by the west door, moving slowly and without any very determined idea of direction. He had a largish brown envelope in his hand.

'Oh...oh, thank you...thanks very much.' Her response at first had been startled, and the words half-mumbled as she put out a hand to take the envelope from him. When she had stopped, and he could see her eyes behind the glasses, it had been clear to him that she had been weeping.

He held on to the envelope for a moment longer than was necessary. 'Look, it's...it's none of my business, but you seem unhappy. Anything I can do? I'm Father Derek, but call me just plain Derek if it's easier for you,' he offered.

Megan stared at him, tried to choke back her distress, but then emitted a strained whimper, before her shoulders and upper body began to heave with sobbing. The first tears that dribbled down her cheek she tried wiping away with the back of her hand.

'Hey, seeing me doesn't usually make people more miserable than they were before,' he said. 'Am I that repulsive?'

'No.' She gave him a pathetic little smile.

He took hold of one of her bent elbows, while offering her a tissue from his pocket with his other hand. 'It's quite clean, honestly,' he said with a grin, 'and by the way, I've just realised we've met before, and where. The Bryntaf grocery store on Friday afternoon, after I'd been to see the church there. You helped me find the stuff for my Saturday picnic. Slice of ham, Cheddar cheese, a roll, and a ripe pear. Isn't that right?'

She nodded slowly. 'And a Diet Coke,' she completed for

him, still in a broken voice, but her tears seemed to be stemmed. 'Did...did you like Brecon?'

'Very much. And the library was still open when I got there as well. There are two beautiful old churches. Different from this one, of course, which is glorious, don't you think? Clifton Cathedral in all its majesty. The finest building in Bristol, I'd say, but I suppose I could be prejudiced.' He turned her about so that they could both admire the impressive outline of what was still one of the newest and unusual modern cathedrals in the Roman Catholic hierarchy, set on a hill top in Clifton which is an inner suburb of Bristol. 'Even if its core is concrete, those big granite facings are gorgeous, and they certainly fooled me. They're Aberdeen granite, by the way. Also I figure the new-fangled steeple would make a great stairway to paradise. As for the interior, it's awesome and highly worshipful. Just as it was designed to be.' He beamed at her. 'O.K., I admit it, I've read the guidebook from cover to cover.' His intentional banter had given her opportunity to further collect herself. 'But this is an occasion,' he continued. 'I hardly know a soul in this country yet I bump straight into an old acquaintance on my first visit to Bristol. So, what are you doing here? Don't you live over the Bristol channel in Wales, in Bryntaf?'

'I live in Llandaff. I just work in Bryntaf.' She swallowed.

The plain envelope was still in her hand. Even though it didn't have 'Pregnancy Advisory Service' printed on it, to her it seemed to be screaming out to him and the whole world why she was here – why she had been seen mid-morning by a doctor and a surgeon who had believed her story, approved her request, accepted the urgency and the fee, and arranged for her foetus to be aborted at 4.15 that afternoon at a nearby nursing home. They'd also fixed for her to stay the night at a local hostel after she left the clinic. It had all been quite easy really – that part. And she'd done it all by herself, without Kevin or anybody else, just the Yellow Pages, the Net, and the loan from Mrs Craig-Owen. She had planned to ring Phil once she had got to the hostel, to tell him what she'd done, that she was all right, and that she'd be travelling home in the morning.

'I'm having an abortion,' she suddenly blurted out, bluntly, even defiantly.

Saying it out loud to someone, to a priest at that, seemed to strengthen her resolution – but only briefly.

'I see. Big step for you.' He might have added 'for your baby as well,' except he knew better. 'Well I said it's an occasion. How about a cup of tea at the Cathedral House over there? There's a coffee shop on the ground floor.'

She shook her head. 'I'm not supposed to eat or drink before...for a bit.'

'Ah. Well let's wander across the park and admire the famous Clifton Suspension Bridge.' He wondered if that was what she'd half had in mind when he'd caught up with her – only not to admire the bridge so much as to contemplate jumping off it, which scores of distressed young women had done in the century and a half of its existence.

'O.K.' It wasn't an enthusiastic acceptance, but she allowed him to lead her across the road to the attractive, open green expanse that led to the bridge and the deep gorge it spanned. Her willingness pleased him – and he sensed that it might be pleasing her even more than it did him.

'So what's your Christian name?' She told him. 'Megan's a nice name,' he said.

'Very common in Wales. I knew your name was Derek. You were in the Eight Bells in Llandaff on Saturday night, weren't you?' she replied.

'Now how ever did you know that?'

'My husband Phil was there. You talked to him and one of our friends. About buying a car from the friend. He thought you had something to do with Llandaff Cathedral.'

'Did he? No, that's Church in Wales, part of the Anglican Church. I'm Roman Catholic.' The last piece of intelligence could have saved the South Wales police a good deal of time and money had they known it when they had started looking for him. 'The church I belonged to never came up in the pub on Saturday. I didn't raise it, not in the shadow of a great Anglican cathedral,' he joked. 'Are you Catholic too?'

She swallowed. 'Sort of. My mother is. My dad's nothing really.'

'But you were brought up Catholic?'

'Yes. I'm...what you call it?...lapsed.'

Oh no you're not, he decided inwardly, while audibly offering: 'But you came to the cathedral here for help over a big decision.'

'I suppose so.' She paused. 'I could see it when I left...left where I'd been, to see the doctors.'

So praise the Lord for high spires, he thought. Since he hadn't asked about Kevin Rees or Phil she assumed, correctly, that he didn't know about the murder. For his part he had more urgent business in mind than a chat about a second-hand car he hadn't bought.

For the time being, and as he saw it, Father Derek was totally engaged in saving a life.

Chapter Eighteen

'Your mother'll stop speaking to me if she finds out I've been here,' Parry announced guiltily.

'Why, Merlin?'

'Because she'll think I came for only one reason, which actually wouldn't be true. To be frank your father wasn't exactly overjoyed about the visit either, but he didn't forbid it.' The chief inspector was seated beside Lucy Lloyd's hospital bed next to the window in the six bed observation ward. She had been transferred here an hour before this from intensive care. Only two of the beds in the ward were occupied, and the other patient was asleep. Apart from a saline drip, inserted on the back of her left hand, Lucy was now free of the attachments to machines that had encumbered her body and movements earlier.

'Go on, Mum knows you've been one of my idols since I was a teenager, and she adores you as well,' she responded in a firm voice. 'Proper fan club you've always had in the Lloyd family. And it's lovely to see you. These flowers are so beautiful. Thanks so much.' She reached out her right hand to clasp his. 'I'm just happy I'm out of hospital drag and into my best sexy M&S nightie. Mum brought it at lunchtime. Do I look pale and wan?'

'No, interesting, and glamorous.'

'Well that's because she brought my make-up case as well.'

'Honestly, you look scrumptious. How're you really feeling?'

'Normal but stupid. Because I brought all this on myself. But I'm a reformed character, cross my heart and...no, not that.' She winced. 'I'm giving up smoking from today. No yesterday. And I'm going on a strict diet as well. Cold turkey. That's the only way with smoking, or so they say. It'd better be as well, because I've tried all the others. As for the weight loss, I'm determined to drop two stone and then stay that way.' She gave a rueful chuckle. 'Ifan is getting us application forms for a tennis club in Cowbridge. They have a pool and a gym as well. We should both have joined ages ago instead of talking about it. He needs toning up too.'

'Don't over-do it at the start.'

'No fear. Shan't have the energy anyway. The doctor says I should be out of here by the end of the week, and they'll have me on gentle physio well before that. I'll be off work for a month. Pity Perdita isn't around doing her phsyio thing in Cardiff still. But she'll be a qualified doctor in two months, won't she?'

'Hope so. I was with her last night in London.' He pulled a face. 'She's talking of specialising again.'

'Gynaecology?'

'That's right.'

'I guessed that might happen after the miscarriage. That was lousy luck. Perdita was mulling it all over the last time I saw her, before you went on holiday. Temperamentally she's made to be a gynae, of course. The gynae consultant she's worked for in London said that, didn't she? Means more study and training, of course, but it'll be worth it in the end. And think of all the oodles of extra money it'll bring in.' She frowned. 'On second thoughts, don't do anything of the kind.' Lucy gave a short sigh before she continued at an increasing pace. 'It's those oodles of money, and the over-work and the late nights it takes to earn it that've got me into the mess I'm in now. I don't even have the consolation that I've been saving lives in the process. Not like a doctor. Or done anything remotely virtuous, unless you're ready to argue that lining my own pockets comes under that heading, which it doesn't.'

'Oh, come on,' Parry interjected. 'Accountancy's a pretty necessary profession, and moral with it.'

'Is it? All I do is keep our company clients' accounts on the straight and narrow, and stop them having to pay out more of their profits in tax than the government's strictly entitled to. And the last bit is pretty mean when you think how much more money the country needs to run hospitals like this one, and schools and…and the police forces and – '

Parry laughed out loud. 'Oh dear, you are in a parlous state. I'd guess you'll change your mind about the need for higher taxes when you're back to rude health. In the past I've heard you give very different views to the ones you've just expounded.'

'Maybe. But I tell you, I was lying awake at dawn this morning thinking it'd be much healthier if Ifan and I gave up the fleshpots and bought a small-holding in rural, idyllic Pembrokeshire where we'd till the soil, milk a cow or two, and produce dozens of babies like my mother wants.' She plucked at the lace top of her frilled nightdress. 'Or perhaps it wouldn't be healthier. Not in times of pestilence and famine, and we do so enjoy our tropical holidays.' She gave a mischievous smile before changing the subject. 'So, you drove back early this morning did you?'

'After I'd interviewed someone in Earl's Court.'

'To do with the Howell Clinic murder? Was it a suspect?' Her free hand, with the drip attached to it, flew to her mouth, if with some difficulty. 'Damn, I shouldn't have asked that, should I?'

'No harm in asking. But I'm not giving you any answers because we mustn't talk about the case for your own good, as your mother would confirm with vigour if she was here.'

'Mustn't hell! I want the latest fast track info as soon as you can give it to me. Of course, you know Daddy and I nearly came to blows about it last night?'

'Sadly it's hard to keep him off the subject. You know he feels entirely responsible for what happened?'

'Yes, but I kept telling him this morning he shouldn't. It was my fault for trying to interfere in his work. I'm a know-all, that's my trouble, and bossy with it. But I'm in a reforming mood today. So take advantage, Merlin boyo. As you just said, I may not be so virtuous and pliable when I start getting better, and you're making me feel a bit that way already.' She squeezed his hand. 'You want to know what I was going to tell Daddy when the grim reaper nearly reaped me, don't you?'

'In your own good time, yes,' he replied, failing to disguise that he could hardly wait. He had been trying since the start of the visit to gauge whether she was up to unburdening, and by now had decided that she was.

'Good time, indeed! Like me, you need to know now, and you have a legal right too, I expect. Except it was something I'd sworn to Megan I wouldn't tell Daddy anyway. I was in such a temper, that's all.' She undid the bow of the blue ribbon at the neck of the nightdress and began to re-tie it to give it more flounce. 'Not that I think what I know is going to solve the case for you,' she continued. 'But at least it should get Phil Collit off the hook. That's why I'm going to spill the beans.' She fluffed up the completed bow. 'You know Megan and I were mates at school?'

'Your father told me, yes. Also that she approached you yesterday pressing you to take up her cause.'

'Pressing wasn't in it. At the time it was more like bludgeoning. To me it did seem Phil had a case against the police as things stood. But since thinking about it in the chaste loneliness of my hospital bed things look a lot different.' She moved her lower limbs under the light bedclothes with energy before adding. 'So even if I risk losing Megan as a friend, which I'm probably going to, at least I'll have served to keep her husband warm in bed next to her. Really, the way I see it all now, the two of them brought the problem on themselves in not coming clean with you in the first place.'

*

'Good afternoon, doctor. Lucky to run into you. I was hoping you could spare me a minute.' It was a little after 3.20. DS Gomer Lloyd had just parked his Rover and had been heading for the main entrance to the clinic. At the same time, Edwin Howell had appeared from his cottage and was moving in the same direction.

Howell halted and smiled. 'Of course, Mr Lloyd. I can even do you for five minutes if you want. Shortly after that, before tea, I'm due to give what young Peter Smith, one of my promising patients, calls a tutorial. I believe we'll soon have that one back on the road to becoming a very distinguished investment banker. Have you noticed that stars in that firmament are getting younger all the time?'

'And prone to what used to be older people's complaints like heart attacks and strokes, sir?'

'You're quite right, of course.' The speaker raised a cupped hand to his forehead. 'Oh lord. My dear chap, I've just remembered, it's your daughter who's had the heart attack isn't it?'

'That's right, doctor. Lucy. She's our oldest girl.'

'I do apologise, and I'm so very sorry. How old is Lucy?'

'Twenty-six, doctor.'

'With plenty of vigour then. Sounds trite, but youth has a head start when it comes to recovery. Doing well at the Heath is she? It's a fine hospital with an excellent cardiac team.'

'She's making good progress, sir, yes. Seems it was quite a small heart attack, but she's taking it very much as a dire warning.'

'Good.' The doctor briefly took the other man's arm. 'Why don't we stretch our legs on the lawn? That way you'll get some healthy exercise from the encounter if nothing else.' He directed their steps to the left, away from the front door. After they had rounded the corner of the building, and were passing the tool-shed and the greenhouse, it was evident that both structures were deserted. The door to the tool-shed was secured with a padlock. 'Hm. I assume Collit's wife is still missing, so Collit is too,' Howell observed. 'We've given him time off to try tracking her down. I've no doubt she'll show up soon. They say she's not given to…to what you might call extravagant gestures.'

'I'd agree about that, sir, from what I know of her,' except the sergeant was a touch more concerned about the young woman than he felt his companion seemed to be.

Howell nodded. 'Her unexplained absence must be worrying for her husband even so,' he said, as though he had sensed the other's assessment of his own apparent coolness. 'Most probably taken herself off somewhere to get away from the inevitable intrusions of a murder investigation.' He gave a sideways glance at Lloyd. 'I mean nothing personal in that, of course. You chaps have your jobs to do, and very tactful you are in the way you do them too, but I gather the Collits have been pretty much in the centre of the enquiries.'

'Ah, you might think that if you hadn't been involved in the other nine-tenths of them, sir.'

'Point taken, Mr Lloyd.' The speaker chuckled, then

looked up and spread his arms apart as they moved down the front terrace and onto the grass. 'Now isn't this a fine sward in magnificent condition? Not a weed in sight. Great credit to Phil Collit. It's not an old lawn by, say, Oxford college standards, of course. Part of a cricket pitch for half a century though, which must have given it a sound base. I know very little about gardening, I'm afraid, but there's something very British about a good lawn, don't you think?' He nodded his own head in vigorous affirmation. 'But now then, tell me what I can do for you? Seems we have the place to ourselves so we shan't be overheard.' It was true that there wasn't another human being in view, a fact that related, the sergeant thought, to the intensity of the therapeutic regimens being followed inside the clinic, and which the director was given to advertising so fulsomely.

'It's quite a small point, sir, really.' The sergeant smoothed the side of his moustache. 'We've been wondering again about your movements after ten o'clock on Saturday night.'

Howell's expression changed to one of enquiry rather than surprise. 'But haven't I given you them already?'

'You have, sir, yes, but you mentioned you'd returned to your cottage for the night after leaving Mrs Ingram at the main door of the clinic.'

'That's quite right,' the doctor replied, then stopped abruptly in mid-step. 'Hang on, though, didn't I say I'd needed to return to the clinic a little later?'

The sergeant beamed. 'Well that's just it, doctor. You didn't mention it, not according to what DCI Parry remembers, or the notes he took at your meeting. He believes –'

'Silly of me, of course, and remiss as well.' Howell had interrupted in an avuncular manner. He began moving forward again. 'What I told Mr Parry makes me guilty of what

234

we call in neuro-speak "a wish compensating negative".' He beamed benevolently at his somewhat boot-faced companion who was not exhibiting any understanding of the phrase just proffered nor, judging from his so far mute reaction, any particular desire to work one out for himself. 'You see, Mr Lloyd,' the other continued, 'after leaving Mrs Ingram I'd really meant to go home to bed after a fairly gruelling day. Having, to all intents, done just that, after a certain passage of time my mind chose to obliterate, to temporarily obliterate at least, the fact that earlier indolence had been the cause of my needing to go back to the clinic.' After delivering this soliloquy he took a deep, self-satisfied breath.

'I see, sir.' Lloyd sniffed. 'You mean you forgot you went back?'

Although Howell's lips moved quite actively against each other, he emitted no words aloud, while seeming to debate with himself for several seconds. 'In very broad terms, yes,' he said eventually quite slowly, and with a frown, while his elongating of the word 'broad' had given it an intellectual sort of emphasis. 'Though to me it's a little more complex than that.' He moved a touch closer to his companion in a somewhat conspiratorial fashion. 'To be frank, my friend, I'm a slave to discipline. A slave,' he repeated with more depth in his voice. 'In my subconscious, sometimes I would actually prefer not to admit to an event rather than concede it happened if it did so because I was dilatory in observing…an obligation. In other words, I might choose to forget it,' he had continued ahead of allowing the sergeant to supply the simple extrapolation of this newest piece of existentialist rationale. 'Hm. Quite pointless, of course, but then we all have our frailties, don't we?' Again he didn't wait for Lloyd to accede to a universal truth. 'In any event, as you implied earlier, it was a small omission. I have to assume,' he added quickly, 'that someone saw me return to the clinic later, minutes later....mm...three minutes later?'

'That's about right, doctor, yes.' After offering an excuse for not telling the truth as circuitous as it had been unconvincing, Lloyd felt that Howell had hardly strengthened a dodgy case by adding such an exact timing to an event whose existence he had earlier claimed to have eradicated from his memory.

'And this is important in view of what happened to poor Rees between ten-thirty and...was it midnight you said?' They had reached the far end of the lawn and on Howell's instigation they turned to retrace their steps.

'Ten-thirty is the start of the time period we're concentrating on at the moment, sir,' the policeman replied without actually answering the question.

'Even so, I assume there's no suggestion that I was involved in the murder?' After this, the speaker immediately bared his teeth and exercised his mouth and jaw in such an energetic way as almost to suggest that his lower face was being subjected to some kind of minor convulsion.

'Of course not, doctor.' The sergeant construed, if not too seriously, that his companion may just have undergone some nervous physical reaction explicable only in what he called neuro-speak. 'It's just that we need to have an accurate record of the movements of everybody in the vicinity of the crime,' he added.

'I understand. Of course, whoever it was who saw me come out of the cottage...?' At his point Howell paused briefly but pointedly, with sufficient interrogative stress to his words to encourage Lloyd to volunteer the identity of the individual involved. Since no such admission was forthcoming, and since the doctor was certainly not intending to ask for one outright for fear the disclosure would be refused, he went on. 'Whoever told you that he…or, I suppose, she saw me must have reported that I went back to the clinic not round to the pavilion?'

'Quite right, sir.' Lloyd rubbed one side of his moustache. 'Only there are quite a lot of ways for anyone going into the clinic by the main door on the west side to come out again from exits on the east side, aren't there? I mean, from here I can count…' he began making short nods with his head like a clockwork toy, his eyes scanning the long eastern frontage as he did so. 'I can count,' he repeated, 'as many as nine of them, not including windows.'

'Ah, I see what you're getting at. Of course, all…all eight ground floor patient rooms on this side have doors onto the main terrace, and there's the double door from the corridor in the centre making nine, as you say.' Even so he had gone through the process of counting them all himself, as though the actual number was something quite new to him. 'So you think the murderer could have emerged from inside the clinic?' he added.

'It's one of the possibilities, sir, yes,' and such an obvious one, the sergeant thought, as hardly to need labouring. The distance from the furthest of the doors that he had indicated to the steps of the pavilion was barely a hundred yards – to be exact, ninety-eight yards and six inches. That had been a measurement made by a SOCO team member the day before, and officially recorded in metres as well as yards, although, wherever possible, Lloyd still preferred to ignore metric calculations. 'It'd be simple enough for the murderer to have come out onto the terrace, gone over to the pavilion, done for Mr Rees, and returned by the same route, sir. The possibility of being observed after dark would probably have been smaller than if the person had come round from the other side of the building.'

The doctor gave a satisfied kind of snort. 'Well at least, sergeant, I can put your mind at rest about my own innocence on that count. You see, after I came back to the clinic, I went straight up the stairs to the second floor. Later I left again by the front door, and returned directly to our cottage. No doubt I can find witnesses to that if need be. My wife – '

'Good lord, doctor, no one's questioning your innocence, I assure you.' The sergeant had broken in with a gusto that bordered on the obsequious. Even so, in his own mind he was well aware that there was no evidence yet, one way or the other, as to whether the murderer had come from inside or outside the clinic, let alone about whether he had approached the scene of the crime from the west or the east side of the building. 'If you could tell me, sir, just for the record of course, what time it was when you left the clinic again?'

*

'So DC Alison Pope apprehended a wanted fugitive by mistake, Gomer?' Parry questioned with a chuckle before lifting a pint glass of Brain's Best Bitter. 'Cheers, then,' he added.

'Yes, and she wasn't over pleased at the time, boss, either. She thought she'd found the missing clergyman – '

'The one called Derek?'

'That's him. Only the alleged clergyman up in the bedroom with the fourteen-year-old Phoebe – '

'Fourteen!' Parry nearly choked on his beer.

'Well, that was alleged as well, by Phoebe's younger half-sister Jessica. Phoebe's actually seventeen. Jessica was jealous and stirring it up.'

'You mean trying to con our admirable but shockable Alison Pope?'

'Yes. It's a long story, boss. The bloke with Phoebe was called Derek all right, except he wasn't a clergyman. He was a young tearaway from Swansea who'd done a runner when he was in transit between Swansea Crown Court and the nick.'

'And was shacking up with Phoebe?'

'Seems so, yes, except her mother denies it, only she's no better than she should be, either. Seems they're a problem family. This Derek had just got six months for robbery with violence. Second similar offence this year. Anyway, when he heard DC Pope coming up the stairs he did a flyer through the window.'

'And she took him on single-handed after he'd landed?'

'She was ready to. Down there in a flash, only she could have come off worst. The reports say he's a savage swine and big with it. Except this time it was no contest. He dislocated an arm falling out of a water butt and onto a sizeable cucumber frame, then busted an ankle trying to get out of the frame. Cut himself as well. She had him cuffed and was providing first aid before assistance arrived.'

'That's our Alison. Like your Lucy.'

The two men had just seated themselves at a table in the garden at the rear of the Dunraven Arms, a pub midway between the Fairwater police station and the Howell Clinic. They'd arranged the meeting by telephone. It was still Monday, and five-thirty p.m., close to what the chief inspector regarded as the end of day two of the Kevin Rees murder case. Although the body hadn't been discovered until 7.30 in the morning of the previous day, he had been determined to squeeze every particle of witness out of those competent to give it before trails got any colder.

Irritatingly for Parry, since leaving Lucy at the hospital he had wasted nearly two hours in court, waiting to be called to give five minutes worth of evidence as the officer in charge of an armed robbery investigation.

He had then spent another fifty minutes at a meeting in the Crown Prosecutor's Office trying to persuade a senior lawyer to proceed with a prosecution where part of the evidence was wobbly. This was because of a palpably lying and unsupported witness, and where the guilt of the accused, a three times convicted felon, was toweringly obvious to every policeman involved, based on well corroborated testimonies. For the moment Parry had failed to win his argument, but he had gained extra time in which to disprove the rogue witness's story. He was confident this could be done, eventually justifying his police team's round-the-clock effort to bring a dangerous criminal to justice – and ultimately winning plaudits in court for a currently over-cautious barrister who would end up with most of the credit.

Parry had got back to his office just before five o'clock, missing Lloyd there, but with time to catch up on progress reports, written and verbal. The sandwich he had just bought at the bar was to be his lunch, and probably also his supper.

Lloyd had spent a lot more of the day than his chief on the Rees murder, the investigation that was challenging both of them the most, in the sergeant's case not least because of his daughter's involvement. He had called in at the hospital briefly on his way back to meet Parry. 'Lucy said you let her down lightly,' he remarked, sipping through the froth on his own overflowing beer glass.

'What else did you expect, Gomer? I wouldn't have gone near her today without your say-so. As it is, I'll bet my name's mud with Gracie.'

'No. She understands. They both do. The flowers helped as well. My wife's always been a knock-over for roses in the expensive season.' He wiped his moustache with his forefinger.

'Well my visit with Lucy was worth diamonds. Did she repeat to you what she told me?' Parry looked around. Although the sun was shining fitfully between light clouds, it was a cooler evening than expected, and so far the policemen were the only customers drinking outside.

'No. Seemed like half the family were at her bedside, or waiting in the corridor. That's why I didn't stay long. I told her I was meeting you. She did say you'd surprise me.'

Parry nodded firmly. 'Would you credit Megan Collit told Lucy that Phil Collit never went to the clinic after he left the Eight Bells on Saturday night?'

Lloyd looked more perplexed than surprised. 'No, I wouldn't credit it.'

'Well it seems to be true, Gomer. But so far only you and I know it, plus Lucy, of course. And that's the way I want it kept until we've got hold of the Collits.'

'Understood.' The sergeant leaned across the table as he continued quietly, 'So who's supposed to have turned up the heating in the greenhouse and closed those cold frames on Saturday night?'

'No one, probably. We only have his word for it that those things happened.'

'Except he said he'd told Dr Janet Howell he'd be doing both?'

The chief inspector paused for a second's reflection before replying. 'Still doesn't mean he did tell her, of course. Anyway, we have to assume that Megan Collit, when she re-appears, may now be ready to admit her husband never left the house again after he came back at 10.25.'

'Question is, which story will Phil Collit be backing, boss?'

'Presumably we could bring on his mother to support the

new one if he doesn't, and if there's any doubt about who's telling the truth.' Still burning about the single witness who was spoiling the other case with the Crown Prosecutor, from what he'd seen of Mrs Collit senior he believed she could be relied upon honestly to substantiate the movements of her own son, not least because it would extricate him from a sticky situation.

'It doesn't make sense yet, does it?' Lloyd gulped down some beer. 'I mean, why did Collit lie to us from the start about his movements on Saturday night? And why did he go to the clinic on Sunday morning when he didn't need to?'

'That's what I've been trying to figure off and on since I left Lucy. Could it be he somehow knew Rees had been murdered, and he needed to find the body?'

Parry shook his head as if to refute his own proposition before he added slowly, 'But when we have the answers to both your questions, of course we'll know who did the murder.'

'Well when we get hold of Collit again, he can't stick to a story his wife's rubbished can he?' the sergeant stated, but with some uncertainty. 'You know, don't you, he's been out looking for her since mid-morning?'

'Mm.' Parry was swallowing a mouthful of prawn sandwich. 'If he hasn't found her, he probably doesn't know she's in effect changed their story. That's why I rang from the hospital ordering a watch on the Mary Street house.'

'I wondered about that,' the other man put in.

'If one of them turns up there without the other, I want him or her brought straight to the nick for interviewing. It'll be good if we can get to either of them before he or she know their main story's had a hole blown in it.'

Lloyd frowned at his beer. 'Funny she chose to trust Lucy with the truth, assuming it is the truth.'

'She was obviously desperate at the time, Gomer, and in a panic. If Lucy hadn't lost her rag with you, I don't think she'd have given Megan away either, not unless we'd actually arrested the husband. I think Megan was counting on that. She pretty clearly deluded herself into thinking you could be persuaded to let him off the hook for no convincing reason.'

'Well delusion was right, wasn't it?' the sergeant offered. 'I mean if she was daft enough to believe a detective sergeant had that much power or influence in any case. Of course, since we don't know where either of them is, could be the whole thing was a delaying tactic while they did a runner together.'

'Possible but not likely, Gomer. It'd mean leaving his mother on her own. Lucy says they'd never leave her by herself overnight. They take her with them whenever they go away, even for a night at her parents' house.'

'I see,' the sergeant answered, but without sounding wholly convinced about his daughter's reasoning.

'You saw Dr Howell. Did he say why he went back to the clinic on Saturday after saying goodnight to Mrs Ingram?'

'Yes, boss. He'd forgotten he had to see the matron about a patient.'

'Was he with her long?'

'Some time, he said, yes, but he couldn't remember exactly when he left. When he first went back he joked with the night sister about his forgetfulness, and he thinks she probably saw him leave again. I'm having that checked out with her.'

'Perhaps we should ask the matron as well, Gomer.' Parry made as if to add something else, then didn't.

'Right, boss.' The sergeant made a note, then looked up. 'So what did Mrs Ingram say when you saw her at Blycot Manor?'

'From what she admitted this time around, I don't believe

she or her husband were even indirectly involved in Rees's death, not knowingly anyway. I as good as told her that, too.'

'Of course she'd have been scared it'd set him back medically if he was caught up in a murder enquiry, boss. Well that's understandable. By the way, she took him out of the clinic this afternoon.' This time Lloyd's comments sounded broadly sympathetic as he continued. 'I expect she was relieved when you said they're not on our wanted list. But that wasn't the reason you said it,' he completed bluntly, pronouncing the last sentence as a statement not a question.

'No, it wasn't. And perhaps it wasn't strictly true either. But I needed her to admit Rees was blackmailing him through her. It worked too. She really let her hair down.' He grinned. 'I mean metaphorically. She admitted Denis Ingram was a deeply closeted gay, that outing him would wreck his recovery, and, worse, his whole mental equilibrium. That was quite apart from what it might do to foul up his promised knighthood. She even insisted it could be the end of him.'

Lloyd made a pained face. 'By that she'd have meant suicide, I should think. Anyway, the honour's to be a knighthood, not one of the lower gongs?'

'That's right, Gomer, and despite the grief Rees was causing her, because of what she told me I really don't believe she had a hand in his murder. It wouldn't have been her style, and she wouldn't have had the contacts to lay on a hit man.'

'Had she told anyone else about the blackmail?'

'Yes. Jeremy Jackson, the bloke in Earls Court. She knows him all right, and all about Denis Ingram's er...close friendship with him. He'd rung to alert her about her husband's stroke when it started, but she was out. At least he got hold of her a bit later to tell her where they'd taken him. She rang him yesterday to warn him he might be interviewed by the police if we found out Rees was in the ambulance crew.'

'That was pretty acute of her,' said Lloyd.

'Yes, I thought the same. Jackson put up a good performance, too, as I told you. She admits he'd do anything for her husband.'

'Anything except commit murder just to stop him from being outed as gay, boss?'

'Well not without a hell of an argument against, probably. As an ex-gay-lib demonstrator, I'd say Jackson would find it hard to treat staying in the closet as a life or death matter. Anyway, I see from the faxes that the Met have checked his alibi, and he's in the clear.'

'So Mrs Ingram's on calling terms with her husband's lovers?'

'As her husband may well be with hers. I think that's part of the understanding between the two of them, and I'd say it's applied for years. Socially and commercially they're a team, a very successful one, and to all appearances they're a devoted couple with a son they both dote on. But when it comes to sex, they have quite separate arrangements, and it all worked perfectly before Rees came along.'

'She didn't tell you this, boss?'

'She didn't need to. Well, not all of it. Incidentally, her boyfriend, or one of them, stayed last night with her at Blycot Manor. I must have scared the hell out of them arriving at nearly no notice, but he did a bunk in a new Aston Martin DB7 right under my nose. Not that it mattered.'

'You know who it was, boss?'

'Yes, I've had the car number checked to be certain, but she'd told me anyway, implying he'd driven down from London this morning. He's unmarried and chief executive of your Gracie's favourite charitable trust.'

'Go on?' Lloyd wondered if Gracie would approve. 'Could he have been her hit man?'

'Unlikely since she swears he doesn't know about the blackmail. To be on the safe side, I'm having his movements on Saturday checked.'

'So you think we're back to the Collits, boss?'

Parry finished his pint. 'The Collits or someone close to them. Is there any information on the mystery woman Mr A.J.Claverhouse saw from his window on Saturday night?'

'When he wasn't wearing his glasses, boss?'

'Is that right?'

'Yes, and he didn't have his hearing aids in either.'

'Pity. All that'll need disclosing to any defence lawyer, I suppose. That was the time he thought he might have heard but never saw a car?'

'Right, boss. A car with a quiet engine, so it wouldn't have been an Aston Martin,' Lloyd offered gratuitously.

'Well maybe – ' The chief inspector didn't finish what he was saying because his mobile phone had started to bleep. 'Hello?' He waited to hear what was a lengthy message from the caller, and from the increasing interest on his face, an important one. 'Right, make them comfortable,' he responded eventually. 'I'll be there in two minutes…Yes, DS Lloyd is with me.'

'The Collits have turned up, have they?' Lloyd enquired hopefully.

'One of them has, Gomer. Megan Collit, with the Reverend Father Derek at the nick. That was DS Norris. She thinks Megan is probably ready to tell all. If you go to Mary Street I'll call you there after we've seen her. I don't know where the husband is, but we still need to keep them apart.'

Chapter Nineteen

'Like the good Christian she is, Mr Parry, Megan wants to tell you all she knows about Saturday night,' Father Derek announced with authority. He had hesitated to describe her as a 'good Catholic' since he felt there was more work to do on that score. 'We know we're a bit late,' he continued, 'and that Megan got a few things a touch wrong last time she was interviewed, but the circumstances have been... extenuating. Isn't that right, Megan?'

Megan Collit, in the chair beside him, nodded nervously. She and the Australian priest were on one side of a small oblong table in an interview room at the Fairwater police station. Parry and DS Mary Norris were seated opposite. The cream painted room was sparsely furnished and window-less. Apart from the four black plastic chairs and table already in use, and the two illuminated ceiling light fittings, there was another chair near the door, and a table, the same size as the other next to it, supporting a tape recorder. The machine was not switched on.

'Well, that's all good news, Father,' responded Parry, 'and we appreciate your coming over with Mrs Collit from Bristol. As DS Norris told you, we'd been trying to contact you as well, except we'd got your denomination wrong I'm afraid, also the address where you stayed Saturday night.'

'That was my mistake, Mr Parry, and I'm sorry. It was in St Fagan's Road, just around the corner from Ely Road. The bus stop is in Ely Road which is why I got mixed up. The clergy secretary at St David's Catholic Cathedral in Charles Street, Cardiff, she could have told you where I was. Anyway, I'm here, better late than never.'

The chief inspector smiled agreement, then turned to Megan. 'And we were worried about you, Megan. So was your husband, of course.'

'We caught up with him at Megan's parents, sir, in Treorchy,' the woman sergeant put in. 'Megan's since talked to him on the phone, and he should be back at their Mary Street house in about half-an-hour. Dr Edwin Howell lent him a clinic car this morning.' She didn't add that he would find DS Gomer Lloyd waiting for him at Mary Street on Parry's instructions.

'Good. So you were in safe hands in Bristol, Megan?'

She lifted her head. 'I went there to have my pregnancy terminated. I thought that way no one locally would know. Phil didn't really want a baby yet because we can't afford it.' There was a pause before she added. 'Except in the end I've decided to keep it.' She gave a sideways glance at Father Derek.

'And you got details of the Pregnancy Advisory Service from Kevin Rees?'

'Only the phone number, yes, so I could ring for an appointment if I wanted. When he'd read my note, he tried ringing me at the store. That wasn't till Saturday morning. But his mobile was on the blink. He rang again, at lunchtime, from a phone-box. I'm sorry I didn't tell you that before.' There was another fleeting glance, this time at DS Norris.

'Don't worry,' said Parry, 'nothing you told us earlier is hewn in stone yet, but we must try to get everything right this time. So you and Kevin arranged to meet?'

'Yes. At the pavilion, between 10.30 and 10.45 Saturday night. Depending on when Phil got home.'

'Had you met there before?'

'I don't…yes, only once though.' Her voice had lowered on the admission.

'He gave you the pregnancy service number when he called from the phone box?'

'Yes. It was…it was the last time I ever talked to him,' she responded sorrowfully. Then her expression seemed to harden as her delivery quickened. 'Phil never went to the clinic after he got home Saturday. It was me who went. When he came in I told him I'd just rung Kev who'd agreed to meet me at the clinic straight away to talk about the lottery winnings. Phil had already told me on his mobile from the pub that Kev wasn't giving us anything. I said I was going to ask him to give us half and that I thought he might if it was me who did the asking, like. Phil didn't believe he would, but he said it was worth a try.'

'He didn't go with you? He was supposed to raise the temperature in the greenhouse wasn't he?'

She shook her head. 'After we'd heard the frost warning on the telly, I said I'd do that, and close the frames as well. Otherwise we'd have had to leave his mother alone. Phil would never do that at night. We always got a sitter. Anyway, he…he didn't really want to see Kev again.'

'I understand. Have either of you since told anyone else it was you who went, not your husband?'

She hesitated. 'I don't believe Phil told anyone. I told one friend who could have helped us.' She looked shyly at Parry. 'That was after I thought you'd arrested Phil. I didn't know what to do. I think my friend tried to help, but…but she's been taken ill. Do I have to say who it was?'

'Not if you don't want,' Parry replied, happy that Lucy Lloyd was still regarded as a trusted friend by Megan Collit as he continued. 'At this point, of course, Phil didn't know you were thinking about an abortion?'

'He didn't even know I was pregnant. And anyway, on Saturday I wasn't certain about having the abortion.'

Parry looked puzzled. 'And when you arranged to meet Kevin Rees, you didn't know about the lottery win either did you?'

'No. Like I said yesterday, we watched the draw at 8.15 on telly. Like we always do on Saturdays.'

'Even though you hadn't put any money on for two weeks?'

The young woman swallowed. 'Phil said if our numbers came up it wouldn't be too late to give Kev the twenty pounds owing, as if we'd always meant to. He'd only mentioned we'd given up to one person, Mrs Radcliffe, and he thought she'd taken it as joking. He was sort of joking himself when he said it wouldn't be too late about the twenty pounds, but when four of the numbers came up a minute later he got serious. So did I, except I wasn't so sure Kev would go along with sharing the winnings, not...not with the other, like.' She looked briefly confused before carrying on with: 'Anyway, it was why Phil went to the pub. To see Kev.'

'But before you knew about the win, how were you going to explain to Phil about meeting Kevin later?'

Megan glanced at Father Derek before answering Parry. 'I wasn't. I was going to say I was taking Waldo for his walk. I often take him out if Phil comes back late from a darts match, or one of his evening classes.'

It was Mary Norris who next put in. 'And Phil still thought you might do better with Kevin than he had?'

'He thought it was worth me trying, yes, like I said.' The other woman frowned. 'Remember we'd been going halves with Kev week after week since November. And they'd got me to pick the numbers at the start. We never changed them.'

'So you felt that if it hadn't been for you there wouldn't have been any big win?'

'Well there couldn't have been, could there?' said Megan without emphasis.

Father Derek chuckled loudly. He had been purposefully silent since his first statement. 'I think that's a point of view that might have been accepted by a friend with a charitable inclination,' he offered, while beaming goodwill at everyone.

'Anyway, Megan,' said Parry, 'you felt one way and another that you and your husband were entitled to something?'

'I didn't see why not, and that's the truth.' This came with more spirit than before.

The chief inspector leaned forward across the table. 'But we know the lottery win really wasn't the original reason you had for seeing Kevin Rees, after all. Accepting you and Phil might have had a case for getting a share of the winnings, your main purpose was to get Kevin to give you the cost of a private abortion, wasn't it? Or lend you the money for it?'

There was a prolonged silence, broken after Megan and the priest had exchanged further glances. 'That's right,' she answered quietly.

'So was the money to be a gift or a loan?'

'A gift.'

'And he'd promised to give it to you when you met?'

She took a deep breath. 'Yes. In cash.'

'He had nine hundred pounds on him when he died. Was that the figure he'd promised?'

She nodded. 'Seven-fifty for the nursing home...for the two doctors who...who had to give permission, and for the operation...plus a hundred for the agency, oh, and fifty to cover the hostel overnight, and the train fare to Bristol.'

'That was pretty generous of Kevin, wasn't it? So in a way he was accepting responsibility for your...your situation?'

Megan sighed. 'Sort of...as...as a friend, yes.' After this somewhat enigmatic reply she stared down at her clenched hands. 'He said if I didn't want the baby he'd pay for me not to have it.'

Parry wasn't prepared to press for a stronger admission about Kevin Rees being the father. Even if Collit had been aware that his wife had been unfaithful to him with Rees, and that itself was not completely resolved, the likelihood of the outraged husband having taken his revenge by murdering the other man now seemed remote. The point could be left hanging in any case, and what was left of Megan Collit's reputation and self-respect hanging with it.

The woman in question blew her nose on a tissue before suddenly announcing: 'The termination was to be by suction. I…I didn't want that, not really…not at all…it sounded so…' She was stumbling over the words before she suddenly burst into tears.

Father Derek put an arm around her shoulder. 'This is obviously very painful for Megan, Mr Parry,' he said. 'Since she's answered all your questions frankly and very truthfully I'd like to take her home now. Miss Norris here said we'd be allowed to go whenever Megan wanted.'

It was Megan who answered before the policeman. 'It's all right, Father.'

She was wiping her eyes. 'I'd rather get it all over with now. I want it cleared up before I see Phil.' She turned her gaze back to Parry 'He doesn't know about Kev's part in it all. Not any of it. You understand that, all of you?'

'We do, yes, Megan,' Mary Norris replied, and pleased that her chief had earlier made the decision not to impute the young wife's conduct without need.

'And in the end it was my money that was going to pay for the abortion, not Kev's,' Megan went on. 'After I knew he was dead, I borrowed it from Mrs Craig-Owen. She owns the supermarket where I work. It was a pay advance.'

'Which praise be has been reimbursed by the pregnancy advice people,' the priest put in with great satisfaction.

'I'm glad about that, Megan,' said Parry. 'And you can rely on what you've told us staying confidential. It was information to help with our investigation into Kevin's murder. We've not been trying to pry into your private life.' He added a reassuring smile to his statement before finishing with: 'So, if you can spare us just two more minutes, I'd be grateful.'

From what Megan had given away earlier, it seemed clear to Parry that Rees had been ready to pay dearly for what most likely had been a single experience in unprotected sex with his best friend's wife. The cash he had been intending to give her covertly explained why Rees had been so obdurate about not sharing the lottery winnings with Collit. The dead man's attitudes fitted with most of what Parry had learned from Stacey Fowler and others about his curious, ambivalent moral stances.

Even if Rees had been ready to offer a share in the winnings to pay for an abortion, Phil Collit might perversely have seen it as enough to make it possible for them to afford a child at last. This in turn was something that would not have suited Rees if it meant that he ran the risk later of it proving to be his child.

'So, are we right in thinking you went to the clinic Saturday night on your moped, Megan?' asked DS Norris, looking at the check-list in her notebook.

'Yes. But I parked it just inside the gate, because of the engine noise. The matron, Miss Oswald, she doesn't like anything that can wake up the patients at night.'

'I see. The gate would have been locked, of course,' the sergeant continued. 'According to the night sister, no one rang the bell all evening. So you knew the entry code, did you?'

'Always did. Phil had it for his job, didn't he?'

'Of course. And so far as you know, did anyone see you while you were inside the clinic grounds?'

'Don't think so.'

'And what route did you take to the pavilion? Did you walk past the main door of the clinic, or along the terrace on the garden side?'

'I went past the main door.'

'When you got there – '

'I never got there,' Megan interrupted. The questioner looked surprised. 'How do you mean? Did you turn back for some reason?'

'Yes. When I got as far as the greenhouse I saw the door was half open, and the cold frames were closed. They're just outside the door.'

'Was there anyone inside the greenhouse?'

'No. Well, the light wasn't on in there, but I could hear Dr Howell and Kev talking further along the path, by the pavilion.'

'Dr Howell? Which Dr Howell was that?'

'Dr Janet Howell.'

'And you left, went home again, because of her?'

'That's right. I didn't want her to see me meeting Kev there again.' Megan hesitated, wetting her lips with her tongue. 'I think she could have seen us that night in March, when Kev and me left the pavilion. It was dark, but she must just have gone into the greenhouse. She switched the lights on as we were going past. We ducked and ran for it, but like I said, she could have seen us.'

'And guessed at what you might have been doing?' the woman sergeant commented flatly.

'Yes. But if she did see us, she never told Phil.' The speaker was kneading the tissue grasped in her hand. 'He's her favourite,' she continued, 'and…and she's always been very good to us. Well, to Phil anyway.'

Parry cleared his throat before he interjected: 'Why do you think she didn't tell Phil she'd seen you with Kevin that night? Was it because it would have upset your marriage?'

'I expect so, yes. She's not interfering…or spiteful. I don't think she likes me. Not good enough for Phil, I expect, but she wouldn't want to start a row between me and Phil. She values him, not that she overpays him. She never valued Kev. He told me so.'

'Did he say what she had against him?'

Megan hesitated. 'I don't know for sure. He told me once he'd found out Dr Edwin was having an affair with the matron, and the matron could never sack him because he knew about them. He said she paid him to keep it quiet. Perhaps Dr Janet knew he had a hold over the matron without knowing what it was.' She shrugged, then gave a half-apologetic glance at Father Derek. 'I didn't know whether to believe Kev or not. He loved gossip. Liked you to think he knew everything about everybody, except I think he…he sort of invented most of it, to make himself look important.'

*

'I don't believe she realised the significance of what she was telling you, boss. Couldn't have done,' Gomer Lloyd stated firmly, sucking hard on a mint. 'To Megan Collit and her husband, Dr Janet Howell is a sort of saint. Pure and above sin. Megan wouldn't credit she was capable of doing the smallest wrong, let alone committing a murder. Neither would I, come to that.'

Parry sniffed. 'Certainly Megan described what happened in a very matter of fact way. Totally unsurprised.'

'Mostly in awe, I should think, boss. To her Dr Janet would be like Caesar's wife, beyond reproach. She's half of the clinic's top medical team. A famous doctor despite her infirmities. And as well as all that, from what Megan told you, the doctor had once caught her with Kevin Rees right after they'd probably had a roll in the hay, like. Well, no wonder Megan was bothered on Saturday. What if the doctor saw her going to meet him in the same place again? No wonder she didn't hang on to find out what Rees and Dr Janet were talking about.'

The two were seated in the chief inspector's office. Lloyd had just arrived. It was 6.50, and three-quarters of an hour since Parry's encounter with Megan Collit had ended. That had been a few minutes before her husband had got back to the Mary Street house. Lloyd had been waiting outside to see him there, briefed by Parry in a hurry on his mobile about Megan's disclosures. She had reached the house with Father Derek ten minutes after her husband. Parry's own pressing need to see Dr Janet Howell had so far been thwarted.

The matron, Eve Oswald, had told him that the doctor had appointments at the University Hospital running from 6.30 through to eight, and couldn't be interrupted.

'So, did Phil Collit swear he hadn't gone to the clinic? I mean after Megan got back to Mary Street from there on Saturday, Gomer?'

'Yes, he was adamant about it, boss. Which is what his wife told you. And as well as her, he's got his mother to prove it. I spoke to her. Not that they're exactly disinterested witnesses, of course. But Megan says the old lady was really groggy and needed a lot of attention from both of them till well after midnight. If you remember, it was the same reason Megan had given us for her not going to the pub earlier. According to Collit, he didn't need to go to the clinic because his wife had noticed the cold frames had been closed, she thought by Dr Janet. He says he assumed the doctor would have turned up the greenhouse thermostat as well, thinking he'd forgotten, or hadn't heard the frost warning.'

'That could have been why she bumped into Rees, I suppose,' Parry observed thoughtfully.

'And the doctor raising the greenhouse heating herself explains why Collit still went there early in the morning, to lower it again,' Lloyd enlarged. 'After all, it was part of his job not hers, and he'd be sensitive to that.'

'Hm. It also explains why at the start Megan first wanted everyone to think it was her husband not her who'd been there the night before,' said Parry. 'It all fits in a clumsy way, of course. But why didn't the doctor tell us she'd been there, and met Rees in the process?'

Lloyd gave a pained grimace. 'Because no one asked her, perhaps?'

'Possibly, Gomer, yes. Well, I can tell you, I'm going to ask her as soon as we can get hold of her, which won't be for another hour yet.' The chief inspector glanced at the time. 'I suppose she does a neurological clinic at the hospital on Mondays.' He looked up at the sergeant. 'By the way, Megan Collit's most astonishing revelation was that Rees told her he had evidence to prove Dr Edwin Howell was sleeping with your paragon Eve Oswald.'

'You don't say?' The sergeant crunched hard on a nearly new mint, an exceptional action on his part, though it wasn't clear whether it was prompted by his dismay at the disclosure, or his lack of trust in the probity of the discloser. '

Even so, she implied she didn't believe him,' Parry continued. 'He also told her it was the reason he'd never be fired, and that the matron was paying him to keep the affair quiet.'

Lloyd's eyes narrowed. 'In other words he admitted he was blackmailing her?'

'Yes, Gomer, and that's the bit I find uncomfortable but just credible.'

'So Rees could have been telling Megan the truth, I suppose,' the sergeant admitted in a begrudging tone. 'By the way, DC Alison Pope has seen Ruth Tate, the night sister. The sister confirmed speaking to the doctor when he came back into the clinic, but she never saw him leave again.'

Parry gave a sardonic chuckle. 'Well I doubt he'd have stayed with the matron all night, Gomer, whatever their relationship may or may not be,' he remarked cynically.

'Well, Sister Tate said she'd been busy with a patient between 11.30 and midnight. She could have missed seeing him if he left between those times. And she volunteered he often goes in to see the matron after he's done his night rounds.'

The two men looked at each other for a long moment. 'In other words the two of them could have been popping into bed nightly,' said Parry. 'On the other hand, his seeing the matron after what he calls his informal after-dinner rounds is a perfectly proper, professional thing to do. But if Rees really did have tapes and photos – '

'Which I know for sure haven't materialised, boss, following a pretty thorough search of his belongings including his two cars,' Lloyd broke in, then added, 'But I still don't understand why the doctor had to make such a performance, and that frankly cock-and-bull story about forgetting he'd gone back to see her. I found it …diminishing in someone of his importance.'

'Hm. My guess is he was confused over being seen to do something he'd decided not to admit to me earlier.'

'Why, boss?'

'In case I misunderstood, probably. Anyway, it doesn't sound as if the good doctor could have done in Rees before 11.30 at least, which probably means not at all.' He was aware, even so, that Edwin Howell could have managed to slip out of the clinic and even back again without the night sister knowing, and with a colluding Eve Oswald prepared to vouch that he had been with her during the relevant period. But for the moment the chief inspector returned to the notes he had been fingering. 'We agreed the head of the Ingram's trust, Oliver Grant, needed an alibi for Saturday night. Anything further on that?' he asked.

'Yes, he's in the clear, boss. He was playing in an open squash tournament in Peterborough all Saturday and Sunday morning. Seems he's a dab hand at the game. County standard and all that. He stayed Friday and Saturday nights close by in Stamford, with a friend and his wife. The friend was also playing in the tournament. He left mid-afternoon Sunday –'

'And drove his speedy Aston-Martin cross country to Chepstow,' Parry put in, 'spending Sunday night with another friend's wife there.'

Lloyd looked up. 'There's nothing in the report about what he did after Peterborough, boss, but I should think you're right.'

'Not that it matters, Gomer. He couldn't have been Angela Ingram's hit man.'

'Which narrows the field of other takers, boss.'

'Mm.' Parry had got up and moved to the window. 'And there's no doubt it must have been Megan Collit that Claverhouse saw going toward the pavilion and returning so fast, even if he short-sightedly mistook her tin-lid for a scarf.'

'There could have been doubt, boss. After he told Mrs Radcliffe what he told us, she reported there was a young woman kitchen helper it might have been. She's since checked with the girl, though, who left early at ten and was picked up at the gate by her boyfriend on his motorbike.'

Parry acknowledged this with a slow nod. It seemed to him that the noose was tightening – and perversely he'd begun to wish it wasn't.

Chapter Twenty

'Yes, this is my private snug, Mr Parry. It's very cramped, but with room enough for me to reach everything, or remotely control it, without my needing to manoeuvre this chariot much, or having to be levered out of it. I can even make palatable coffee from that ingenious dispenser, or pour you a noggin of Scotch. Would you care for a spot of either beverage?'

Janet Howell smiled at her visitor from where she was seated in her 'chariot' which, after she had let him into the cottage, she had drawn up behind the angle of an L-shaped wooden desk-top. The short side of the L was an extension of the windowsill, and supported a computer terminal, keyboard, and printer tiered above a clear under-space. This still left a pleasant view from the window onto a flowerbed, part of the clinic driveway beyond, and, to the right, a glimpse of the main lawn.

The longer side of the desk-top butted against the wall with, above and below, cupboards with sliding glass fronts as well as open shelves housing an impressive and, for a seated person, accessible selection of files, reference books and more pieces of office equipment, including a complicated-looking electronic coffee machine – and a defiantly un-regenerated bottle of Macallan's single malt whisky on a tray with two glasses beside it.

The owner of all this equipage presently had her back to it and was turned to face Parry. The chief inspector was seated in a business-like, upright, well padded armchair with a hinged, adjustable side-panel on which the user could rest notes, or take them. The chair was the only additional piece of furniture in the room besides the light fittings.

It was 9.15 on Tuesday morning. The doctor's appointments the evening before had over-run. She had explained as much then on the telephone and begged to be excused this meeting – her first with Parry – until the following day.

'Nothing to drink for me, thank you, doctor,' he replied. 'But don't let me stop you having your coffee.'

'I'll wait a bit, I think. Too much caffeine isn't appropriate on my...my present diet. I don't care for the decaffeinated stuff either. Sadly, I'm required to be on the wagon for a bit as well. Heigh-ho.' The response came with a vocal liveliness that was not matched by the drawn appearance of the speaker's face. Her eyes seemed tired, something that was reflected in the heaviness of her movements. Only her black hair was as well presented as if it had just been styled and set. 'You didn't want to see my husband too, did you?' she continued. 'I'm afraid he'll be walled up with patients until noon. It's my fault because I've begged a morning off to...to catch up with correspondence. He's filling in for me. I didn't tell him I was seeing you. He's got so much on his plate today.'

'That's fine. It's just you I wanted, doctor, and I'm sorry to use up precious free time. Anyway, I'll try to keep this short.'

'That's helpful, but, in any event, it's very good to meet you. By the way, I'm glad to hear that Megan Collit is back in the fold, and is not having her pregnancy terminated.'

'You knew about that?'

The doctor made a tolerant head movement. 'News travels fast in a small community like ours. Eve Oswald told me last night, and about the police interviewing Megan and her husband. Eve and I had both figured Megan's disappearance might have boded an abortion. My husband wasn't so perceptive. Phil Collit is a sober and sensible young man, but his insistence on their putting off starting a family because he says they can't afford the extra expense is ridiculous. They have money enough, well, relatively so. I arrange his salary which is quite substantial, and I've no doubt hers is reasonable at least. She was obviously bowing to his wishes, but without telling him.'

Parry hesitated for a second before deciding to say: 'There may have been another reason why Megan Collit was contemplating an abortion. One she wouldn't have admitted to her husband.'

'Yes, and I believe we can both guess what it was without naming it,' the doctor responded, before adding: 'It was more important before Kevin Rees's death than after it, perhaps. Incidentally, I don't believe their...their rumoured liaison was a very serious one. Of course, Rees was a good deal livelier than Phil...but a good deal less desirable in the moral sense, if possibly not so in a strictly carnal one. From what I hear of her, Megan is easily led.'

'Can I ask, doctor, did you ever see her and Kevin Rees alone together?'

'Yes, they knew it too. It was one evening in...in March when I surprised them, quite unintentionally as it happened. They were scuttling away after a...after a cuddle, shall we say, in the pavilion. Of course, seduction was possibly the least of Rees's sins.'

'Blackmail being the worst of them, doctor?'

Janet Howell frowned as she moved both her open palms along her trousered thighs as though needing to relieve some discomfort in them. 'Blackmail and drug trading are abhorrent. I learned recently that Kevin Rees was guilty of practising not just one but both. Using our pavilion as a wholesale store for illegal drugs was inexcusable.'

'I agree. He...he didn't try to blackmail you?'

'No.' The speaker paused, pursing her lips while she was

evidently debating whether to go on, and before she related, slower than before, 'In confidence, he tried to blackmail Eve Oswald who is devoted to me and to my husband, as we both are to her. The three of us have a…a very close relationship, Mr Parry, extremely close, which that evil man claimed involved a clandestine sexual relationship between Eve and my husband. Rees threatened Eve that he would tell me about it, unless she paid him not to. I forget how much he demanded. He claimed he had tapes and photos to prove what he said. Huh! Very sensibly, Eve countered by saying she'd tell me about his unfounded allegation immediately. That saw him off in short order, I can tell you.'

'I'm sure it did, doctor.'

'Of course there were no tapes or photos. He'd made up the whole thing. Incidentally, this certainly means that Eve had no reason, no motive, for killing Rees. Otherwise I wouldn't have told you about the incident.' She took a long breath. 'Rees was a fool. Eve must have been the most sympathetic employer he ever had in a highly chequered career.'

'But she didn't sack him?'

'Not straight away, but there was a sound reason to delay. He'd so ingratiated himself with one of the patients – '

'Would that be Denis Ingram?'

'Yes. You know the story perhaps? I'm sorry to give Rees credit for anything, but he was heavily involved, with many others of course, in bringing about what amounts to Mr Ingram's quite exceptional recovery. Without consulting my husband, who knew nothing of Rees's treachery, Eve and I decided that dismissing him summarily might risk reversing Denis Ingram's, at the time, perilously fragile recovery, with the possibility even of making him worse than he'd been when he came to us. You've no idea how very, very fragile these things can be.'

'You mean if Rees had gone to Mr Ingram and told him you'd fired him, and the reason why?'

'Precisely, Mr Parry. It could have resulted in all kinds of unpleasantness. So Eve and I decided to hold off getting rid of the creep until the summer, by which time – '

'Mr Ingram would have that much more confidence in himself, and a knighthood to go with it,' the chief inspector put in, nodding his head.

The woman doctor looked up sharply. 'So his wife has taken you into her confidence over the honour?'

'Yes. She's also admitted to us that she told you Rees had been blackmailing her over her husband's...secret proclivity.'

The doctor chuckled. 'That's very nicely put, Mr Parry. Angela Ingram confided in me, yes. She pleaded at the time that we shouldn't tell my husband about Denis being gay. I agreed, partly because I guessed that Mrs Ingram rarely pleads for anything with anybody, and it must have been quite an exercise in humility for her to do so with me.' The speaker gave an impish grin before she continued. 'I also went along with her because they've kept his secret for so long one can't help feeling it's due to their never ever having shared it with anyone at all unless absolutely necessary. When you think about it, that shows she's exercised an astonishing degree of loyalty. Well, at least in one connection. In fact, of course, my husband had figured Denis was gay within about an hour of meeting him. But Angela is still unaware that he knows. I was against such a silly subterfuge at the time. Practising deceit is a fool's game, especially in medicine. Now, in this particular case, I've agreed they should keep things the way they are, for fear Mrs Ingram loses belief in the digestibility of humble pie.'

Parry grinned, then leaned forward in his chair. 'Could we switch to Megan Collit, doctor? On her own admission she came to the clinic to meet Rees on Saturday night. Their rendezvous was to be the pavilion. Although she nearly got there, she says she never did meet him. From the cover of the greenhouse she was frightened to see him talking to someone near the pavilion. She insists she then immediately fled, scared that the person he was with would see them together and tell her husband.'

'So it was another lovers' tryst,' the doctor announced flatly.

'Not according to Megan, no. Without her husband knowing, Rees had promised her some money. It was to pay for an abortion, and she'd come to collect it. Rees had the necessary cash on him. Phil Collit knew they were meeting, except his wife had told him she was going to beg Rees to give them part of the lottery winnings. At the time he didn't know she was pregnant. Another…piece of deception, I'm afraid,' the chief inspector ended.

'All very interesting, Mr Parry. I suppose it's heartening to know Rees had a conscience of sorts. Presumably he was responsible for her pregnancy? Or thought he was?'

'I can't say, doctor,' he answered truthfully. 'Of course, we only have her word for it that he was with someone else when she arrived. While there's some slim circumstantial evidence that another person was there, it's equally conceivable that there wasn't anyone else, that Megan and Rees did meet, that he said he wasn't going to give her the promised money without concessions. Perhaps he was demanding sexual favours there and then? She could have stabbed him in a fit of rage and disappointment, though if that was the case it'd be difficult to credit why she didn't just take the money from his pocket after she'd killed him.'

'She really was there, was she, Mr Parry? I mean, she wasn't fabricating again?'

'She was there all right, doctor. We have a witness who saw her walk round the house toward the pavilion at the time she says.'

Parry had no inhibitions about offering A.J. Claverhouse's testimony as something more specific than it had really been, particularly since Annie the kitchen helper had been eliminated. 'Unless we find the other person, or a witness besides Megan Collit to prove that such a person existed,' he continued, 'we have enough evidence to indicate Megan's lying, and to justify our arresting her on suspicion of murder.' He paused before completing more slowly and pointedly than before. 'And if we do that, I believe it will almost certainly end in her conviction.'

Janet Howell had listened impassively to Parry's account. 'This slim circumstantial evidence you have about the other person, what does it amount to?' she asked.

'It was the sound of what might have been a car approaching along the clinic drive just before Megan arrived, but which stopped some distance short of the building,' he replied. 'Except it could just as easily have been the sound of a much quieter vehicle, like her own moped which she parked at the gate, or even something electrically operated, for instance a wheelchair like this one of yours, and which actually drove past the building and went on to the pavilion area. In both cases the volume of sound to the hearer who was indoors could have been similar.'

'But not that similar,' the doctor commented dryly. 'And since I'm the only owner of an electrical conveyance in the vicinity, I ought to be delighted your circumstantial evidence is so pathetically slim as to be positively emaciated.' Her gaze was holding his firmly as she went on: 'I'm not delighted though, and that's as you expected, of course. My nature wouldn't allow it, as I suspect you're aware. Am I right?'

'Quite right, doctor,' the policeman replied. 'Your reputation is a very enviable one.'

She returned his smile. 'I don't buy all of what you've said, but I do accept the premise that Megan Collit could be convicted on the strength of it.' The speaker pulled the edges of the cardigan draped over her shoulders closer together as though she might be feeling a draught from somewhere. 'Rather than have a pregnant woman suffer for a crime she didn't commit,' she went on, 'I'm ready to admit that...that I was the other person, the one Megan saw with Rees.' Her gaze didn't falter as she ended. 'But I imagine Megan herself will already have told you as much.'

Parry's impassive expression betrayed nothing of the relief her admission had supplied. Without affirming her last supposition he began: 'then you must realise, doctor – '

'I'm afraid I realise only too well, Mr Parry,' she interrupted, lifting her chin and moving her head slowly from one side to the other. 'It follows, of course, that it was I who stabbed him.'

There followed a moment of dead silence in the room before the policeman declared. 'In that case, doctor, I'll have to caution you formally, and my advice would be that you say nothing more until you have a lawyer present.'

'How very considerate of you, chief inspector, but that may not be necessary when you've heard what really happened.'

He hesitated before replying. 'If you're sure that's the way you want it – '

'It is the way I want it.' She relaxed a little in her chair. 'I was coming out of the greenhouse when Rees half tumbled down the steps of the pavilion. He fell against the handrail, part of which came off in his hand. I must have looked surprised. I'd thought I might run into Collit who'd said he'd come back if there was a frost warning on the television. There was. I tried to call him to say I'd do the necessary myself, about the thermostat and so on, except all I got was that irritating message about the line being engaged and to try again later.' She cleared her throat, then added, 'Rees was in a thoroughly arrogant mood. I thought straight away he was on a high, with whatever drug he'd ingested on top of alcohol. He and I had never spoken of his attempt to blackmail Eve Oswald, but, of course, he knew she'd told me. Instead of his usual cringing attitude he was positively aggressive, asked me if I could guess why he was there and who he was meeting. Then he told me without waiting for an answer.'

The speaker breathed in and out, this time very slowly indeed before continuing. 'He said he was waiting for Megan Collit to...to pleasure him, as she'd done so many times before as I well knew. Those were his exact words. He added there was no harm in my knowing since he was going to be sacked as soon as Denis Ingram left the clinic.'

'So he'd worked that out for himself?'

'Mm. Without too much effort, of course. He then informed me that it was in both our interests that Ingram should be returned to full health and not upset in any way. This was because he, Rees, would be making Denis provide the capital for his expanding drug business. Not content with that, he announced that he already had enough crack-cocaine on call to satisfy half the needy population of Cardiff, and that he and Megan were about to indulge in a smoke together. He then added that he didn't expect I'd want to join them, but there was nothing I could do to stop them unless I wanted the *News of the World* to get the story of my husband's affair with Eve.'

'There were no drugs found on him,' Parry put in.

'Really? So that bit was just to goad me.' The other shrugged.

As she had been speaking, Sister Tate, as pretty as she'd been described to Parry, came out of the clinic opposite, hesitated, then waved as she saw Doctor Janet through the window, who waved back.

'Such a nice girl,' the doctor remarked with a smile. 'Should have left an hour ago, but she's so conscientious. Now, where was I? Oh yes. My first inclination had been to humour Rees, but I'm afraid outrage got the better of me. The prospect of this unspeakably foul person undoing all the work we'd put in to get Denis Ingram well made me more angry than I can say. I wasn't so much riled at the intended blackmail as I was about what it was going to do to the victim mentally, psychologically. Denis, a man who's done, and will do again, more real good in the world every week than the fraudulent, self-deluded Rees will do in a lifetime. And I said as much to him, though not in such polite terms. That was a mistake of course. It put him in a boiling rage. But he didn't scream abuse. He advanced on me hissing menacing obscenities, and brandishing that piece of handrail he was still holding.'

'In what way brandishing, doctor?'

'Slashing the air with it in front of my nose. Very close to my nose. I thought he was going to knock my head off with it. And I think so still.'

'You didn't attempt to drive away from him?'

'No, nor to scream my head off either and scare half the patients to death. At the critical moment I admit I was thoroughly frightened though. I couldn't gauge what was behind me, so I did the opposite, Mr Parry. I ducked, and put the chariot in fast forward in an attempt to run him down. He side-stepped, and made an almighty swipe at me with the stick, this time really aiming to hit me. I swivelled the cart and tried again, catching him behind the knee with the top of the footrest. He stumbled away from me. The dibber was the only weapon handy. It was here, in the right side-pannier. Been there a week since I'd borrowed it to do some potting. As he fell forward, I had my only chance, I thought, to stop him from bashing my head in. Yes, I struck him hard. Very hard. Intentionally, where it'd do the most damage, and accurately, because he expired on the instant.' She swallowed. 'Satisfied he was dead, I went back to the cottage. So far as I know my...my excursion was not seen by anyone, including my husband. He had gone over to the clinic just before I went out, to see Eve about a patient. By the time he returned, just after eleven, I was virtuously reading in bed. By the way he knows nothing of what happened. I made sure not to involve him in any way.'

There was silence in the small room for several seconds, except for the sound of the doctor's breathing.

'That's it, doctor?' the policeman questioned quietly.

'Apart from what motivated me and...and the floorshow.' She leaned backward in the chair, heavy perspiration glistening on her brow. 'Have you ever planned what you'd do to improve the world if you knew you mightn't have long to live, Mr Parry?'

'No, doctor. I've never had the excuse.'

'I'd always been the same,' she nodded to impress her agreement. 'Then I had something of a shock.' She lifted both her hands before adding: 'And here's the striptease I promised. The floor show – '

To conclude

'And with a flourish,' Parry exclaimed, 'she took off the wig she'd been wearing. Underneath it she was completely bald.'

'Chemotherapy is it?' But Lloyd's first question had come more as a statement.

'That's right, Gomer. The cancer was diagnosed five weeks ago. They've kept mum about it. That's she and her husband, and Eve Oswald, so as not to depress the clinic patients. No wonder I'd thought her hair-do was the liveliest part of her. She wasn't at the hospital running a clinic yesterday, of course. She'd gone there for her own regular treatment. I gather chemotherapy really takes it out of you. That's why she put off seeing me till this morning. Yesterday was her third dose.'

The two detectives were in the Porsche. Parry was driving them away from the police station where Dr Janet Howell had been formally charged with withholding evidence affecting a suspicious death, and for failing to admit involvement in a suspicious death. At her solicitor's instigation, and with no objection from Parry, the arresting officer, she had then been released on police bail pending the verdict of the coroner's court on the cause or causes of Kevin Rees's death. The court had previously been convened for the next morning.

'Did she say why she hadn't owned up earlier, boss?'

'Yes. She'd waited in the hope his murder would never be solved. That it'd be put down to a vagrant or one of his drug customers who'd never be traced. She said that wasn't as much to protect herself as to preserve the good name and reputation of the clinic.'

'Well, she was right there too, in a way,' put in Lloyd. 'Having one of the owners do in a member of staff doesn't sound like a commendation, does it? Still, from what she said in her statement, there's no doubt it was self defence, is there?'

'I'm sure that's right, Gomer.' Parry responded with sober confidence. He had halted the car and was waiting for the chance to join the easterly heading, lunch-time traffic along the wide Western Avenue. Any doubt that did exist in his mind was something which, for strictly legal reasons, he had no intention of sharing with anyone, not even DS Lloyd. The notes on the interview which he had purposely conducted alone with Dr Howell at the cottage would bear official scrutiny in this respect, as surely as would the lady's later recorded formal statement at the station in the presence of Parry and DS Mary Norris. DS Lloyd hadn't come on duty until noon.

There was little doubt that most juries would exonerate a half-paralysed and seriously ill, 56-year-old woman for defending herself by any means available from a murderous assault by a drug and drink-crazed criminal. The only weakness in that scenario lay in the fact that she had stabbed him in the back – indicating that he was probably moving away from her at the time. Parry was hopeful that her panicked and difficult-to-retrace manoeuvering of the powered wheelchair would explain that consequence, particularly since he had convinced himself it was the truth.

The doctor's query to Parry, about whether he had ever considered what he might do to improve the world if he knew he might have little time to live, had not been stricken from his record – for the reason that he had never entered it on his record in the first place. There was no point in muddying what promised to be clear waters – clearer, almost certainly, than the ailing doctor's troubled mind when she had asked the question, and before he had advised her not to repeat it to anyone else.

'At least the Collits are going to be pleased,' the sergeant observed, smacking his lips as he sucked on a fresh peppermint.

'Let's hope so. They're having their baby after all.'

'What if it's Rees's.'

'He won't be around to ask, Gomer, will he? And no one else has reason to, come to that. I doubt if anyone knows his blood group.'

'That's true enough.' Lloyd seemed pleased with the conclusion.

Except, in due time, Megan Collit obtained the answer to the sergeant's question without her husband's knowledge. She didn't know Rees's blood group either, but she knew her husband's – and the baby had been his.

'They haven't got that share of the lottery win, of course,' Parry went on, 'but I never believed they were entitled to it anyway.'

'And she told me she's giving back the loan from Mrs Craig-Owen, boss, so they're not in debt.' Not being in debt used to be the virtue the Lloyds instilled into their daughters as being next in importance to the one about retaining their virginity until marriage.

Parry chuckled as he moved the car onto the inside lane, while calculating the rough cost of the maternity leave payments Megan would ultimately be receiving from her devious employer.

Policemen were rightly disgraced for manufacturing evidence to secure a conviction. Parry could never have been charged on such a count. On this occasion he had solved what had seemed to be a murder case in exemplary time. His object had been achieved by leaning on the person he'd calculated was responsible for the death to confess as much, in the belief that, after the coroner's court's expected verdict, all charges would be dropped against her. His other hope, rather than solid expectation, that Janet Howell would overcome her cancer was also to be fulfilled, though it took longer to obtain than the dropping of the pending charges against her, and her acquittal, which happened next day.

There was little doubt in the chief inspector's mind that the tranquil, contented and very possibly innocent *ménage a trois* existing between the Howells and Eve Oswald would continue undisturbed. The secret that governed the Ingrams' way of life was more complicated. It had survived Sir Denis Ingram's stroke, his recovery, and Kevin Rees's death, an event partly precipitated by Rees's avaricious threat of exposure. But Ingram remained obdurate about sustaining the deception. So Jocelyn Jackson in Earls Court and Oliver Grant at the Housing Trust continued to play their well-cast and adequately remunerated parts in the undisturbed saga.

Lucy Lloyd recovered from her heart attack before the end of summer, slimmer and altogether healthier than she had been before it. She and her boyfriend Ifan married in September to the immense satisfaction of her parents. Lucy may have lost her virginity before she was wedded, but, as Gracie kept reminding Gomer unnecessarily, their oldest daughter wasn't pregnant before she reached the altar – something Gracie described as 'a sound moral fall-back position', an axiom which, perhaps, she might have fashioned with more delicacy if she had thought about it.

Indeed, there was nothing on Parry's mind affecting the case he had just completed which presently, or for that matter in the year ahead, was to loom larger than his concern about whether Perdita Jones would pass her finals in the following month. In fact she did so easily. This, of course, did present the problem of whether she should return to Wales as soon as possible, or accept the offer to specialise at St Mark's Hospital in London.

But then, that's quite another story.